More books in
The Lost T
The One-Ey
The Black P

Also by Eric T Knight

Immortality and Chaos

(epic fantasy series)
Wreckers Gate: Book One
Landsend Plateau: Book Two
Guardians Watch: Book Three
Hunger's Reach: Book Four
Oblivion's Grasp: Book Five

Chaos and Retribution

(sequel to Immortality and Chaos)
Stone Bound: Book One
Sky Touched: Book Two
Sea Born: Book Three
Chaos Trapped: Book Four
Shadow Hunted: Book Five
Book Six – Winter 2018

THE ACTION THRILLER
Watching the End of the World

Follow me at:
ericTknight.com

All books available on
Amazon.com

ACE LONE WOLF
and the
Hidden Fortress

by

Eric T Knight

ISBN: 9781731453549

Author's Note: The Lone Wolf Howls *series does not need to be read in order.*

Foreword

If you've read any of the other Ace Lone Wolf books, you know that I have strenuously hewn to my belief that facts should never, never get in the way of a good story. (Please be aware that you don't need to have read the previous books to enjoy this one. All of Ace's stories stand alone.) Which explains historical figures who sometimes lived decades apart appearing in the same scenes, geography that doesn't quite fit the real world, etc.

However, sometimes facts can make a story much better. (Who knew?)

This is one such story. This story is based on fact. The general events in this tale actually happened.

If you're interested in how much of this story is factual, there's an Afterword at the end that should answer all your questions.

I hope you enjoy the ride!

1

Coyote and I ride into San Diego. It doesn't look like such a bad town. I pass by a saloon and I don't hear a single gunshot coming from it, even though it's almost sunset. Up ahead, on the corner, is an actual, honest-to-goodness brick building. It's even two stories tall. And somebody planted a tree out front. Nobody on the street is drunk or waving a gun around. Shoot, some of these people aren't even wearing guns.

The people I pass seem friendly enough. No one curses or points a gun at me. That's always a good sign. A well-dressed woman wearing a ruffled dress and a big, lacy hat even nods politely to me.

Of course, it probably helps that before I rode in I tucked my hair up under my hat. I usually do that when I ride into a new town. I'm half-Apache—my grandfather was the great chief Cochise—and with my hair hidden most people take me for a Mexican.

"I have a good feeling about this town," I tell Coyote. "I think my luck's about to turn."

He turns his head and gives me a look.

"Don't look at me like that," I tell him. "I know I've said it before, but it's different this time."

I know why he's skeptical. Things have been...*rough* ever since Boyce shot that marshal and I got blamed for it. Since then it's been nothing but people chasing me, shooting at me, trying to hang me. Hell, I even got staked to an anthill once and that's a lot less fun than it sounds.

"Besides, I'm due. No one can have bad luck all the time." This time Coyote completely ignores me. It's a sad day when a man's horse loses faith in him.

I see a man looking at me strangely and I decide to stop talking to Coyote until after we leave town. Best not to draw any more attention to myself than I have to. Attention is something I don't need. I'm a wanted man just over the border in Arizona. I'm wanted in Colorado too. Probably Texas still also.

My luck better turn around. I'm running out of places to go.

San Diego's the biggest town I've ever been in. A lot bigger than Phoenix or Tucson, which I guess isn't saying much. Its size and the fact that I'm not wanted in California is why I'm here. I'm hoping there's someone here who wants to buy these black pearls I'm carrying.

I'm way past ready to get shut of them.

The thing is, the pearls are giving me bad dreams. In my dreams I'm on that rotted Spanish ship again and there's terrible things coming out of the shadows to get me. It doesn't matter how many of them I gun down, they just keep coming. There's someone laughing in the background the whole time too. It's not what you'd call a pleasant experience.

Last night I thrashed around in my sleep so much I rolled into a cholla cactus. I'm going to be picking spines out of my behind for a while.

Over the tops of the buildings I can see a handful of what looks like tall trees with no leaves on them. It takes me a minute to realize those must be masts, which means the harbor is over there. I've never seen the sea before. I hope I get a chance to take a look at it before I leave town.

I see a livery stable down a side street and mosey on over that way. There's a wooden corral, a small barn, and a long, low building with a hand-lettered sign on the side that says "Offise". I put Coyote in the corral and strip off his saddle and bridle. He glares at me when I close the gate.

"I know you don't like being locked up like this, Coyote, but we're in town now and I don't think people want you wandering around getting into whatever you feel like." Coyote has been known to raid gardens. He also likes to pick fights with other horses, especially if they're taller than he is. Which is pretty much most of them.

"You want your feed, don't you? You're not getting them if you're not in the corral."

He lays his ears back.

"Don't get all snarky on me. It is how it is, and that's all there is to it."

I head over to the office hoping no one else shows up to stable their horse while I'm gone. With Coyote in a mood like this, there's no telling what will happen. I don't need some man hot to shoot me because Coyote walloped his favorite stud.

A man comes out the door of the office. His face is leathery and seamed by the sun and the years. His hair is pure white and hangs down to his shoulders. Strangely, he's not wearing a hat. If there's one thing I've learned in the years since I left Pa-Gotzin-Kay, the Apache stronghold in northern Mexico where I grew up, it's that in the white man world, every man wears a hat. I'm not sure why, but that's how it is. I've known men who'd sooner go outside buck naked than without their hat.

The old codger spits on the ground, takes a glance at me, then looks over at Coyote.

"I'll tell you straight off that I won't give you much for that ugly hoss you're riding, mister," he says, spitting again. "Got a couple of goats and a swaybacked donkey, but that's as high as I go."

Coyote puts his head over the corral fence and fixes the old man with a hard look. I give him a hard look too. While it's true that Coyote is ugly—he's a dirty yellow color, with a jug head and crazy eyes—that doesn't mean I stand by and let people bad mouth him. The old man ignores both of us and bites off another plug of tobacco.

"I'll have you know that horse isn't for sale," I say. "Not for all the tea in China." I don't know much about tea and less about China, but I heard the saying somewhere and it seems to fit here.

The old man peers up at me with his beady little eyes and his mouth turns down. "Well, they ain't no need to go and get your dander up. I was only opening negotiations as it were."

I fish some coins out of my pocket and drop them in his hand. "Can you put him up for the night? I want some oats for him too."

He squints at the coins and rubs one between his thumb and finger like he's trying to see if the color will come off. "It's an extra two bits for the oats." I drop another coin in his hand. "Ayuh, that'll do," he allows. He jabs a thumb over his shoulder. "You can drop your rigging on any empty saddle tree you find in there. It'll be there in the morning when you come for it."

He starts for the barn, but I stop him. "Is there a goldsmith or a jeweler or something in this town?"

He picks a piece of tobacco out of his teeth while he considers my words. “Feller down the way who sells rings and necklaces and such,” he says finally, looking at whatever he picked out of his teeth. He flicks it away and looks back at me. “You in the market for a wedding ring? Looking to marry that horse of yours?” He chuckles a bit at his joke. It’s a dry, rasping sound like he swallowed a handful of gravel and never spit it back up.

“I don’t expect it matters to you why I’m looking for him,” I reply. “You want to tell me where he is?”

“He’s at the end of the street down by the docks.” He shakes his head and walks away. “Awful touchy for a young feller.”

2

I walk down to the docks. There's a half dozen ships anchored in the bay. From what I understand you can get on a ship and sail clean around the world if you want to. I can't imagine why anyone would want to. As I see it, any place you can't get to on a horse isn't worth going to in the first place.

A couple of seagulls fly overhead, squawking at each other. There's a sailor working on the side of one of the ships, chipping away at some stuff growing on the hull. Two other sailors are rolling a barrel of something toward one of the docks and arguing while they go. A man in a fancy hat stands on the deck of one of the ships, peering through his looking glass out to sea.

The building at the end of the street is painted blue. There's a sign hanging out front with a picture of a necklace on it. I hope it's still open. Once I sell these black pearls, I'll have money in my pocket again. I'd like to sleep in a bed and eat someone else's cooking. Buy some new duds. Mine are looking a little tattered, after all I've been through lately.

I get almost to the shop when this boy pops up about out of nowhere and starts tagging along. "You going to the jewelry shop, mister?" he asks. He's not wearing a shirt and he's barefoot. He's probably about ten.

I nod.

"Buying or selling?"

I look down at him. "You ask a lot of questions."

"That's how you learn things, isn't it?"

"Why do you care what I'm doing?"

"I think you're selling." He looks me up and down. "You don't have enough money to buy anything he's got for sale in there."

"Then you didn't need to ask me, did you?"

"You'll get cheated," he says confidently. "You got no idea what you're carrying is worth."

He's got me there. I really don't have any idea what the black pearls are worth. I know they're rare, but that's about it. I also know what they're worth to me, which is just on the south side of nothing.

"Don't you have somewhere to be?" I say to the boy.

"I warned you," he says. "Don't say I didn't." He runs off.

I open the door and walk into the shop. The door has a glass window set into it and a lacy curtain. A little bell tinkles when I open the door. Glass cases line two walls, jewelry sparkling within them. Behind a desk in the back of the room is a man in a brown suit. He's sporting a thick, walrus mustache and an extra chin. He's bent over something, looking at it with a magnifying glass. I walk over to him.

"Not hiring," he says without looking up. Up close I can see that he hasn't got enough hair to cover the whole top of his head, but that hasn't stopped him from trying. He's brushed everything up from the sides and greased it down pretty solid. I reckon he could come through a tornado without any of that hair moving.

"I'm not looking for a job," I say.

The man sets the glass down, rests his thick hands on his desk, and looks up at me. "No offense, stranger, but I don't believe you can afford what we're selling here."

That strikes me as odd. I look around the shop. There's no one else here but us two. I look back at the man. "You said 'we.'"

"So?"

"Seems strange is all, saying we when it's just you. You have a partner somewhere?"

"Is there a point to this?" he asks. "I'm a busy man."

"Then let's do this fast. I got things to do too."

He raises an eyebrow as if he finds the idea of me having things to do questionable. "As I said before, I don't believe you have enough money to shop here."

This man is starting to get under my skin. "Mister, you don't know what I have or don't have," I say. "Besides, I'm not here to buy. I'm here to sell."

His eyes tighten a little. "It is doubtful you have anything to sell which we would be interested in purchasing. If you've picked up some gold nuggets somewhere, you'll want to take them to the assay office."

"You did it again, talked about yourself like you were two people."

"I'm afraid I'm going to have to ask you to leave," he says.

"Got it right that time at least."

He stands up. "I bid you good day, sir."

"But you haven't seen what I have to sell."

"This is a respectable establishment. We don't traffic in stolen goods."

That does it. Now he's gone and got me all riled up. I stick my chin out and in a low voice I say, "You're calling me a thief."

He takes a step back in alarm and waves his pudgy hands. "Now, now. Not in so many words."

"Thief is only one word."

His eyes fall to my twin Colt .45s, which he can see now that I've pulled my duster back. He licks his lips. "The sheriff here is a personal friend. If you harm me, it will not go well for you."

"I have no cause to harm you unless you give me one. I'm here to sell something and that's all. I was told you were the man to talk to in this town. Now are you or aren't you?"

He sighs and rubs his forehead like I'm giving him a headache. I know he's giving me one. "Let's see it already." He folds his hands over his belly. His tone says he already knows he won't like what I have.

He's wrong.

I pull out the leather pouch from the inside pocket of my duster, untie the drawstring and dump the pearls on the desk.

His eyes get real round. "What the…? Are those real?"

I shrug. "You tell me."

He reaches into the pocket on his vest and pulls out a little round thing with a glass lens in it. He puts it to his eye, pulls the lamp on the desk closer, and picks up one of the pearls. He looks at it for a minute or so, turning it this way and that, and whistles.

"Black pearls," he says. "I've heard of them, but I've never seen them."

"So they're something you want to buy?"

He takes out the eye piece. "Where did you get these?"

"A friend gave them to me." Which is true. Beckwourth did give them to me. I leave out the parts about the skeletons and the ghost ship. I'm pretty sure that would only complicate things.

"A friend," he says skeptically.

"Yep."

He taps the desk, thinking. "Is your friend here in town with you?"

"Nope. He went home." Also true.

He comes to a decision then and his suspicion and hostility slide off him like oil off a skunk. He swaps them out for a big, greasy smile that I don't trust at all. If a snake could smile, this is exactly how it would look.

"It seems I have misjudged you, my friend, and I want to apologize for that. Of course I wish to buy your pearls." He gestures toward a door at the back of the shop.

"Why don't you come into the back? We'll sit down. Get comfortable. I don't like dickering on my feet and my mouth is uncommonly dry. I could use a little toot to wet my whistle. What about you?"

I'm not sure what he's talking about. I don't see a whistle anywhere and I'm not sure what a toot is, but I follow him when he picks up the lantern and heads into the back.

3

In the back room there's a table and a couple of chairs. Against one wall is a sideboard with several bottles of liquor and glasses on it. There's a safe in the corner, the door closed.

"Please, sit down," the man says.

The chair is upholstered in pink fabric and padded. "What's your offer?" I ask him.

"First, I must apologize for my earlier rudeness."

"Okay."

"It also occurs to me that we have not been properly introduced. I'd like to remedy that. My name is Pierre LaChance." He holds his hand out to me.

Reluctantly, I take it. It's soft and moist. I wipe my hand on my pants once I get it back. "Ace."

"That's it? No last name?"

"Ace Lone Wolf." Lone Wolf isn't really my last name. It's something I added on after leaving home. People seem to want me to have more than one name for some reason.

"If I may venture, you are an Indian, are you not? One of the local tribes I suppose?"

"Maybe. I don't see what this has to do with anything."

One eyebrow rises. "I was only curious." He gets up and goes to the sideboard. "Let us have a drink before we begin," he says. "A drink to a profitable business association. Perhaps some friendly conversation as well?"

I sit back in the chair and cross my arms. "Let's get this over with. I'm not in the habit of chewing the fat with people who call me a thief."

"Yes, yes, I can understand that," he says placidly, completely unperturbed by my words or angry tone. "But surely you will join me in a small glass of sherry before we start. Clearly you have come far. You must be thoroughly dried out."

He picks up a bottle and pours two glasses of some yellowish liquid. He comes back to the table and sits down, then pushes one glass over to me.

I eye the glass suspiciously. "What is it?"

"Sherry. The very finest quality. One of the sea captains I am acquainted with brings it to me."

I've never heard of sherry, but I am thirsty. However, I'm not a fool. I've been drugged before. I push the glass back and take his before he can pick it up.

He smiles. "Not the trusting sort, are you?"

"People aren't always what they seem."

"No, they are not." He raises his glass and takes a sip. "Here's to the black pearls."

Once he takes a drink, I have some of mine. It's not bad, if a bit too sweet for me.

He pours the pearls out of the bag and holds one up. "Beautiful," he sighs. "Before I make you an offer, I want to look over them individually. Make sure they are all as flawless as the one I saw before. You understand, of course?"

I shrug and take another drink of the sherry.

"I'll need better light." He opens the cabinet underneath the sideboard. "I purchased this when last I was in India," he says, taking out an odd-looking thing and bringing it over to the table.

Despite myself, I'm curious. I've never seen anything like it. It looks almost like a squat pitcher, with a curved handle on one side and a spout on the other. It appears to be made of brass. "What is it?" I ask.

"It's a lamp," he says. He takes a packet of matches from his pocket.

"Not like any lamp I've ever seen."

"Yes, well, they do things differently in India." He strikes a match and holds it to the spout. "You're not an actual Indian, you know that?"

The lamp smells odd. It has a heavy, cloying scent unlike anything I've ever smelled. It also doesn't put out very much light. I look over at him. "What's that you said?"

"You're not really an Indian. I know. I've been to India. I've tried to tell people, to correct their errors, but they insist on calling your people Indians." He holds his hands up in defeat. "What is one to do? Ignorance is a heavy stone to move."

"Can we get down to business here?" I say. My head feels kind of funny. I rub my eyes. I notice that he's smiling. His teeth look very yellow. He pulls a large kerchief from his pocket and holds it over his face.

"What's going on?" I demand, rising from my chair.

"Only a few more seconds." His voice is muffled by the kerchief. "Try not to get too excited. It won't hurt."

I stagger back from the table and knock over my chair. Everything is swimming before my eyes. "What did you do to me?" I pull one of my guns and point it at him, but there's something wrong with my muscles. The barrel of the gun is wandering all over the place and I can't feel my hand.

"Here, let me take that before someone gets hurt." He looms up before me and takes hold of my gun. I try to pull it away, but my arm betrays me and a second later my legs do too. I slump to the floor.

"There, there," he says, patting the top of my head as the lights go out for me.

4

When I wake up the first thing I notice is that I'm all wet. More than wet. I'm standing in water up to my neck. Waves are splashing against my face.

Where am I? How did I get here? I have a vague memory of going into a shop to sell the pearls, but after that things get fuzzy.

I try to move, but I can't. I'm tied hand and foot to some kind of post. In the water. All at once it hits me.

I'm in the *sea.*

Why?

I think I'm alone, so I'm surprised when I hear LaChance's voice right near my ear.

"You're awake," he says. "Pity. I was hoping you would sleep through this next part. I'm afraid it will be rather unpleasant."

"What…how…?"

"It's normal to be confused," he says. "It was quite a powerful sedative I used on you. I'd tell you the name, but you won't have heard of it anyway. It's not your normal sort of substance, being something brewed up by the monks in an otherwise insignificant Hindu mission high in the Himalayan mountains and nowhere else."

Pieces are starting to fit together for me now. "The lamp. There was something in the lamp."

"Indeed there was."

I struggle against my bonds but get nowhere.

"I'm afraid that won't work, my friend. I have done quite a lot of sailing, you see, and along the way I learned a few things about knots from the sailors. Those knots will never fail."

"Where am I?"

"Oh my, you *are* confused by the drug. Otherwise I should think you'd have figured it out already. You're under one of the docks."

The final piece clicks into place. "You're killing me for the pearls."

"*Moi*? Perish the thought. I am no murderer. I am simply tying you under the dock as the tide comes in. It will be up to the ocean to kill you."

"Sounds like murder to me."

"All a matter of perspective, I assure you."

Perspective? If I had one of my guns right now I'd show this man some perspective.

"I don't really know what the pearls are worth. You could have just cheated me, you know, like a normal person would."

"I suppose I could have, but it's a little late for that right now, don't you think?"

"Not really. I'm still alive. You could let me go."

"And then what? You'd either try to shoot me or you'd go to the sheriff. Either choice would lead to unnecessary complications. No, this way is much cleaner."

"Not for me."

"No, not for you. Not everybody wins in business. That's how it goes."

"You seem pretty calm about this. I'm glad to see my death isn't going to trouble you too much."

"Not too much, it's true. You're a drifter and a savage. I doubt there was much contribution you were going to make to the world."

"But you are."

"Naturally. I am quite the gifted jeweler, actually. The money from the pearls will allow me to open a shop in Paris or London. A proper shop, a place the rich and powerful will frequent. My creations will be worn by all the best people."

"You're a special kind of crazy, you know that, LaChance?"

"Again, all a matter of perspective. I don't expect you to understand. Your aboriginal mind is necessarily quite limited."

I'm not quite sure what he said, but it sounded like an insult. "It's not bad enough you have to kill me, but do you have to insult me too?" I ask him.

"Don't take it personally. It wasn't meant that way."

"Can I take the whole murdering thing personally?"

"If you wish. Now, I must be getting along. I dislike being wet. Time for the final step, the gag. Do you have any last words before I gag you?"

"Only this: I'm going to get out of this. And when I do I'm going to come for you. You're not going to like it."

"I don't suppose I would. However, since you won't be getting out of this it doesn't matter. Well, it's time for me to go. Thank you for the pearls. They're really quite lovely." I try to fight the gag, but he simply holds my nose until I have to breathe then, when I open my mouth, in it goes. He ties it tightly.

"It will probably take about an hour for the tide to rise enough to drown you," he says, "so you have time to make peace with whatever god it is you worship." He pauses. "That is, unless you have any open cuts on you, some place where blood is leaking out. You don't, do you? Because blood attracts sharks. They simply go mad for the stuff. Sometimes, if there is more than one, they will bite each other in their frenzy to get at their prey. It's quite horrifying, actually."

I've heard of sharks before. A cowboy I worked with up in Montana told me about them. Big fish with huge teeth. I thought he was having me on. Now it looks like I might get eaten by one.

"Well, I'll see you on the other side," he says lightly. "If there is another side. I've no idea, really. The Hindus believe we are reborn. If that is true, perhaps you will have a chance at revenge in your next life, assuming you aren't reincarnated as a worm or some such thing." He chuckles. "Listen to me, rambling on. I must have inhaled more of the drug than I realized. I have to go now. There is a ship sailing on the morning tide and I intend to be on it, but I have some packing to do first. *Ciao*, my friend."

He splashes away and I am left alone.

But not for long.

I feel something bump against my leg.

5

Okay, that can't be good. Maybe it was only a piece of driftwood. Or some other kind of fish. Surely it's not a shark. I'm not bleeding anywhere.

There's not a lot of light under the dock. What little there is comes from the lanterns hanging on a ship anchored nearby. Turns out it's enough to see a triangular-shaped fin slicing through the water.

Definitely a shark.

This just got a whole lot more interesting. Instead of drowning, I'm going to be eaten.

Then I start to feel angry. I'm getting really sick of this. Once again, I'm going about my life, minding my own business and something bad happens to me. If it's not someone abandoning me in an ancient temple, it's someone trying to frame me for murders I didn't commit.

All I wanted to do was sell some pearls that I nearly got killed over. Is that too much to ask?

The fin starts moving toward me.

Enough complaining. Time to do something.

I brace myself, but the fin veers off at the last second and all the shark does is bump me again. Like he's trying to get my attention.

For some strange reason it reminds me of a dog the foreman had on the Bar T ranch where I used to work. The dog loved nothing better than playing fetch. It was always following me around with a stick in its mouth, trying to get me to throw the stick for it. When I didn't cooperate, the dog would bump me with his head. I get a bizarre image of me throwing a stick for the shark to fetch.

Which is a whole lot better than the image of the shark chewing me up into small, bloody pieces.

I have to get out of here. Fast.

Fortunately, I'm not helpless. I carry a knife in my boot. Hopefully LaChance didn't take it when he took my guns.

All I have to do is get it out and cut myself free. It would be a lot easier if my legs weren't bound too.

It would also be easier if I wasn't tied up under a pier with a shark nosing around my nether regions.

There's only one way I can think of to get hold of the knife. If it doesn't work I'll probably drown before the shark eats me, so there's some silver lining in all this.

Taking the biggest breath I can, I push back with my hands to create some space and slide down the post. The log the post was made from wasn't hewn very carefully so there's plenty of broken-off limbs and knots sticking out of it for the rope to catch on, but it's also thickly coated with slimy moss or something and that helps the rope slide.

Now I'm crouched underwater, quickly running out of air, fumbling in my boot for my spare knife. This better work. I don't have a lot of wiggle room here.

At first I can't find it and my heart kind of stops, but then my fingers touch on the carved wooden handle. I can only get two fingers on it and the water makes it slippery.

I have to hurry because I'm running out of air at a rapid rate and the urge to panic and thrash around wildly is strong. But I also have to be careful, because if I drop the knife I'm truly doomed.

I manage to ease the knife out of my boot without dropping it. So far so good. Carefully, trying to ignore my lungs and their desperate demands for air, I work the knife around so I have a good grip on it. Once I do that it takes only a few seconds to slice the bonds holding my feet.

But now I really, really have to get to the surface and get some more air. I flex my legs and push upwards…

And go nowhere.

Those broken-off limbs I mentioned? The rope is hung up on one. I can't get past it.

The shark bumps into me again, but this time I don't actually care. All I care about is air and getting more of it. A shark's nothing next to that.

I start to give in to panic a little bit, flailing around trying to get the rope free. The rope stays stuck and I almost lose hold of the knife. A terrible thought flashes into my mind—

I'm not going to make it. First time I've ever seen the sea and I'm going to drown in it. How's that for a happy ending?

I force myself to calm down. It's not easy. My heartbeat is like a herd of wild mustangs galloping between my ears. Flashes of yellow light are bursting behind my eyelids. The urge to open my mouth and suck something, *anything*, in is almost unbearable.

I push it all away and focus on the rope, feeling around with my fingers for the problem.

There it is. This particular broken-off limb is pointing downwards. I need to go back down, then push outward further with my hands to get the rope around the limb. Then I can stand up.

It feels like it takes forever, but finally I get the rope up over the limb. Gasping, I break the surface and suck in as much air as I can. Which isn't all that much on account of the gag.

You're going to pay for this, LaChance.

It takes a couple of minutes of gasping and choking before I start to feel a little bit normal again. That's when I notice two things.

One, the water is higher than it was. It's up to my chin now. In a little bit I'll get to experience the joy of drowning again.

Two, my favorite shark is back and he brought a friend. I can see two triangular fins sticking out of the water. One of them bumps into me hard enough to hurt. As it passes by it kind of rolls on its side and I see a large, unblinking eye staring at me.

In order to cut my hands free I need to reverse the knife, so the blade is pointing upwards. When I do this the knife starts to slip out of my grasp and I have a sick moment when I think I've lost it, but then I manage to get hold of it again. I start sawing at the bonds.

It's not easy. In fact, it's downright hard. In order to cut the ropes on my wrists I have to hold the knife by the blade. Right away I cut the ball of my thumb.

So now there's blood in the water. I'm sure the sharks will love that.

On top of that, waves keep hitting me in the face. I can't actually close my mouth because of the gag and so every time a wave hits water goes down my throat, making me choke.

Also, did I mention that it's hard to cut ropes off your wrists when your hands are behind your back? Because it is.

I wonder where the sharks will bite me first. I wonder if I'll be the first Apache ever to get eaten by a shark.

Lucky for me my knife is sharp and the sharks leave me alone for a minute. Probably arguing over who gets to bite first.

Suddenly the rope parts. Quickly I cut the gag as well. I spit the gag out and look up to see two fins slicing towards me. It looks like the sharks got over their differences.

One fin is closer than the other. When it's a few feet away the shark lifts his nose up out of the water and opens his mouth. Now I'm staring at a terrifying number of triangular teeth.

A couple of options flash through my mind, none of them good. I settle for the most direct one and stab him right in the nose. The knife slams in up to the hilt.

The shark doesn't seem to like that. I guess. Hard to tell with a fish. Anyway, instead of biting me in half, he kind of slams into me. Caught between a giant, toothy fish and a wooden post, I lose most of the air in my lungs.

The shark is thrashing around in the water in front of me so I up and stab him again, aiming for where I hope his eye is.

And here comes the other shark. I'm off balance and trying to get myself turned so I can stab him too, but I know there's no way I can react in time. He's going to take my head off. There's nothing I can do.

Except that, instead of biting me, he bites the other shark.

I've definitely used up my luck. It's time to leave.

I put the knife between my teeth and shinny up the post as fast as I can. It's not easy. The thing is slippery with moss or whatever, but I have a whole passel of motivation on my side and I manage to overcome that little obstacle.

I get up out of the water a couple of feet. I should be safe now. I mean, fish like to stay in the water, right?

Not all fish.

The water boils and one of the sharks leaps into the air, mouth gaping wide. Clinging to the post with one arm, I stab him in the snout. The blade sinks in and he tosses his head, which rips the knife from my grip. He goes back into the water, my knife still sticking out of his nose.

I shinny up higher, but I can only go a couple of feet before I reach the underside of the dock. Now what? There's no way to climb over to the edge. I could wait here and hope my new friends can't reach me, but by now I'm not sure they won't follow me clear into town. Who knows what these things are capable of? Besides, I'm itching to have a long talk with LaChance.

Up it is.

I start banging on the boards overhead. The first couple I try are solidly nailed down, but the third one moves a little. I bang on it for a minute and it gets looser. Then it rips free and I knock it up and out of the way. I'm able to worm my way through the opening and climb up onto the dock.

For a few seconds I lie there and catch my breath. A light comes toward me. I blink against the brightness before I see that it's a man carrying a lantern. He holds the lantern up and squints at me. He looks down at the new hole in the dock and then back at me, confused.

"You should get someone to look at that hole," I tell him. "A body could fall right through. Sharks down there, you know."

I walk by him and leave him there, staring after me. Time to go see LaChance.

6

The front door of LaChance's shop is locked, but the one around back isn't. That's careless of him. He's got no idea who might wander in.

He's in the back room where he drugged me, filling a carpet bag with jewelry. The safe is standing open and there are stacks of bills on the table. Hanging off one of the chairs is my gun belt, both Colts in their holsters, my Bowie knife in its sheath. My duster and hat are on the table.

"Packing light, are you?" I say.

He jumps and spins toward me. His face drains of color when he sees who it is.

"Oh dear," he says. "You got free. That wasn't supposed to happen." He scurries for my guns.

But he's not nearly fast enough. I trip him and he goes down hard. Groaning, he rolls over onto his back. I draw one of my Colts and shove the barrel into his nose. His eyes cross, trying to stare at it.

"Get up."

I grab his tie and jerk him to his feet. He straightens his jacket and tries to gather himself.

"What will you do now, I wonder?" he says.

"Shooting you comes to mind."

He shakes his head a little sadly. "Alas, I don't believe you are a killer."

I jab the gun into his chest. "You sure about that?"

"You could turn me over to the sheriff, I suppose, but it will be your word against mine and I am an upstanding citizen of this town, while you are merely a drifter. An Indian no less."

He does this thing where he puts the first two fingers of each hand in the air and waggles them while he says Indian. I have no idea what it means.

"You're making a powerful good argument for shooting you." I make a show of cocking the pistol slowly.

I'll give him credit. Most men get all rattled when they're staring down a cocked .45. Some cry. Some wet themselves. He does neither. Instead he strokes his mustache, thinking.

"Perhaps the best thing would be for you to take your pearls and leave. We'll simply chalk up this little mishap as a learning experience."

"Except I don't feel you've learned anything, and all I've learned is that you're a low-down skunk," I say.

"It is what it is," he says solemnly.

"I have a better idea."

He raises an eyebrow. "Do tell."

"First, you go ahead and finish packing that carpet bag."

He nods like I said something he was expecting. "So you *are* a thief after all."

"How about you stop talking before I change my mind about shooting you?"

He sighs and continues packing the bag. I put my gun belt on and make sure my Bowie knife is secure, then check the loads on both pistols. Finished, I holster both pistols and put my duster and hat on.

"Why'd you take my duster off before hauling me out into the water?" I ask him. "It wouldn't fit you."

He shrugs. "It seemed a shame to waste a nice jacket." He looks puzzled. "How did you get free anyway?"

"Knife in my boot."

"Oh. I suppose I should have thought of that. This is awkward, isn't it?" The jewelry is all in the bag now. He reaches for one of the stacks of cash.

"Leave those out." I walk over to the table and pick up the cash. There are three stacks, held together with string. I flip through them. "What is there, about fifteen hundred dollars here?"

"Closer to two thousand."

"That's a fair price for the pearls, don't you think?"

"Actually—"

"That wasn't a real question." I stuff the bills in the inside pockets of my duster. "Pick up the carpet bag."

"What are you about?" he asks curiously.

"You're right, I'm not a killer," I tell him. "Awhile back I found out I'm not really much of a thief either. And, like you said, turning you in won't do much but maybe land me behind bars. But at the same time, a thing like this, it rankles, you know? You tried to kill me."

He holds up one finger. “Technically, the ocean—”

“Save it. That kind of talk makes my trigger finger itchy.”

He lowers his finger. I point to the door. “Let’s go.”

As we head out the door, I draw a gun and press it into his back. “You won’t go hollering for help, will you? I may not be a killer, but I have killed men before.”

“Quiet as a church mouse,” he says.

The street in front of the shop is empty and so is the dock where he tried to drown me. I prod him with the gun and he stumbles out onto it. “Watch your step,” I say softly. “There’s a board missing up ahead.”

A moment later he sees it and steps over it. “A person could take a nasty tumble there.”

“Someone should do something about it,” I agree.

I march him to the end of the dock. “What now?” he says.

“Dump it in.”

“What?”

“Empty the carpet bag into the water.” I punctuate my request with another jab from the pistol.

“Why?” For the first time he sounds shook up. His voice has a quiver in it that I find I like.

“It strikes me that the best way to get to a man like you is to take away what he values most. You sounded like you really hate living here. That jewelry is your way out. I’m taking it away.”

“You’re a monster,” he says shakily.

“I’ve been called worse. Do it. Now. Or I’m throwing you in too.”

Reluctantly, he upends the bag. There’s a bunch of splashes down below. He turns to me, defiance creeping back into him.

“I can swim, you know. And the water here isn’t that deep. I can retrieve that jewelry in the morning.”

“Go ahead. Of course, before I leave town I’m going to stop into one of the local saloons and start a little rumor about the lunatic I saw dumping jewelry and gold off the end of the dock.”

“You wouldn’t,” he says, alarmed. “Why, they’ll be swarming everywhere.”

“I would and I will.” I start to turn away, then stop like I just thought of something.

"An ambitious man would beat the rush and start diving tonight," I say. I draw the Bowie knife, grab his hand and, before he can react, I slash him across the palm. He shrieks a little and jerks his hand back. Blood is dripping from his hand. I grab his hand, hold it out over the water and give it a good squeeze.

"But before he does, he should know that there are sharks down there already. And I hear blood gets them all worked up."

He glares at me. "You're a horrible, horrible man, you know?"

"Not a man, a savage, remember? And a drifter. But what I'm not is someone who murders people to steal from them. Which is what you are. How's that for a learning experience?"

As I turn away I deliberately hit him with my shoulder, hard enough that he loses his balance and falls down, nearly tumbling into the water as he does.

I leave the dock feeling a whole lot more cheerful. I'm a little wet, and I lost a good knife, but other than that I'd say my first trip to San Diego came out all right.

I stop in at the Busted Saddle Saloon to have a quick whiskey and spread my story. Before I'm done with my drink half the place is empty, men with lanterns heading down to see for themselves.

I fetch Coyote from the stable and light out of town. There's no sense in sticking around and pressing my luck. I ride most of the night, lost in my thoughts, and by the time I stop to make camp about sunrise I've come to a decision.

It's time to go home.

7

Home means Pa-Gotzin-Kay, an ancient Apache fortress in northern Mexico, on the slopes of the Sierra Madre mountains. I grew up there. But I left a few years back because I wasn't sure I belonged there. See, my mother's a full-blood Chiricahua Apache, daughter of the great chief Cochise, but my father is a white man, a drifter and a gambler. He's the one who named me Ace, which he probably thought was pretty funny, though it's not so bad as names go.

I got called half-breed a lot of times while growing up and most times people didn't mean it in a friendly way. There came a time when I started wondering if my place might be out in the white man's world. So finally I lit out on my own, going to see where I did fit.

This latest incident proves that my home isn't out here. You'd think I'd have figured it out before this, what with all the bad things that have happened to me since I left home. I've been sent to prison, sentenced to hang, chased by the cavalry, poisoned, almost scalped, shot, stabbed and beat up more times than I can count. Why I didn't go home before this I don't know. I guess I'm slower than a three-legged mule.

I pat the bundles of bills in my pocket. At least I won't have to show up empty-handed. I can stock up on supplies before I go. Flour, coffee, sugar, beans, cloth, tools. Weapons too, if I can get my hands on them. I'm sure my clan can use whatever I bring.

There's only one little problem.

I'm a popular man in the Arizona Territory these days. Popular with the law anyway, which isn't a good kind of popular. That popularity is on account of me escaping from the Yuma Territorial Prison a few weeks back. The Yuma prison is the most notorious prison in the West, tall stone walls sitting in the middle of brutal desert. People who build prisons like that generally do so with the intention that the men they put there will stay put. Which explains why those people get heated when that doesn't happen.

So by now every jail and post office in the whole Arizona Territory has got my face plastered on it. That by itself isn't such a big problem. I just need to avoid the towns and I can do that. I know how to live off the land. But it will make buying supplies a lot harder. It'll be too risky to buy them myself. I'm going to need someone to buy them for me.

I could hire someone. There's always people who'll do a job for a dollar. The problem is I've got no way of knowing if I can trust whoever I hire. Look at what happened with LaChance. If I go hand a fistful of dollars to a man I don't know, the likelihood is he'll try to double cross me.

Then it hits me.

I can ask Tom Jeffords to help me. If the Chiricahua Apaches can be said to have a friend amongst the white man, it's Tom Jeffords. He and my grandfather, Chief Cochise, were blood brothers. He was the one who worked the middle to get the peace treaty done between my people and General Howard of the US Cavalry, a treaty my grandfather wouldn't sign unless Tom was named Indian Agent in charge of the reservation. The treaty didn't hold up all that long, but that wasn't Tom's fault.

I feel better knowing there's someone I can go to that I can trust. It seems crazy that I never looked him up before. I haven't seen Tom since I was still a kid. I wonder if he'll recognize me.

For the next few days I travel mostly at night and keep my head down. Except for taking a ferry across the Colorado River—which I do very early in the morning when the ferryman is still half asleep and nursing a hangover—I avoid people and towns altogether and don't have any problems.

One morning as the sun is coming up I see the Owl Head Buttes in the distance and know that I'm getting close to Tom's spread. Rather than stop and camp like I usually do when daylight comes, I push on. Coyote's not happy about it. This is his time to graze. Hopefully Tom has some hay laid by.

The desert around Owl Head Buttes is pretty flat, not much more than cactus and greasewood bushes, with a few patches of mesquite and palo verde trees here and there lining the washes. Tom's house and barn sit up against the west side of the buttes where the land starts to rise a little. It gives him a lot of view so Tom sees me coming some way off and he's standing out by his rickety pole corral with the gate open when I ride up.

"You look like you rode long and hard, mister," he calls out to me. He's in his late fifties, wearing dungarees, a patched rawhide jacket and an old straw hat that's seen better days. His thumbs are hooked in his belt and there's a big smile on his red-bearded face. "You're welcome here. I don't have much, but I'm happy to share it."

"Much obliged," I say. I stop and take my hat off. I've been wearing my hair tucked up under my hat and it spills down around my shoulders when I do so.

Tom does a double take and blinks a few times. "Is that Niño I see?" he asks. Tom has always called me Niño. "Damned if it isn't."

I drop down off Coyote and he grabs my hand and starts shaking it heartily. "Well, cover me in lard and set me to running with the hogs. I never expected to see you come riding out of the morning like this. You've sure enough grown, haven't you? You were only about knee high to a jackrabbit when I last saw you."

"It's been awhile," I say.

He looks me up and down and then looks at Coyote. "Times a bit tough, I see." He gives Coyote a friendly slap on the shoulder. "Better than no horse at all, I guess, right?"

Coyote's head whips around and Tom jerks his hand back about an eyeblink before he loses part of it.

"Careful," I tell him. "Coyote's a might sensitive." I whack Coyote on the nose before he can go after Tom again. "Easy there, Coyote. Tom's an old friend."

Coyote glares at me and stamps his foot. I turn back to Tom.

"I know he doesn't look like much, but he's got more heart than any ten horses put together."

"If you say so," Tom says, though he looks dubious. "It's none of my business what horse you own anyway."

"I don't own Coyote. Coyote owns himself. He's free to leave whenever he wants."

"Is that so?" Tom asks. I don't usually tell people about the arrangement Coyote and I have. The few times I do, everyone looks at me like I'm crazy. But not Tom. He looks thoughtful. "How did that come about?"

"Awhile back I helped him out of a tight spot and he decided to throw his hand in with mine for a spell. But it's his choice. He's free to leave if he wants."

Tom is watching Coyote while I speak and now he says, "He looks like he knows what you're saying."

"Maybe he does. It's hard to tell how much Coyote knows. He keeps his thoughts to himself mostly."

"I'm sorry for my words, Coyote," Tom says earnestly, a serious look on his face. "I spoke before I knew."

"Your words will go a lot further if you have something for him to eat."

"Got some hay in the barn, probably a few oats as well. Also, there's this." He reaches into his pocket and pulls out a withered, sad-looking carrot. "Still not much of a hand at gardening," he says. "This is the whole of this year's carrot crop so far." He holds it out to Coyote.

Coyote takes a sudden step closer, and before I can warn Tom to step back, Coyote up and knocks his hat right off. The hat falls on the ground and when Tom bends over to pick it up, Coyote puts his foot on it.

Tom straightens and looks at Coyote. "That ain't too neighborly. I said I was sorry."

"Give him time," I say. "He'll get over it. Coyote doesn't usually hold a grudge for too long."

Tom says to Coyote. "Can I have my hat back now?"

Coyote stands there staring at him, ears back slightly, his eyes narrowed down.

"Try giving him the carrot again."

Tom holds the carrot out gingerly, careful to keep his fingers well away from Coyote's teeth.

Coyote munches the carrot, keeping an eye on Tom the whole time. When he's finished he gives a big old horse sigh and picks up his foot.

Tom looks down at the hat. "Is he going to kick my head off when I go to pick it up?"

"He might. Let me unsaddle him. You go get some of that hay. It should be safe enough then."

I unsaddle Coyote and brush him down. Tom returns with a big pitchfork full of hay and tosses it over the fence into the corral. Coyote perks up his ears, gives Tom one last look—not so mean this time, more like he might have misjudged Tom—and trots into the corral. When Tom starts to close the corral gate I stop him.

"He doesn't much like being penned up."

Tom shrugs and picks up his hat. There's a big hole in the crown where the brittle old straw cracked away under Coyote's hoof. "It's ruint," he says. "This was my favorite hat."

"Don't worry, Tom. We'll get you a new one."

He looks at me and raises an eyebrow.

"I need your help," I say.

8

"Let's go up to the house," Tom says. "You look like you could use some grub." Hitching up his pants, he heads for the house and I follow.

It's a little one-room place, unpainted, the boards coming loose in the sun. The whole thing leans a bit to the left. But it's got a porch all down the front with a couple of chairs on it. Tom points to an old gunny sack that's hanging under the porch roof. "Cool water in that *olla*," he says. "Help yourself and I'll go in and get something going. You like corn dodgers, don't you?"

Not really. But I haven't eaten since yesterday morning, so they'll have to do.

Inside the old gunny sack is a clay jug, the *olla*. Water seeps through the clay slowly and keeps the gunny sack damp. Breezes blowing across the porch keep the water inside cool. I take it down off the nail it's hanging on and have a long drink. There might not be anything better in this world than cool water on a hot day.

After I've chipped my teeth a few times on the corn dodgers we sit on the porch and Tom puts his feet up on the railing, tilts his chair back and rolls a cigarette. "What's going on, Niño? How can I help you?"

"I'm headed down to Pa-Gotzin-Kay."

"Been gone a while, have you?"

"What makes you say that?"

"You have the faded look of a man who's been driftin'."

"Before I head down, I want to buy some supplies. Coffee, beans, flour, you know."

"You short on coin?"

I open my jacket and take out the bundles of bills. Tom's eyes widen and he whistles. "Damn, Niño, did you rob a train or what?"

"I tried. Once. It didn't work out so good," I say, thinking of wet dynamite and Boyce shooting a marshal. "No, I earned this. Or found it really."

"I'm not calling you a liar, but no one finds money like that lying around."

"Sometimes they do. You ever hear of the black pearl treasure?"

He nods. "A legend. And a crazy one too. What would a Spanish ship be doing out in the middle of the desert?"

"Looking for more black pearls," I say.

"A man would have to be crazy as a bedbug to think he'd find pearls on land."

I think of the vision I had while locked in solitary confinement in prison. "The captain of the ship didn't know he'd end up on land. But he angered the wrong god."

Tom's eyes widen. "It sounds to me like you've been having yourself some adventures."

"Some would call them that. Beckwourth for one. I call them a pain in the neck."

I tell him the short version of what happened, how Beckwourth and I found the old Spanish ship, how Beckwourth managed to come away with a handful of the pearls, which he gave to me. I leave out the parts about the skeletons and the ship vanishing at the end. Even Tom wouldn't believe that. Sometimes I'm not so sure I do either, and I was there.

"So you sold the pearls and that's where you got the money?" he asks when I finish.

"I tried to. But the man I tried to sell them to thought he'd rather feed me to the sharks instead."

"That sounds downright unfriendly. What did you do?"

"I threw all his jewelry into the sea. Took his money as payment."

"You tossed the pearls into the sea too?"

I nod. "It seemed to me those things have been nothing but trouble for everyone. I figured it would be best to put them back where they came from."

"Well, it sounds like you sewed everything up right nice. What do you need me for?"

"I need your help buying the supplies. I'm kind of a wanted man."

He takes his ruined hat off and scratches the top of his head. He's lost most of the hair up there and all he's got left is a kind of a frizzy cloud of red curls. "Do I want to know what you did?"

"I escaped from the Yuma prison."

"You've sure been through the mill, ain't you?"

"The cavalry thought I killed some settlers. But it wasn't me. It was the Apache Kid. He set me up. Then he turned into a raven and left me to face the cavalry—"

"Stop right there." He stands up and squints up at the sun. It's late morning. "It's a mite early, even for me, but I can see you've got some tales to spin and I think we're going to need some cactus juice to get through this."

There's a hand-dug well off the corner of the house with a little stone wall built around it. A rope is lying there, the other end disappearing into the well, and he picks it up and hauls on it until a copper jug appears, dripping wet. He comes back to the porch, pulls the cork with his teeth and spits it into the yard. He takes a long drink and hands the jug to me.

I take a drink and start to cough. "That's truly awful," I say, wiping my chin. "What is it?"

He grins and takes the jug back. "Cactus juice. My own invention."

"Think I'd rather eat the cactus." I have another swig. It's worse the second time.

He puts his feet up again and pushes his hat back. "Go on. Spill."

So I do. I tell him all of it. About being accused of rustling horses in Texas. How I fought for Coyote and he followed me when I left. The botched train robbery. Almost getting hanged and then going after the lost temple of Totec with Victoria and Blake. Doc Holiday and the shootout at the OK Corral. I tell him about Lily Creek and the Hashknife Outfit. Beckwourth. The crazy man with his cabinet of curiosities who wanted an Apache scalp. Mickey Free saving me so he could chase me. I've never told anyone the whole story before and it feels strangely good.

By the time I'm finished the jug is too and we're both drunk as three-legged skunks.

For a long minute he says nothing. Then he belches and sets the jug down. "You sure do get yourself into some scrapes, don't you?"

"It's bad luck is all."

"Uh-huh," he says, but I can see he's skeptical. "I can see there's only one thing to do," he drawls. "I'm going with you. Not just to buy supplies, but all the way down to Pa-Gotzin-Kay."

"You don't have to do that, Tom. Once I get the supplies and get down into Mexico, I'll be fine."

"Really?" he says. "From the rattles on that tale you just told me, I'd say the likelihood is that you'd get yourself into…" His words trail off. "I don't know what you'd get into. I can't think of anything more unlikely than what you already told me. No, I need to go with you. It's the only way I can be sure of getting you there in one piece," he says. "And I'd like to see your mother again. It's been too long. She's a fine lady. The finest."

He looks out over his spread. "Nothing much keeping me here right now anyway. What cows I got are wilder than jackrabbits with a fever. Don't think I could gather them if I tried. I have a little silver mine over in the buttes, but it's about played out. The change could be good for me."

"I can't tell you how glad I am to have you along," I say, and stand up and shake his hand.

Or I try to. For some reason the porch bucks like a spring bronc right then and I trip and somehow fall over the railing.

On my back, I look up and see Tom leaning over looking down at me. "That cactus juice has a hell of a kick, wouldn't you say?"

9

"I was gonna suggest we pick up your supplies in Tombstone," Tom says the next morning, "but we're likely to run into one of the Earps if we do and there's no way to know how old Wyatt will react if he sees you. That man is as ornery as a bull with a bee in his butt. So we'll go to Bisbee instead. Also, it's closer to Pa-Gotzin-Kay than Tucson is, so we won't have to tote the supplies so far." He pauses. "You aiming to empty my well or what?"

I'm busy draining my second bucket of water. My head is pounding from the cactus juice and I feel like I swallowed every sand dune in Yuma I'm so thirsty. I haul up a third bucket and dump it over my head before I answer.

"I'm never drinking that stuff again. If I was still sheriff I'd arrest you for trying to poison me."

Tom's bearded face splits in a big grin. "You give up too easy, Niño. Only one round with my cactus juice and you're already throwing in the towel?"

"Damn straight I am. Let's go already. If I'm going to feel like dying I might as well get somewhere." Why do my eyes feel like they're too big for my head?

"That's the spirit," he says. He's got a lariat in his hand and he shakes out a loop. "That broomtail nag of mine must be around here somewhere. She usually comes nosing around in the morning hoping for a handout."

I whistle for Coyote, but he doesn't show. I whistle again. "Not today, Coyote," I mutter. Right then I feel a sharp pain in my gut and put my hand on my stomach, which gurgles loudly.

Tom gives me a sympathetic look. "Stomach feeling poorly, is it?"

"It's the cactus juice," I groan.

"You may experience the backdoor trots," he says. "Unfortunately the juice sometimes has that little side effect on people with weak constitutions."

"It doesn't feel little. It feels like I swallowed a racoon and it's trying to get out. And I don't have a weak constitution."

"Sure. Whatever you say. Look at it this way. We can all use a good cleaning out now and then, right?" He winks at me.

Another pain goes through me and I bend over, both hands on my stomach now.

"Don't feel too bad," he says sympathetically. "That ol' prickly pear does the same thing to my cows. Goes right through them. Doesn't seem to stop them from eating it though!"

"Urg," I say, and take off at a trot for his outhouse.

When I come out Tom is saddling his horse, a short sorrel mare with a blaze on her face and one eye set lower than the other.

"Looks like Coyote has taken quite a shine to my mare Sheila," he says cheerfully. Coyote is sniffing around his mare, who aims a kick at him that he dodges. "Back off there," he tells Coyote, swatting at him with what's left of his hat. "You go too fast, it makes the ladies skittish."

Coyote snorts at him and tosses his head. While he's distracted, Sheila kicks at him again and this time lands a solid one on his ribs. Coyote throws up his head and dances sideways, looking surprised.

I grab his mane. "Looks like you finally met your match," I tell him with a chuckle. I've seen him tackle stallions twice his size and here a little mare hardly taller than a donkey has put him in his place. This I can enjoy.

Coyote gives me a sour look and bares his teeth at me. I whack him on the nose.

"I keep telling you, Coyote. Horses don't do that."

He makes a rumbling sound in his chest that lets me know he does whatever he wants and I give up ribbing him. He's patient and smart. If I get into it with him I'm the one who'll end up losing. Coyote plays to win.

"You should feel honored that Coyote is sweet on your mare," I tell Tom. "He hates most other horses as bad as he hates people."

"Well, I'd rather he wasn't," Tom replies, tightening his cinch. "Don't take it poorly, Ace, but I don't want Sheila popping out a colt that looks like Coyote. I'm afraid it'd look too much like the father. Hard to sell an ugly horse."

Coyote lays his ears back and goes very still, staring at Tom. "It's not me you have to worry about taking it poorly, Tom. It's Coyote. He heard what you just said."

"Now, Ace, that's just foolishness. A horse can't understand people talk."

"Are you sure?" I ask him.

Tom glances over at Coyote, who still hasn't moved and is still staring at him. An uneasy look crosses Tom's face. "Maybe you're right."

"If we're going to be spending some time together, you need to get right with Coyote. Otherwise you're likely to end up missing some bits and pieces after a while," I say.

"Probably not a bad idea. Do you have any suggestions?"

"Tell him you're sorry."

"You think that'll help?"

"Probably not, but it's a start."

Tom looks at Coyote. "I'm sorry, Coyote. I truly am. I hope we can leave our differences on our back trail." His eyes slide back to me. "What do you think?"

"It's as much as you can do for now." I grab Coyote's nose and shake his head a little to get his attention. "He's a friend. Remember that."

We hit the trail a few minutes later and head southeast toward Bisbee. We haven't hit full summer yet, but the day feels like it's going to be a hot one. The sky is perfectly clear, with not a single cloud showing even over the tops of the Santa Catalina mountains. We make good time even though Coyote is still distracted by Tom's mare and manages to get himself kicked again for his troubles.

Tom looks at my twin Colts at one point and asks, "So when did you start carrying a pair of barking irons?"

"Since about the time I left home."

"The other one for show, or can you actually use it?"

Instead of replying I drop my left hand and draw. The Colt comes out smooth. I point and squeeze the trigger. A neat round hole appears in a prickly pear pad a few dozen paces away. I drop the gun back in its holster.

"Not bad. If that's what you were shooting at anyway," he says. When I don't reply he asks, "Was it?"

I draw the pistol again and put another hole right next to the first one.

"I'll take that as a yes," he says. We ride a few more minutes and then he asks, "Why?"

"Why what?"

"Why carry two guns?"

I shrug. "Twelve bullets instead of six."

"And that's good?"

I give him a funny look. "What kind of question is that?"

"An honest one."

"I don't have to reload as often so, yeah, that's good."

"You ever think that maybe the reason you have to reload so often is *because* you're carrying two guns?"

"What kind of fool question is that?"

"It's not a fool question at all. You can't be that ignorant, Ace. You have to know that carrying two guns marks you as a gunslick."

"So? That means folks leave me alone, right?"

"Ordinary folks, anyway. But the West is full of bad *hombres* itching to make a name for themselves. They see those twin guns of yours and some of them are sure to make a go at you. In other words, maybe having two guns gets you *more* trouble instead of less. You ever consider that?"

I haven't, but I don't like letting on that I haven't, so all I do is grunt in reply.

"I've been chewing on this ever since you told me about all the troubles you've had out in the wide world. You seem to think it's all bad luck, but I'm not so sure about that."

"What are you saying?"

"I'm saying that maybe you're bringing your troubles on yourself."

"I never heard anything so foolish."

"It's got me wondering. Maybe you're *looking* for trouble."

"Why would I be looking for trouble?"

"I don't know. Maybe you got something to prove."

"How long are we going to keep talking about this?" I'm feeling a little peevish. This conversation is making me more uncomfortable than I'd like to admit.

"I guess we can stop talking about it now. But give it some thought, will you?"

I don't want to think about it, but I do anyway. For longer than I'd care to admit.

10

When we get to Bisbee I tuck my hair up under my hat, pull my hat down low over my eyes and try to look as invisible as I can. I ride behind Tom with my head down. Most people will think I'm his hired hand and not give me a second look. At least that's what I'm counting on.

We ride up to the Phelps Dodge general store and go on in. The man behind the counter is tall and lean. He's wearing a crisp white shirt and a bow tie. An unlit cigar is sticking out of his mouth. He smiles when he sees Tom.

"Well, Mr. Jeffords, it's been a while." He comes out from behind the counter and pumps Tom's hand enthusiastically. He barely even glances at me.

"Howdy, Gerald," Tom replies. "How's the wife and pretty little daughters doing these days?"

"Not so little and too pretty for my comfort, I'll tell you," Gerald said, his smile dimming. "I've got young fellers sniffing around the house all hours of the night and day. I'm starting to think that I'm going to have to shoot a couple of them so's the others get the idea."

Gerald looks pretty mild mannered. In fact, he looks exactly like what he is: a store clerk. But the way he says that makes me think there's a good chance some unlucky kid is going to get his britches full of buckshot before this is over.

"So, what can I get for you, Tom?" Gerald asks, his smile returning.

Tom looks around. We talked this over before we got into town and settled on what we'd need and how much. I handed all the money over to him too. It would look strange if I was holding it. "Some of about everything, I think. I need a half dozen of those fifty-pound sacks of flour, a half dozen sacks of beans and seed corn. A hundred pounds of coffee, five pounds of sugar…" While he talks Gerald scribbles furiously in a little notebook.

"…two bolts of that calico cloth and…" Tom looks around some more. "A pound of that horehound candy."

Gerald finishes writing and looks up. "That's quite a haul. If I didn't know better, I'd say you're buying to outfit an army."

Tom snaps his fingers. “That reminds me. Six of those Winchester carbines and two dozen boxes of cartridges.”

Gerald raises an eyebrow. His eyes go to me and for the first time he really looks me over. He gets a thoughtful look on his face. “You know I’m not the kind of man who pries into the affairs of others, but does this have anything to do with the trouble brewing in Mexico?”

“What trouble?” Tom asks.

“Word is that a general name of Torres is gathering soldiers. Some say he’s got fifteen hundred men under him now.”

Tom goes very still. We’re both staring at Gerald. This is the first I’ve heard about it.

“You think Torres is raising the red flag?” Tom asks. In Mexico, raising the red flag means revolution.

“It looks that way.”

“Where’d you hear this?” Tom asks.

“A couple of cowboys came in from the Slaughter ranch a few days ago to stock up on supplies. Kind of like you’re doing. That’s what brought it to mind.”

“Are they reliable?”

“They were salty types, men who looked like they’ve been in a scrape or two. Maybe men who were hired because of the scrapes they’ve been in. And you know John Slaughter isn’t the sort to spook at the first sight of lead.”

Tom considers this. “Better throw in another half dozen boxes of shells then.”

Gerald totals up our purchases and while Tom is counting out the money he pauses. “Throw in a couple of apples too would you?”

“Apples?” Gerald says skeptically. “It’s a little early for apples, Tom.”

“You don’t have any? Even some withered ones left over from last year would do.”

“I’ve got a tree out back with some apples on it, but they’re rock hard and sour still.”

“That’ll do fine.”

Gerald gives him an odd look, then shrugs and heads out back to get the apples. Tom turns to me. “They’re for Coyote. He likes apples, doesn’t he?”

Gerald comes back in with two tiny green apples and gives them to Tom. Tom pays up and we leave the store. Coyote looks at Tom suspiciously when he holds out the apples.

"Go on, eat them," Tom says, shaking them under Coyote's nose. Coyote sniffs them but doesn't take them. "Consarn it, horse!" Tom snaps. "Just eat the durned apples already."

Coyote sneezes on Tom's hand.

Tom looks at me, disgusted. "What's wrong with—"

"Watch out!" I say.

Tom jerks his hand back just in time to keep all his fingers and jumps back. Grumbling, he tosses the apples down on the ground and stumps down the street. I follow.

"So much for trying to make amends," he grumbles. "What kind of horse doesn't like apples?"

I look over my shoulder and see Coyote eating the apples off the ground. "He likes apples all right, Tom. He doesn't want to make it too easy for you is all."

We stop into a saloon and Tom orders a couple of kegs of whiskey. Dee-O-Det will never let me hear the end of it if we show up without any whisky. Then we head for the livery to find some mules to tote all the supplies.

"I'm worried," Tom admits later while we're loading everything on the mules. "If Torres is waving the red flag, that could mean real trouble for your clan."

"We'll be okay," I say. "So long as we stay low and stay out of it."

"You might not have a choice."

"The stronghold is well hidden. Not many people know where we are. And if they try to come up there, well, there's a reason my people have used the place for centuries. We can defend it."

"I hope you're right about that," Tom says, but he sounds doubtful.

The truth is, I don't feel nearly as optimistic as I sound. If there's one thing I've learned in my time out in the world it's that trouble has a way of finding a man whether he likes it or not. Suddenly I'm really glad I've decided to go home now. If a revolution really is brewing, my clan is going to need all the help they can get.

11

We head out of town late in the day. Normally we would have stayed overnight in Bisbee, but Gerald's words are weighing heavy on my mind and I want to get to Pa-Gotzin-Kay as fast as I can.

We ride until well after dark and then camp in a wide swale beside a mesquite thicket. Once the mules are unloaded, hobbled, and turned loose to graze, Tom and I build a small fire and cook up some eggs and beans.

"I'm looking forward to seeing your mother again," Tom says, finishing the last of his beans. "It's been too long."

"I know she'll be happy to see you. She speaks highly of you."

"She's some woman, your mother. History won't remember her—a woman in a man's world—but by rights she should go down as one of your greatest chiefs, right up there beside her daddy, Chief Cochise."

That surprises me. I've never heard anyone say that before. "Why do you say that?"

"Because it's true." I must still look puzzled because he says, "You don't know the story, do you?"

"What story?"

"About how your clan escaped and fled to Mexico."

"Sure, I know the story. Every child in the clan hears it growing up."

"Ah, but you don't know the *whole* story."

I settle back against my saddle. "So let's hear it."

"It was almost winter when the army rounded up all the clans on the Chiricahua Apache reservation and began moving them north to the San Carlos reservation."

This part of the story I knew. When my grandfather signed the treaty with General Howard ending the war, my people were given the lands around the Chiricahua mountains as our home forever more. In truth, forever turned out to be only a few years. Then our lands were taken and we were told we were being moved. I was only a baby then.

"Your mother realized that their best chance to escape was during the move. Once they got to the San Carlos reservation it would be too late. The problem was that she couldn't get any of the clan chiefs to listen to her…"

"No," Klan-o-tay said. The old chief was sitting beside a tiny fire of sticks. His hair was white and spilled around his shoulders. A moth-eaten bearskin was wrapped around his shoulders. He looked at her with his rheumy eyes. "We are done. No more fighting."

"I'm not talking about fighting," Nod-Ah-Sti said. The baby in her arms cried out in his sleep and tried to squirm free of her grasp. She stroked his cheek to calm him. Ace was a restless, fussy baby. "We run to the old stronghold and hide. We stay out of sight. Let the world forget about us."

"It's too far," the old chief said. "And winter is coming. Maybe in the spring." He pulled the bearskin tighter around him. The fall night was chilly and there was a sharp edge to the wind.

"That won't work and you know it," she said desperately. Klan-o-tay was making the same objections that the other clan chiefs had made. "By then we'll be too far from Mexico. The soldiers will chase us. We'll never make it."

"They'll chase you now."

"But not right away. There aren't enough of them. Some have to stay and guard the rest of the tribe, keep them from scattering, make sure they make it to San Carlos. They'll have to get reinforcements before they can chase us. That will give us a few days at least. We'll almost be there by then."

"And then what?" he asked her. "How will you raid? The warriors are all gone." It was true. Their tribe numbered several hundred people, but very few of those were warriors. Too many had died in the wars against the white man's armies.

"No raiding," Nod-Ah-Sti said. "Our only chance is to disappear. If we raid, more soldiers will come."

"Then how will you live?"

"We'll hunt and trap what we can. We'll grow crops. I have a small bag of seed corn stashed away, and some beans and potatoes. If we can get a few cows and goats we can raise them as well."

The old chief spat on the ground and gave her a contemptuous look. "Apaches are not farmers. We are warriors."

"Maybe it's time we became farmers," she shot back. "What other choice do we have?"

"We do not scratch the ground like the white man or the Tohono," he said.

"It's better than living as a prisoner in a place we do not belong," she replied.

The air went out of the old man then and he sagged inside his bearskin. "We are nothing. They have taken everything from us."

"Not everything. We still have Pa-Gotzin-Kay. It has sheltered us before."

"Pa-Gotzin-Kay belongs to the past. It will not save you from the Mexican soldiers or the cursed Yaquis. It will be your grave. If you make it there at all."

"So you won't come."

The old man looked down and away. Nod-Ah-Sti knew he would not speak again. She stood abruptly and headed across the camp toward where her clan had built their fires and made their beds. It was late and the tribe was tired from the day's hard walking. Most of the fires had burned down to coals and only a few people were still up, talking in low voices.

There were a handful of soldiers standing guard around the perimeter of the camp, but they had their rifles slung over their shoulders and barely glanced at the young woman carrying the baby. They knew the fight had gone out of the Chiricahua Apaches and they expected no trouble.

The wind gusted then, cutting through Nod-Ah-Sti's coat and ruffling the thin blanket she had Ace wrapped in. She looked up at the thick, dark mass of clouds overhead. They had already swallowed the moon and most of the stars. Only a sliver of clear sky was visible to the east. There was a smell of moisture in the air. In the distance, thunder rumbled. Rain would come this night. Which was why she'd spent the whole evening since they made camp talking to one clan chief after another. The storm would provide the perfect opportunity to slip away. If they missed this chance, they might not get another. Every day they walked took them farther from the Mexican border and increased the chance that reinforcements would come to join the few soldiers who were herding them to the reservation.

She reached the fire where her sister and Dee-O-Det were sitting.

Dee-O-Det squinted at her and grunted. "They said no." It wasn't a question. It was a statement. The old shaman had told her what to expect.

"I thought Nanay at least would go," she replied, sitting down, "but he's given up too." She set Ace in her lap and held her hands out to the fire. "I think they hate the idea of farming more than anything else."

"It is how the men are," her sister said. "They are not practical like we women." She waved a hand like shooing away flies. "We are better off without them."

"You still mean to go," Dee-O-Det said. Again, it was not a question.

"I won't go meekly to San Carlos," Nod-Ah-Sti said with some heat. "It is not our home. We do not belong there. I won't raise my son there."

"You are your father's daughter," Dee-O-Det said. "If only you were his son, perhaps they would listen to you." He rubbed his gnarled old hands together. "Life has gotten too easy for us. We have gotten too fat living off the white man's handouts. It will be good to live by our own hands once again."

The words were said mockingly. The Chiricahua Apaches were far from fat. The rations allocated to them by the government were never quite enough to feed everyone, and that was even when they received the entire shipment. Clum—the agent who stepped in after Tom Jeffords resigned in protest after the government reneged on the treaty—was a greedy, grasping man. He stole half the supplies before the people had a chance at them.

"Live or die, we will be free," Nod-Ah-Sti said to the baby in her arms. "This I promise you."

The storm struck around midnight. Lightning flashed and rain poured from the sky. Those unfortunate soldiers on picket duty huddled in whatever shelter they could find and so it was that none of them saw thirty-eight of their prisoners—mostly women, children and the elderly—rise up from their blankets, slip away into the darkness and disappear.

In the morning the remaining Chiricahua Apaches were rousted and set back on the trail leading north. The captain in charge of the operation was sitting on his horse, trying to light a cigar, when a young corporal hurried up. The corporal saluted and said, "Captain, I think some of the prisoners escaped during the night."

The captain ceased in his efforts to get the balky match to light and turned a hard stare on the young man. "Well, which is it? Did they, or didn't they?"

"What?" the corporal said, not sure what was being said.

"You said 'I think'. I want facts. Did some escape or didn't they?"

The corporal swallowed nervously. "Some escaped."

"How many?"

The corporal winced. "Thirty or so."

The captain thought about this for a moment, then said, "Okay. Carry on."

The corporal blinked at him, confused. "Shall I gather some men and chase them, sir?"

"And leave me here short-handed with hundreds of Apaches on my hands? Are you mad?"

The corporal nodded. "I hadn't thought of that, sir." He started to go, but the captain stopped him.

"Who else knows about this besides you?" he asked the corporal.

"N-nobody. I came straight away to tell you."

"Good. Keep it that way."

"Sir?"

"Don't tell anyone. Do you think I want this going on my record, that I lost thirty old men and women?"

"No, sir. Only…"

"What?"

"Is that a good idea, sir, leaving thirty Apaches loose out here?"

"Nope." The captain finally got the match to light and he puffed on the cigar for a moment before replying. "But I'd be surprised if they survive the winter. They don't have any guns. All their braves are gone. I say this is a good thing. A few less worthless mouths for Uncle Sam to feed."

12

"It was a hard time," Tom says. "They almost starved before they got to Pa-Gotzin-Kay because they were worried the soldiers would catch them so they couldn't stop to forage properly. Not that there's much to eat that time of the year anyway. Your mother told me that they ate whatever they could get their hands on, prickly pear, pine nuts, acorns, even skunk cabbage roots. It got a little better once they got to the stronghold. They had no guns, but they had their belt knives and so they were able to make lances, clubs, traps, bows and arrows. They were able to hunt and trap small game. They built wikiups for shelter. But then the snows came. Most of the game disappeared. Everything was buried under snow. That's when it really got rough."

Tom stares into the fire for a few minutes. When he speaks next it's in a low voice. "If only I'd known. I could have done something…" He clenches his fists and stares helplessly at them.

Then he looks back at me. "It's not glamorous like being a warrior or a war chief, but what your mother did, holding those people together through that first desperate winter…" He shakes his head in wonder. "She's a true hero, Niño. Don't you forget that."

I nod, feeling too choked up for a few moments to speak. "She never told me. She doesn't like to talk about the early days."

"It's not her way to talk about herself, but your clan wouldn't have made it without her. I don't think your clan would have survived with any male chief. It's too ingrained in them, the warrior way, raiding and fighting. And if they'd done that, they would have brought the wrath of the Mexican and probably the American governments down on them sooner or later. You'd have been wiped out or hauled off to a reservation. But she understood that if your people were going to survive, they had to stay out of sight. They had to disappear from the world."

"When I was growing up she often called us the Nameless Ones," I say.

"And the name fits. There's no record of you anywhere. I checked one time with a friend who still works for the government. Your clan is assumed dead."

Something occurs to me that I've never thought of before. "That explains why it always upset her so much when the *Netdahe* warriors showed up in Pa-Gotzin-Kay." *Netdahe* means "death to all intruders." The warriors who took the *Netdahe* oath vowed to fight until they died. "She never turned them away. She always gave them a place to stay and heal and recover, but she was on edge until they left. I was always excited when they came, even when they were led by Golthlay, my uncle."

"The man we know as Geronimo," Tom says grimly.

"The same. I thought they were exciting. I thought they were true Apaches, living free, raiding, fighting. Not scratching the earth to grow potatoes and corn like we were. But now I see that we were the ones who were free." I'm stunned into silence then, struck by the enormity of my blindness. Part of the reason I left Pa-Gotzin-Kay was because I felt suffocated there. I thought we were wasting our lives being farmers, hiding from the world. Now I understand for the first time that it was the only way left for us. I feel very small and stupid.

"To think that one woman got a clan of fierce Apaches to do what the entire might of the US Cavalry couldn't do: give up the warrior life and become farmers." Tom chuckles a little. "Now you see why I admire her so. She's Cochise's daughter in every way."

His chuckle fades away and his seriousness returns. "I'm worried about this revolution. I'm afraid this won't be something the Nameless Ones can hide from. It may be time for the Chiricahua Apaches to become warriors again, and they're going to need you for that."

His words hit me hard. I hadn't considered that. The thought makes me uncomfortable. I don't want anyone counting on me. I like that it's just Coyote and me. Life is simple that way.

"We'll do what we've always done, stay low," I say. "We don't care who rules Mexico. If we don't take sides, they'll leave us alone."

"I wish I could believe that," he replies, "but I know something about this Torres."

"But if we—"

"You don't understand. Torres is hungry for power and he's ruthless. He'll stop at nothing to get what he wants. He'll cheat, backstab, whatever it takes."

"So?"

"Don't you see? It's not that Torres won't believe that your people will stay out of the fight, it's that he *can't* believe it. A man like Torres looks at the world and sees that everyone is like him. They just haven't shown it yet. If he doesn't own you, if he's not sure you're in his pocket, then you're a threat, which means you have to be eliminated. Your clan has done a good job of hiding, but they're not invisible. People know you're up there, which means Torres knows you're up there. Sooner or later he's going to come root you out."

I lie awake for a while that night, thinking about what Tom said. Is my clan really in that much danger from Torres? I wish I could convince myself that Tom doesn't know what he's talking about, but I have a sick feeling he does. And haven't I seen enough proof of the sort of thing he's talking about since I left home?

I don't think I ever realized how good I had it growing up. Sure, we faced danger from bandits and thugs like Mustang Grey and his Scalphunters, but we had each other to count on. We had the security of knowing that there was a whole clan at our backs that we could count on. How many people have I met since leaving home that have that? Most of the people I've met are making it on their own.

13

The next day we cross into Mexico. I leave Tom to handle the mule team and ride ahead to scout our path. With General Torres gearing up for war, a mule train loaded with supplies makes a tempting target. I didn't almost get killed on a ghost ship in the middle of the desert just to let some power-hungry general steal my clan's food.

I find plenty of tracks and when I study them it looks to me like there's a couple different teams of rustlers operating in the area. Strangely, they're not taking the stolen cattle and horses back into the US to sell like they usually do. Instead, they're driving the livestock southeast. What's that way? The General's headquarters maybe?

In the afternoon I rejoin Tom. He's stopped at a watering hole and is letting the livestock drink. I tell him what I found. Tom takes off the new hat I bought him in Bisbee and wipes the sweat from his forehead with the back of his wrist. "Torres is stealing cattle to feed his army."

"What I didn't see was any sign of the Rurales," I say. The Rurales are Mexico's version of the Texas Rangers. They patrol northern Mexico, chasing down the various outlaws that prey on the border region. Just about all of the Rurales are themselves former outlaws, given the choice to join up or be executed when they were caught. Their leader, Colonel Kosterlitzky, is a Russian Cossack who deserted the Russian navy and joined the Mexican army. "I feel strange saying this, but I was hoping to run across them."

Tom gives me a look with raised eyebrows. "I thought you had a little run-in with Colonel Kosterlitzky the last time you were in Mexico. If I remember right, he arrested you."

"He did."

He gives me a wry smile. "Trip getting a little boring for you, is it?"

"No. That's not it. He helped us escape from General de la Cruz because he didn't want de la Cruz getting his hands on the Totec treasure and using it to pay for a revolution."

"And you think he'd help against Torres?"

"I think so."

"If he's still loyal to President Diaz, that is."

"He's still loyal," I say. I don't much like Kosterlitzky, but he struck me as the loyal type.

"If we've heard about Torres' plans, it's a sure bet Kosterlitzky has too." Tom shifts in his saddle. "From what I've heard of Kosterlitzky, he's a smart one. Probably he's keeping his head down and an eye on Torres, reporting it all back to Diaz in Mexico City."

Tom gets down off his horse to refill his canteen. I dismount too and while neither of us is paying attention, Coyote makes his move.

As Tom bends over to fill his canteen, Coyote takes a step forward and bangs into Tom with his shoulder. Tom loses his balance and falls face first into the watering hole.

Tom comes up spluttering and red-faced. "By Gawd, I've half a mind to shoot that horse!" he hollers.

I feel bad for Tom. I really do. But it's a couple of minutes before I can tell him that, on account of I'm laughing so hard I can't speak. Coyote stands there with an innocent look on his face the whole time.

"I gave you apples," Tom says, shaking his fist at Coyote. He splashes his way out of the watering hole, sits down and empties water out of his boots.

"Don't take it personally," I say, squatting down beside him.

"How else am I supposed to take it?"

"Coyote does that sort of thing to me all the time. It means he's warming up to you. Keep trying."

He gives me a look like he thinks I'm pulling his leg. "He does stuff like that to you?"

I nod. "Whenever he gets a chance."

"How do you put up with it? I'd've sold that horse to the first person I could find with a dollar."

"He makes up for it in other ways," I say, thinking of all the times Coyote has bailed me out of tough spots. "The thing is, I don't think Coyote knows how to be friendly. This is the best he's got."

Tom grunts and pulls his boots back on.

"Look at it this way. He didn't bite you and he didn't kick you. All he did was have a little fun with you. I think if you keep trying, he'll come around."

Tom mutters something under his breath I can't quite catch and hauls himself to his feet. He gives Coyote a wide berth on the way to get back on his horse.

We make camp that night in a narrow box canyon with a seep in the bottom feeding a couple of big cottonwood trees. After we're done eating, Tom gets out a couple pieces of the horehound candy and walks over to Coyote, who's grazing underneath one of the trees.

"No hard feelings, okay?" Tom says, holding out the candy.

Coyote's ears perk up. He doesn't mess around this time but goes right after the candies and crunches them loudly.

"Well, that's better," Tom says. His hand lifts as he considers patting Coyote on the neck, then thinks better of it. Smart move. Coyote barely lets me touch him.

Tom rolls out his bedroll and then comes to sit by the fire with me. He rolls a cigarette and lights it. "Is that old rascal, Dee-O-Det, still alive?" he asks.

"When I was there last year he was."

"He has to be better than a hundred years old now," Tom says. "I wonder what his secret is."

"He's crazy."

"Hell, Niño, that's no secret. Everybody knows that. I reckon you have to be crazy to be a medicine man, don't you?"

"It helps."

Tom asks me about a few other people from my clan. We sit in silence for a bit. I stand up and pick up my rifle. "I'll take first watch."

"I guess it's time to hit the sack," Tom says, standing and stretching. He heads over to his bedroll and that's when I hear him start swearing.

"What is it?"

He points at the ground by his bedroll. "That damn horse about crapped on my bed!" he squawks.

I walk over to look. Sure enough, there's a fresh pile of road apples right by his bedroll. It had to have been Coyote. All the others are hobbled. Only Coyote is roaming free.

"I told you Coyote is starting to like you," I say.

He glares at me. "You can see the horse shit, can't you?"

"Tom," I say, "if Coyote didn't like you, he would have crapped *on* your bedroll."

14

The next day I scout on ahead again. Before we left Bisbee, Tom bought a pair of Army surplus binoculars and I use them to scan the terrain ahead and on both sides. I don't see anyone but a solitary prospector with his donkey the whole day, but I do find plenty of tracks. The ones that concern me the most I find late in the afternoon.

By then we're into the foothills of the Sierra Madres, the big peaks looming in the distance. The tracks are of a half dozen unshod horses. I follow the tracks and find where they camped. The camp is fresh. Whoever used it was here last night. I climb down off Coyote for a closer look. It only takes me a minute to realize it's a Yaqui camp and that has me worried. What are Yaqui braves doing here? We're close enough to Pa-Gotzin-Kay that this is nominally my clan's hunting grounds. The Yaquis wouldn't come here unless they were looking for trouble, just like my people wouldn't go into their lands unless we were looking for trouble.

I climb back on Coyote, meaning to go back and tell Tom what I found, when up ahead to the south I see buzzards circling.

Normally buzzards don't mean anything. There's pretty much always one or two circling around in the desert sky. But there's a dozen of them at least and some are low down, close to landing. That means there's something dead up ahead. Dead or dying. The buzzards don't always wait. They're known to help themselves to some choice bits once whatever it is stops thrashing around too much.

And for there to be that many, whatever it is has to be large. A rabbit wouldn't draw more than one or two. It has to be a horse or a cow or a deer.

Or a man.

Suddenly, I've got a sick feeling in my gut. That could be one of my people lying up there, ambushed by the Yaquis.

My first instinct is to go and see for sure, but I realize right away that would be foolish. Those Yaquis might still be hanging around. They might be waiting to see who gets drawn in by the buzzards and comes to check it out.

I ride hard back to the mule train. I skid to a halt by Tom. He can see the bad news on my face.

"I saw the buzzards. Is there a body?" he asks.

"I don't know. I haven't checked yet. I found tracks of a Yaqui war party."

Tom doesn't ask any questions, just hops down and starts hobbling the mules in a palo verde thicket. I help and in a few minutes we're riding south. We both unlimber our rifles and check our loads.

When we get to where the buzzards are circling it's near sunset. The buzzards appear to be centered over a dry wash that cuts through the desert hardpan. We split up to come at the spot from two different directions.

Floods have cut the bed of the wash deep into the desert soil. The edges are badly eroded, steep and crumbly. Growing near the edge of the wash is a large ironwood tree. Two buzzards are perched in the tree, watching something on the ground.

Once more I scan the surrounding terrain, looking for movement, a glint of sunlight on metal. There's not a lot of cover here. The desert is pretty barren. Almost all the bushes and trees are growing down in the wash. I look at Coyote to see if he's heard or smelled anything. If there's another horse nearby, he'll know about it. But his ears are forward and he's looking toward the spot where the buzzards are. That means it's probably clear.

I get down off Coyote and creep closer on foot, my Winchester in both hands. The whole way I've got my head on a swivel, watching the bushes, checking the edge of the wash. I'm not walking into an ambush if I can help it.

Still no sign of movement. On the far side of the wash is a big cholla cactus that's fallen over. I see the faintest glint of red through its limbs and know that Tom's hunkered down there, covering my approach with that big Henry rifle he favors. That makes me feel a little better.

I get up close and peer over the edge of the wash, careful not to collapse it. There's a man lying on his face in the sand. I'm relieved to see that he's not Apache. His hat is lying on the sand nearby and there's a pistol by one out-flung hand. There's blood on his back over the right shoulder blade.

I drop down into the wash and scan up and down it. Still no sign of anyone. I walk closer and see the exit wound in his armpit. I put my finger on the big vein in his neck. His pulse is weak, but it's there.

"He's still alive!" I call to Tom.

Tom comes huffing up a minute later. By then I've turned the man over. He's a big man, bearded, with black hair quickly turning to gray. His nose is crooked from being broken too many times. He's wearing a leather vest and leather chaps on his legs, the kind cowboys use for protecting themselves from thorns when riding through heavy brush. Large-roweled Mexican spurs are on his boots. From the look of him he's a cowboy. The little finger is missing on his right hand, which isn't that uncommon among cowboys. Rope enough wild steers and sooner or later a man is bound to get careless while taking the dallies on the saddle horn. When a finger gets caught between the rope and the saddle horn, with eight hundred pounds of red-eyed beef on the other end, well, it just comes right off.

Tom crouches down and takes a look at the man. Right off he says, "I know this man. This here's Buck Green. He owns the Lazy R ranch."

"No ranchers run their cattle this close to Pa-Gotzin-Kay. What's he doing here?"

"I don't know. Give me a hand and let's patch him up." Tom cuts the man's shirt off and splashes water on the wound. "Missed his lung," he says. "Looks like it went through clean." Blood is still leaking from both wounds. "I don't know why he's still alive, but he won't be for much longer if we don't stop the bleeding." He looks at me. "Think you can find a bee hive around here?"

I know immediately what he's saying. It's a remedy we Apaches have used for generations. Pack wild honey into the wound and it stops the bleeding. The honey helps keep out infection too.

I hustle off. I get lucky and find a hive in a gnarled mesquite tree. I get stung robbing it, but not too many times, all things considered. I bring back a good amount of honeycomb and we pack both wounds tight, then cut the man's shirt into strips and bandage him up good and tight.

About that time Buck starts coming to. He moans and his eyelids flutter open. The first thing he sees is me and his eyes go wide. An oath breaks from his lips and he grabs iron.

Only his gun isn't in his holster. It's still lying in the sand a few paces away.

I pick it up and check the cylinder. Every round is spent. I hand him the gun back. He tries to point it at me, but he can't quite hold it up.

"Easy there, Buck," Tom says, pushing the gun down. "Ace is with me."

Buck turns his head and his eyes gradually focus on Tom. "Where the hell did you come from, Jeffords?" He coughs. "Bad time to be taking up ranching in Mexico."

"I don't know about that. Looks like it's working out all right for you."

Buck coughs again and groans with pain. His hand goes to the wound under his arm and he winces. "Goddammit, Tom. This is no time to be making a man laugh. Can't you see I've got a little scrape here?"

"A little scrape, eh?" Tom asks, raising one eyebrow. "Hang on, I've got just the thing for scrapes."

He goes over to his horse, rummages through the saddlebags and returns with a bottle of whiskey. "Have a draw off this," he says. He props Buck up against the side of the wash, pulls the cork and hands the bottle to Buck. "It'll set you right up."

Buck takes a drink, coughs and spits, then takes another drink. This one goes down. "Obliged," he says, handing the bottle back. His gaze turns back to me.

"You got some explaining to do, Apache," he growls.

"Now, Buck, I already told you," Tom says. "Ace here is with me. He's the one who found you and helped me patch you up. We just got into the country yesterday. He's got nothing to do with whatever is going on."

While they were talking I had a minute to look around and read what the tracks have to tell me. I swing back to Buck. "You were tracking stolen cattle."

Buck nods. "Damned Apaches bushwhacked me when I got down to piss," he growls. "I tried to fight back, but I don't reckon I shot any of 'em."

"It wasn't Apaches who shot you. It was Yaquis."

His eyes narrow. "You said you just got into the country. How do you know who shot me?"

I cross my arms and give him a hard look. "Because my people don't ambush men for no reason."

He snorts. "Spoken liked a goddammed bushwhacking Apache."

"Maybe I should have let you bleed out," I say.

"Give me a second to load my gun and we'll see how you do facing me man-to-man. Or do you Apaches only know how to shoot people in the back?"

Before I can retort, Tom cuts in. "Both of you, shut the hell up!"

"This don't concern you, Tom," Buck says. "It's between me and this savage." He starts trying to thumb shells into his pistol but he's too weak from blood loss and he keeps dropping the shells in the sand.

"I say we leave him here, Tom. Let him find his own way home."

"We're not doing any such thing, Ace. We're getting Buck back to his people. Buck, stop trying to load your gun. You're not shooting Ace." Tom leans over and snatches Buck's pistol away from him.

Buck glares at him. "I don't need a gun to kill an Apache anyway," he rasps. "Give me a second to catch my breath and I'll settle his hash with my own two hands."

"Now you're being a crotchety old fool, Buck," Tom snaps. "Stop flapping your gums for a second and listen to what I'm telling you. Ace had no part of this. Neither did his people. I know them and they wouldn't do this."

"I heard you was an Indian lover, Tom, but I never reckoned it to be this bad," Buck growls. "What, did you up and take one of their squaws as your wife? Is that it?"

Tom looks at me and sighs. Then he looks back at Buck. "You are sorely trying me, Buck, you know that?"

"Go on with you, then," Buck growls. "I don't need your help, either of you." He starts trying to stand up.

Gently but firmly Tom pushes him back down on the sand. "We only just got the bleeding to stop. You're going to start it up again."

Buck looks down at his bare chest. "What is this? What did you use?" He dabs his finger in the stuff leaking out from under the bandage and licks it. "What the hell. It's honey."

"That it is," Tom says.

"You put honey on me." Buck seems genuinely confused by this. He doesn't even seem that angry anymore, as if there's not room for confusion and anger at the same time in his head.

"It's an old Apache remedy," Tom says.

Buck looks down at the wound again. "Seems to be working."

"Are you going to listen to me now?" Tom asks him.

Buck gives him a baleful look, but keeps his mouth shut.

"Here's what I think happened," Tom says. "You American ranchers are tight with President Diaz, right?"

"Mostly Slaughter is, but yeah," Buck grunts.

"That makes you a threat to General Torres' revolution." He gestures at me. "Same as the Apaches are."

"Damned Apaches are a threat to everyone," Buck grumbles. I find myself wishing he wasn't injured so badly. I'd like to take a poke at him.

"Sure, Torres could take you both out, but doing so will cost him men and time and he can't spare either. He needs to be focused on Diaz."

"He wrassles with us, he's going to find he caught hold of the wrong end of the lion," Buck mutters. "We've been preparing for him."

"And Torres is smart enough to know that. Which is where the Yaquis come in," Tom says. "The way I see it, he hired them to steal your cattle and drive them into Apache lands, knowing you'd follow. Then they shoot you down. The ranchers naturally think it was the Apaches who did it and they go on the warpath. The ranchers and the Apaches tear each other apart and the only winner is Torres."

His words make a lot of sense. They get me to thinking. I can see they're having the same effect on Buck. He's got a thoughtful look on his face.

"Could be," he allows after a bit. "I wouldn't put anything past that snake Torres. Only one problem. The Yaquis are as bad as the Apaches and they got plenty of reasons to hate Torres. I don't see them working for him. There ain't enough gold in Mexico."

"What if Torres offered them something they want more than gold?" Tom asks.

Buck chews this over too, then nods slightly. "He could give them their lands back."

Like us, the Yaquis have also fled into the Sierra Madre mountains. But their traditional lands were down along the banks of the Rio Yaqui.

"So maybe instead of fighting each other, you two could start working on figuring out how to fight together. It seems to me the only chance you've got."

Neither Buck nor I say anything for a few minutes while we think about it. There's not much thinking to do, really. I don't like the idea, but Tom makes sense. Torres is the real enemy here.

I stick out my hand.

Buck looks at it and shakes his head. "Not so fast, Apache. It don't go that easy." He looks at Tom. "You might have something there, Jeffords. I'll talk to the other ranchers and see what they say." He tries again to get up and fails.

"First I reckon I need some help getting home," he grumbles.

15

I go get the mules and when I get back Tom has a fire going. He stands up and puts his hat on.

"The way I see it, if we try to haul Buck on back to his place on a mule, he'll die. We need a wagon. I'll head on over to the Lazy R ranch and fetch one. You stay here and keep an eye on Buck." He climbs on his horse.

"Hold on there," Buck and I both say at the same time.

"You're not leaving me here with *him* are you, Tom?" Buck asks.

"Sure I am," Tom replies with a wry grin. "It'll give you two time to get to know each other."

"I'll go," I say. "I don't need to know him any better than I already do." We may be allies now—sort of—but I'm afraid if Tom leaves me here with Buck I'll shoot him.

"I don't need no Apache wet nurse," Buck growls.

Tom gives me a look like I turned out to be a whole lot dumber than he thought. "Have you given any thought to how the cowboys at the ranch might react when an Apache comes riding up out of the dark telling them the boss has been shot and they should go with you to pick him up?"

The truth is I hadn't thought about that.

"How many holes do you think they'll put in you, Ace?"

"Okay, okay," I grumble.

Tom stands there for a few seconds, looking from one of us to the other.

"What're you waiting on, Jeffords?" Buck says. "The sooner you leave, the sooner I get out of here."

"You two aren't planning on shooting each other as soon as I'm gone, are you?" Tom asks, still with that odd grin on his bearded face.

"I'm thinking about shooting *you*," Buck says. "I don't like the look on your face."

"You're an ornery old cuss, aren't you?" Tom says to him.

Buck shrugs. "I've been called worse." He waves Tom away. "Now go on, skedaddle."

Once Tom is gone I rummage around in our stores and get out some beans that I put on the fire to cook. Then I get out the coffeepot and put it on. I can feel Buck looking at me. I try to ignore him.

"You put some in there for me?" he asks.

I glance over at him. "Yeah, I put some in for you."

When it's done I fill him a cup and hand it to him. He takes a drink, spits out some grounds and grunts. "I didn't know Injuns drank coffee."

"It's about the only good thing the white man brought with him," I reply.

"How about those guns you're wearing?"

"Before you came along we didn't need them."

Buck finishes his coffee and tosses the cup on the sand. "Can't believe I let an Injun sneak up and shoot me like that."

"I can't believe that Yaqui wasn't a better shot. If it was an Apache who shot at you, you'd be dead now."

"No one's killing me with only one shot," he says. He thumps himself on the chest. "Tough as old boot leather." He coughs a little and spits.

Buck shifts to a more comfortable position and takes a drink from the whiskey that Tom gave him. He doesn't offer any to me. I don't want any anyway. I want my wits about me. I noticed that his gun is back in his holster and there's some empty slots on his gun belt. He probably reloaded while I was getting the mules. If he tries to draw on me, I *will* shoot him.

I have a feeling I might shoot him anyway.

"Your people ain't the secret you think you are," Buck says. "We've known for some time there was a nest of you up there in the mountains. Just never got around to cleaning you out."

"Why?" I ask him, angered by his casual talk of killing off my clan, like we were ants getting into the flour or something. "Why would you do that? We never harmed you. We never so much as stole a steer from you."

"Only a matter of time," he says belligerently. "Once a thieving, murdering savage, always a thieving, murdering savage."

That gets my hackles up. I throw the dregs of my coffee on the fire and stand up. "It seems to me you just called me a murderer and a thief," I say, my voice low and dangerous. I twitch my duster back a bit so I can get at my Colts. "Is that what I heard?"

His eyes narrow and he licks his lips. "You planning on gunning me down, boy?"

"I think that's up to you."

"Huh." His eyes stare into mine. They're hard and nearly gray. Deliberately, he says, "You're a murderer and a thief. It's in your blood."

"You don't know a damn thing about us."

"The hell I don't," he says in a low, dangerous voice. "I know everything I need to know about Apaches."

"You sure about that?" I ask him. My hand feels itchy, I want to grab my gun so bad.

Still glaring at me, he says, "For thirty years I been sure. Ever since the day I rode out to check on my cows on the spread I owned up by Camp Verde. I rode back at the end of the day to find my wife and baby girl dead, my home burned." He bares his teeth. "By filthy, murdering Apaches."

That rocks me back on my heels. I want to argue with him, tell him it wasn't my people who did that, that Camp Verde is a long way from the Chiricahua Apache range. I want to tell him that not all Apaches are like the ones who killed his family, if it even was Apaches and not some other tribe.

But I don't.

What difference does any of that make anyway? When the people you love are dead, what are words but empty sounds? What argument holds any water?

Then, almost without my knowing, two words do pop out.

"I'm sorry."

Something strange passes over his face when I say that. The skin under his eye twitches. His mouth opens and closes. A half dozen emotions flash through his eyes too fast to see.

In a quiet voice he says, "I came to Mexico to get away from Apaches. Now it looks like I got to fight beside one. So be it. But only until Torres is done for. Anything after that is fair game, you hear me?"

I nod.

He leans back against the side of the wash and closes his eyes. He doesn't open them again.

16

The next morning Tom shows up with a couple of hands from the Lazy R ranch. They don't have a wagon. Instead, they've rigged a litter to carry Buck between a couple of mules. He cusses when he sees it and starts hollering that he won't be carried around like a child, but when he tries to stand up he falls over. The hands, a couple of sallow-faced young men who look enough alike that they could be brothers, help him to his feet. From the look on their faces, I'd say they're used to hearing their boss bluster.

"I ain't getting on that damned litter. Tie me to the saddle if you have to," Buck snaps. "The only way I'm getting on that thing is if I'm dead."

That sounds like a good idea to me, but when I open my mouth Tom grabs my arm and shakes his head.

"I know what you were going to say," he mutters. "Don't."

"Easy for you to be so calm. You didn't have to listen to him like I did." But I know he's right so I keep my opinions to myself.

"I ain't riding one of those cursed mules, either," Buck says. He turns to one of the hands. "I'm riding your horse. You ride one of the mules."

The young man's face closes up a little when he says that—most cowboys wouldn't sit on a mule even if it meant walking ten miles after a cougar chewed their leg off—but he knows better than to argue with his boss and he goes and gets his horse.

Buck growls at the hands when they try to help him on his horse, but no matter how he tries he can't climb on by himself. Which for some reason he makes to be their fault. His face gets all red and he cusses them up one side and down the other. I get the feeling I'm not the only one here who'd like to shoot the man.

Finally, Buck is in the saddle. There's some more blood showing on his bandages and he's swaying a bit, but he's just as cantankerous as ever.

"You'll talk to the other ranchers, right?" Tom asks him.

"I said I'll talk to them and I will," Buck grouses. "But it ain't gonna be today. It'll take time and that's all there is to it." He looks at me. "We'll be keeping an eye on you, Apache. You better hope nothing else suspicious happens."

I open my mouth to tell Buck what I think of his accusations, but once again Tom is ahead of me. He steps in front of me and says, "Everything will be fine, Buck. You have my word on that."

"What the hell good does—" Buck starts, but Tom cuts him off.

"Are you calling out my word, Buck?" he says firmly. There's a hard edge in his voice I haven't heard there before. The calm, easygoing Tom is gone, replaced by someone a good deal harder. Someone you don't want to get crossways of. "Is that what you're doing?"

Buck gives him a gimlet eye, but then shakes his head. "Naw, Tom. I know your word's good."

"Heal up and we'll talk soon," Tom says, his normal voice back.

Buck is still growling like a bear with a sore tooth as he rides away, but now it's directed at his hands and not us. I look at Tom once he's gone.

"Next time I go get help. Even if it means getting shot."

Tom winces. "I take it things didn't get any better after I left."

"Nope. I found out why he hates Apaches so much though."

"He told you about his wife and child."

"He did."

"You have a bit of an idea what it's like walking in his boots then."

"Enough to keep me from shooting him," I say. "Not enough to like him."

"That's good enough for right now," Tom says. "Deal with Torres first, then you two can go all cats and dogs on each other. Keep your eye on what's important, Ace. Put the personal stuff aside."

Tom and I strike camp and head out soon after. I chew over Tom's advice as we ride. I don't like it, but I can see the wisdom of it. If it was just me, maybe I'd brace Buck anyway and the hell with the outcome. But it's bigger than me now. I have to think about my clan and how what I do affects them.

By midafternoon we're well up into the Sierra Madre mountains and I can see the ledge where Pa-Gotzin-Kay is. The sight of it causes an unexpected pang of homesickness in my gut. It feels good to be going home. I think of my mother and Dee-O-Det.

I think of Chee and Hi-okee, my two best friends growing up. My last time through I was gone so fast I hardly had a chance to talk to any of them. I find I'm really looking forward to seeing them.

The stronghold is on a long shelf about a thousand feet up on the side of the mountains. The shelf is about a mile wide and three or four miles long. It overlooks the wickedly steep Nacozari Canyon. Behind it rises the vast bulk of the mountains themselves.

It's virtually impossible to come at Pa-Gotzin-Kay from the rear. That way lies a lot of miles over incredibly rugged terrain that would trouble even a mountain goat. There are really only two ways into Pa-Gotzin-Kay. On each end of the shelf there's a narrow canyon that feeds down into the Nacozari. Those side canyons are narrow, steep, and covered with loose rock. The trails leading up them wind in and out through jutting stone buttes. There's places where the trails are so narrow a loaded mule can barely get through.

That's why Pa-Gotzin-Kay is such a natural fortress. It's hard to make it up those steep trails on a good day. With people up top shooting down at you it's nearly impossible.

Tom rides up beside me and peers up at the mountainside. "Now I remember why I don't come visit more often," he says. "One of these times my horse is going to slip and we'll bounce all the way to the bottom. That'll be the end of me. People will say, that's what old Tom gets for messing about with Apaches." He smiles to let me know he's only joking.

"I hope it's not today," I say. "If I bring you this far and you don't survive to say hello to my mother, she'll never let me hear the end of it."

"I'll do my best," he promises me.

We start up the trail, me in the lead, Tom bringing up the rear. I need to be in the lead because there's sentries posted along this trail. Could be the one posted here today is too young to remember Tom. I don't want anyone getting excited and shooting my friend. That will put a damper on the day for sure.

Halfway up the trail curls around a butte about thirty feet tall. I know there's bound to be a sentry on top of it so I give a coyote howl, which is the signal we use. Coyote lays his ears back when I howl. For some reason it always angers him when I do that.

"You want them shooting at us?" I say, patting him on the neck. Coyote shakes his head irritably and snorts. He always has to get the last word in.

Someone stands up on top of the butte and calls out. "Ace? Is that really you?"

It's Hi-okee. I feel myself smiling.

"Of course it's me," I call back. "Did you go blind while I was gone?"

"I wasn't sure. From the way you're dressed, I thought it was a *Pinda-Lick-O-Ye*." It means white eyes.

He climbs down and trots over to me. He glances at Coyote, but says nothing. I think Coyote bit him last time I was here. He probably remembers that.

"It *is* you," he says, a smile creasing his face. He looks like I remember him. He's wearing buckskin *kabuns*, which are knee-high moccasins, and a patched cotton shirt. A neckerchief is tied around his head. His hair is in two long braids and there's a feather tied in one braid. "It's good to see you. It's been too long."

"It has," I agree. I'm still staring at the feather. "You're wearing a raven feather in your hair," I say.

"Nothing gets by you, Ace," he replies, still grinning.

"A *raven* feather?" I know I'm repeating myself, but I can't help it.

"You're not going to start in on me too, are you?" he asks, his smile fading somewhat. "Dee-O-Det is always after me about it."

"That sounds like Dee-O-Det," I say.

"It's always 'Ravens are bad medicine.' Or, 'You don't want Raven looking your way, do you?' It gets old," Hi-okee says. "He's living in the past. But you, you've been out in the world. You don't believe his mumbo jumbo anymore do you?"

I'm thinking about what happened to the Apache Kid when he jumped off the side of Canyon de Chelly. I'm thinking about the vision I had in prison. I'm not sure what I believe anymore. "I don't know," I reply. "You surprised me is all."

Hi-okee's smile comes right back. That's the thing about Hi-okee. He's almost always cheerful. Nothing ever seems to get him down for long. I'd forgotten how much I missed that about him.

"Your mother will be happy to see you," he says. "Everyone will be."

"Everyone?" I say. Before I left, I clashed with the clan elders several times. I was frustrated by how tightly they clung to the old ways. I also got in more than a few fights with young men closer to my age. Noses were broken. Teeth might have gotten lost. I was angry a lot back then.

"Most everyone," he says. "What's with the mules?"

"Supplies."

His eyes widen. "The white man's world has been treating you well I see."

He has no idea. "It's been up and down," I say. "I'll tell you more later." Probably not all of it, though.

Hi-okee peers down the trail. "Who's the old man with you?"

"It's Tom Jeffords."

His face lights up. "Taglito?" he says. That's our nickname for Tom. "Your mother will be *really* happy to see him."

That sounds to me like she'll be happier to see Tom than her own son, but I keep that thought to myself. It sounds childish even to me in my own thoughts.

Hi-okee runs on ahead of us to tell the clan that we're coming. He can make better time on this trail than a horse can. He leaves us behind in no time.

17

Word spreads fast and when we ride into the *rancheria*—the loose collection of wikiups clustered around the communal kiva—everyone is out waiting for us. A number call greetings to me and I see a few smiles, but mostly all they can see are the mules. They swarm around the animals and start immediately unloading them. The men admire the carbines, the women exclaim over the bolts of cloth, and the children have big eyes for the candy. I'm thinking I bought at least a little popularity right there.

I look around and see Dee-O-Det standing off to one side, watching me. The old shaman looks the same as ever, which is to say like a piece of rawhide left out in the sun for a hundred years or so. He's wearing a baggy old calico shirt that hangs down past his knees and buckskin leggings. A wide leather band is wrapped around his head. There's a withered crow foot sticking out of it.

I ride over to him and dismount. He doesn't say anything, only stares at me. His stare is somewhat unnerving. He's looking at my chest and his eyes are unfocused. I have the odd feeling that he is looking inside me.

I figure there's no point in pleasantries with the old shaman. I might as well get right to the point.

"Danger is coming," I tell him.

"I know," he says, tilting his head to the side, still staring at my chest, as if he can see something from that angle that he can't see otherwise. "That's why I called you home."

"You didn't call me home. It was my decision."

"Are you sure?" he asks, raising his eyes to mine and blinking rapidly. "Then how is it you are here?"

"Sometimes things just happen."

"Is that really what you believe?" he asks. "After all that has happened to you, still you question?"

"What do you know about what's happened to me?" I say. I try to sound skeptical, but I don't really manage it. I wouldn't be surprised if he knew everything.

"The spirits have a use for you. It would be better if you didn't fight them."

"That's nonsense. No spirits are trying to use me."

He smiles hugely and pats me on the arm. "Tell yourself whatever you must if it frightens you that much."

"It doesn't frighten me," I insist. Why am I starting to feel like a little kid again? How come I always let him draw me into arguments like this? "I'm not afraid."

"No, of course not. Not the bold, dashing Ace Lone Wolf with his blazing pistols of fire." Dee-O-Det mimes drawing two guns and firing them, all the while still grinning widely.

"Why do you always do that?" I ask him.

He bobs his head. "A shaman's role is to guide his chief."

The words almost hurt. I get a sense of walls closing in. "I'm not your chief. I'm not anybody's chief."

His eyes grow very large. "Are you sure?"

"I've never wanted to be chief!" I snap, aware that I'm close to yelling but somehow can't do anything about it. "I ride my own trail and no one else's."

"And that's why you're here when we most need you." He pats me on the arm again, like I'm a child who got overexcited and can't calm down.

"Why do I even talk to you?" I mutter and turn away.

"Your mother is waiting for you at her wikiup," he calls after me. "Do you remember where it is still?"

"It's good to see you too," I tell him over my shoulder. I pull the saddle off Coyote and give him a rub down, then turn him loose.

I walk over to Mother's wikiup. She's waiting for me outside. She looks a little older, a little more gray in her long, black hair, but otherwise she looks much the same. She's wearing a gingham dress belted around the waist with a wide, embroidered leather belt. She pulls me into a long hug. I can feel her heart beating.

She releases me from the hug, but keeps a hold of me, as if to make sure I won't float away. "How did it go?" she asks.

I know she's asking how it went with Victoria. She and Blake and I came through here while searching for the temple of Totec.

"Let's say it didn't end very well." Which is an understatement.

Her lips twitch in a little smile and she inclines her head. "As I knew she would."

"What? Really? You already knew? How?"

She smiles again. Her smile is calm and gentle. "A woman can see these things in another woman. If she pays attention. I pay attention."

"Why didn't you tell me?" I feel pretty upset about this. What mother lets her son get cheated without warning him?

She raises one eyebrow. "Would you have listened if I did? You were very set on her. You could see nothing else when you were here."

"I might have listened." I sound sullen, mostly because I know she's right.

She touches my cheek. "It is not my place to interfere with your path, Ace. How am I to know the things you need to learn? Why would I seek to take them from you?"

"Sometimes you sound like Dee-O-Det," I grumble.

"Dee-O-Det has advised me for many years."

"Did he tell you I was coming?"

"Some days ago. We were going to make another trip to Sasabe to buy supplies, but we canceled it because he said you would bring us what we need."

"Come on. You don't expect me to believe he really said that."

"It's the truth."

"Then it was a lucky guess."

"Poor Ace," she says. "Still not sure what you believe."

How come none of this is going like I imagined it would? "Taglito is here."

"I know," she says, and smiles again.

That's when I realize her dress looks almost new and that she's wearing her fancy moccasins with the beads sewn on them. There is a tiny bit of color around her eyes too. Noticing this makes me feel uncomfortable.

Tom comes walking up then. He's got a huge smile on his face. His hair and beard are wet, so he probably just dunked his head in the horse trough.

"Taglito," my mother says, her eyes lighting up.

"Niome," he says. No one calls her that but Taglito.

She hurries toward him. They take each other's hands and then stand there, staring at each other without speaking. I start to feel even more uncomfortable and wonder if I should go.

About the time I can't take it anymore, they release each other and step back. "A steer is cooking over the fire," my mother says. "There are beans and onions and if you have brought flour there will be bread."

"We've got mountains of flour," Tom says, still grinning through his thick beard.

18

As the sun goes down, the party starts. Some rough plank tables are set out and a couple of big pots of beans and potatoes are set on them, along with slabs of beef on wooden serving trays. At the end of one table one of the kegs of whiskey is broached.

I'm sitting down with a plate of food when I hear someone say, "Welcome home, my friend."

It's Chee. I stand up, a big smile on my face. I'm so happy to see him. "I was wondering where you were," I say.

"There were potatoes that needed watering. I didn't want them to wait until tomorrow."

That explains why he looks like he just came from working. Chee is shorter than me, a quiet, soft-spoken young man, fine-boned with gentle, expressive eyes. He looks me up and down and smiles.

"You've done well."

"Uh…sometimes," I say. I look down at myself. I bought all new clothes and a new hat and boots in Bisbee. I wonder now at it. Did I do it so when I got here people would think I was a success in the world? "It's a little more complicated than that," I add.

"I knew you would do well," he says in his soft voice, sitting down on the bench. I sit down again.

"It's funny you should say that. There's been times that I've wondered if I made a mistake by leaving."

He shrugs. The motion says a great deal. It says what is in the past is past and therefore not to be worried about. It says that things happen outside our control and all we can do is ride with it. It's part of what I always loved about my old friend. He's calm and steady no matter what happens. Nothing rocks him.

"You're here now. That's what counts," he says.

"It feels good to be back," I say. And it's true. I look around. A handful of the younger men are gathered around the whiskey keg, laughing and talking. Women move through the group, bringing more food from the cook fires to the tables. Elderly people sit together at one of the tables, eating and talking amongst themselves. Children run laughing through the crowd. These are my people. I belong here. Here I don't have to hide who I am or wonder how people will treat me.

Why did I ever leave?

The food is finished and we begin working on the whiskey keg in earnest. As usual, Dee-O-Det drinks more than anyone else. But, also as usual, it doesn't seem to really affect him. Or maybe it's that he's so crazy all the time that the temporary craziness brought on by the whiskey doesn't change him all that much. Later on, a couple of people bring out drums and Dee-O-Det disappears back to his wikiup.

When he walks back into the firelight, he's wearing his long medicine man robe, a tanned elk hide dyed black and covered in feathers and beads. His face is painted and his long white hair hangs loose around his shoulders. Everyone stops talking and we all move into a big circle around him. We all know Dee-O-Det is going to dance and when he dances, it's something to see.

At first he stands perfectly still, his head down, his body rigid. Slowly he raises his arms over his head, raising the elk-skin robe as he does so. The robe looks like the wings of a giant bird. Suddenly his head snaps up. His eyes are wild and they seem almost to glow.

He starts to turn in circles. The robe flares out around him. As he spins, his feet move in a complex series of steps and his arms fly up and down, causing the robe to undulate. He's moving so fast he's almost a blur. I begin to feel dizzy watching him. Everyone is staring at him silently, as if mesmerized. Even the small children are still.

Somehow, unbelievably, he begins to move even faster. He seems taller now. I can't tell if his feet are still on the ground or if he's floating in the air. The elk-hide robe looks like the wings of a giant raven. I'm having trouble standing up. There's an intense pressure building inside my head.

He throws his head back and howls at the night sky. The sound is sort of an unholy cross between a coyote and a cougar and it's unbelievably loud. The howl goes on and on. A massive shiver passes over my whole body and I go to one knee, the pressure inside my head now unbearable.

As suddenly as it started, the howl ends. Dee-O-Det slows and comes to a halt. The pressure inside my head disappears and I'm left blinking, wondering what happened.

Hi-okee grabs one arm and Chee grabs the other and they haul me to my feet.

"Too much whiskey?" Chee asks, concern on his face.

"Not enough!" Hi-okee yells and sloshes some of the whiskey in his cup into mine.

They're still talking, but I'm not listening. I'm looking at Dee-O-Det. He's standing perfectly still, hunched inside the robe. He's invisible in that darkness except for his face which seems oddly pale. He's staring at me with burning eyes.

Then people move between us and the moment passes. I rub my eyes and drink the whiskey in my cup.

The three of us walk over to the keg. Hi-okee is talking as we go. "Remember the time we caught that skunk and threw him into the communal kiva while the council was meeting?" He laughs loudly. "They came running out of there like they were on fire. I never saw old Guyan move so fast in my life!"

"I remember spending the rest of the summer weeding in the fields every day," Chee says, grimacing. "My mother was so angry."

At the keg the clan's other young men cluster around us, their eyes bright from the whiskey and Dee-O-Det's dance. Alchise, Boa Juan, Kersus, Deya, Chatto. They admire my guns and the new shirt with the shiny silver buttons.

"Are you a gunfighter now?" Boa Juan asks. He's round-faced with soft eyes and long lashes that make him look like a pushover. Which he's not. Boa Juan is one of the best fighters I've ever known and the only one I used to lose to regularly in wrestling while growing up.

"Of course he is," Alchise says. He's tall and kind of bent over, with a long face and morose features. "Who else carries two guns? Is that where you got the money to buy everything, Ace? From gunfighting?"

"It's a long story," I say. "I don't really—"

"Stop right there," Boa Juan says sternly. "If you were about to say that you weren't going to tell us the story, don't. Tell us or else."

"Or else what?"

He cracks his knuckles. "I'll throw you a couple of times and we'll see how your nice new clothes look with some dirt and blood on them."

I look at Chee and Hi-okee for help, but see none there. "I'm not helping you," Hi-okee says. "I want to hear the story too."

"Okay, I'll tell it," I say reluctantly.

Someone refills my cup and thrusts it into my hand. I decide to tell the story of how I got the black pearls. It takes a while to tell it. People keep interrupting me either to howl in disbelief or to ask questions. Other people gather around until there's at least a dozen people listening. When I finish they all stare at me in silence. Hi-okee breaks the silence first.

"Wow." Others nod.

"You're either the biggest liar in the world, or the greatest hero since…since forever," Boa Juan says.

I don't know what to say. I don't really like having everyone look at me. I wish I would've kept it to myself. I wanted to come home and blend in. "Well, I exaggerated a bit here and there," I say. "To make the story better, you know?"

"You had me going," Alchise says. "I believed all of it. I should've known better."

"Tell another one," Boa Juan says.

"Maybe later," I reply.

When the others protest, Chee steps forward, takes my arm and starts pulling me away. "He said later. Give him some air, will you?"

He and Hi-okee hustle me away and we find a quiet spot to sit in the shadows. My friends seem to understand that I don't want to talk and mostly we sit there in silence, sipping our whiskey, watching the party continue. They catch me up on their lives. Chee is married now and has a child. He points out his wife to me. I only vaguely remember her. She seemed so young when last I saw her. She's grown up a lot. She sees us looking at her and waves, but doesn't come over.

"No wife for you?" I ask Hi-okee.

He grimaces. "There's no women to choose from. Chee got the only good one."

"What about Bina? She likes you," Chee teases.

"Ugh. She talks too much. She never stops," Hi-okee complains.

"So do you. That makes you perfect for each other," Chee laughs.

"What about you, Ace?" Hi-okee asks. "What happened to that beautiful woman you showed up with last year?"

He's talking about Victoria. "That didn't end so well," I say.

"Did the big, square man take her?" Hi-okee says. "I never saw anyone so big in my life."

"In a way, I guess," I say. "Can we talk about something else? Where's Nakai? I haven't seen him yet."

"Nakai lives in Basaranca now," Chee says. Basaranca is the nearest Mexican village.

"He married a Mexican woman," Hi-okee says. "They have two children. She's made him into a Mexican. He cut his hair. I think he even started going to her church."

That seems hard to believe. No one wanted to join Golthlay and his *Netdahe* more than Nakai when we were kids. Hi-okee sees the look on my face and laughs.

"It's because there aren't enough women here. That's why Nakai left. Who knows? Next time you come back maybe I'll be living in Tucson and be an American."

Chee gives me a serious look. "How long are you staying, Ace?"

"I don't know," I tell him. "At least until we deal with General Torres."

"So you've heard about him."

I nod, but before I can say anything further, Hi-okee cuts in. "Tonight is for the party. Tomorrow there will be time enough for serious talk." He holds up his cup. "Who's with me?"

We talk about little things then for a while. Eventually my friends drift away and I sit there alone. More people are dancing now. Old women dance with small children. Husbands dance with their wives. Women dance with each other.

I see Tom dancing with my mother. It goes on for some time. For some reason it gets me to thinking about my father, who I haven't seen in years. Where is he now? What is he doing?

And bigger questions. Like why did my mother have to take up with a no-account gambler? Why couldn't my father be an Apache? How different would things be then?

If my father was Apache I probably never would have left the stronghold. He would be chief and no one would be talking about me being chief. He'd know what to do about Torres.

He'd be a far better leader than I could ever be.

19

I wake up in the morning and my mouth tastes like it's stuffed with wool. I can feel every heartbeat behind my left eye and each one hurts enough to make me wince. Maybe it was a mistake to bring so much whiskey. Why did anyone ever invent that stuff? Except that if I'd showed up without it, I'd hear about it from Dee-O-Det forever. I still can't believe that dance he did. How does he do it?

Other memories filter back and they make me wince as much as the pain. I have vague memories of talking with Tom after my mother went to bed. Things are pretty blurry by then, but I recall talking to him about my father. I recall getting angry at one point and waving my pistol around in the air. Why would I do that? My best hope is that Tom doesn't remember any of it. As I recall, he wasn't too steady himself. I'll simply pretend it never happened and hope he does the same.

A few hundred yards from the *rancheria* a spring spills out the bottom of a low bluff. There's a small pool there lined with thick grasses and shaded by a couple of trees. I stumble down there to get a drink and find that Tom is there before me. He's lying on the grass on his back. He has an old shirt that he's dunked in the water and wrapped around his head. As I approach he pulls back the edge enough to reveal one bloodshot eye which fixes on me.

"Feeling a little rough this morning, Tom?" I ask him cheerfully. Strangely, seeing him looking so miserable makes me feel slightly better.

He pulls the shirt back over his eye and makes a sound. It might be a groan. It might be a curse. I find myself smiling.

I dunk my head in the pool. Things start to get better almost immediately. I drink the cool, clear water, slurping it down until my belly is swollen with it and I practically have to roll away from the pool. I lie there in the shade and think maybe I'm going to survive after all.

Dee-O-Det comes bounding up then. He's wearing a tattered old pair of trousers that basically have disintegrated to nothing below the knee. He has no shirt on. Around his head is the leather band with the shriveled crow's foot stuck in it. He has a broad smile on his wrinkled old face, showing off the few teeth he still has remaining.

"It's good to see you two are still alive," he says, nudging Tom with his foot, maybe to make sure he actually is alive.

Tom pulls back the shirt and peers up at him. "What's wrong with you?"

"Nothing," Dee-O-Det assures him.

"That's what I'm talking about. There's nothing wrong with you, but there should be. How do you do it?"

I try to stop Tom from asking that last question because I know what Dee-O-Det is going to say, but I'm not quick enough. Dee-O-Det crouches down next to Tom.

"Magic soup." He says this in a whisper, as if it's a big secret. The truth is that Dee-O-Det loves to talk about his "magic" soup.

Tom perks up a little. "Magic soup?" he repeats.

"You're going to be sorry," I tell him.

"Magic soup," Dee-O-Det assures him.

"What's that?"

"Tom, you fool," I say.

"Once a year I take an entire elk," Dee-O-Det says solemnly. "The *entire* elk, antlers, hide, guts, hooves and all. And I put it in a big pot and boil it down into a soup. It takes days."

Tom's face wrinkles as Dee-O-Det says this. He's imagining what the soup smells like. I don't have to imagine it. I've smelled it enough times. Growing up I spent a lot of time tending the fire. I'll *never* forget the smell.

"Then I drink it. All of it." Dee-O-Det grins and rubs his bare belly.

Tom makes a gagging sound. "That sounds terrible."

"It *is* terrible!" Dee-O-Det cackles. "That's why it's so good!"

Tom's eyes shift to me. "Is he telling the truth?"

"I wish he wasn't, but he is. It's worse than it sounds."

Tom's eyes shift back to Dee-O-Det. "I've always said it and I'll say it again: you're crazy."

Dee-O-Det laughs some more. The sound is somewhere between a crazed donkey and a dying chicken. "Yes, I am!" he howls. "But I have also seen more than a hundred winters and look at me!" He jumps up and does a little dance, really kicking up his heels. "And it's all because of the magic soup."

"Could we stop talking about the soup?" Tom asks. "It's making me feel worse."

"I can't tell you any more about it, anyway. The soup is an old secret of the Apache shamans, handed down from the beginning of time. We're not allowed to share the secret with anyone, especially not palefaces."

"I think you already did," Tom says.

"I came looking for you because we're having a council meeting and we want you there," Dee-O-Det says, poking Tom in the ribs with his toe. He looks at me. "You too." And he calls me a name that doesn't really translate into English but basically means He-who-wanders-foolishly-without-purpose. Then he trots away.

Tom sits up. "I'll never understand that man," he says, taking the shirt off his head. His red hair is all standing up and pointing in every direction. "But maybe he's onto something with that magic soup. I've known him for over thirty years and he hasn't slowed down at all."

"He doesn't live completely in our world," I say.

"What does that mean?"

"I don't really know."

It's hard for me to be around Dee-O-Det sometimes. It's like I get confused. I've spent enough time in the white man's world and seen enough modern inventions that I think most of what Dee-O-Det believes in is superstitious nonsense.

At least that's what I think when I'm out in the world.

As soon as I'm around him, everything starts to go sideways. Too many weird things happen around him. Things I can't explain. Even now, thinking about it makes my headache worse.

Tom and I walk up to the council circle. The council is already gathered there, my mother, Dee-O-Det, several elders, Hi-okee and Chee, all sitting inside a circle of stones laid out on the ground. In cold weather the council meets in the communal kiva, but since it's warm they're meeting outside. I'm curious why Hi-okee and Chee are at the council meeting. The meetings are for elders and chiefs. They must be chiefs of something.

Tom and I enter the circle. Dee-O-Det shuffles around the circle, sprinkling *hodenten*—a powder made from ground *tule* pollen—and chanting softly. When he is finished the circle has been blessed and we can start.

I look around the circle and see that everyone is looking at me. "I think Tom knows more about what's going on than I do," I say. But everyone keeps looking at me. I look at Tom for help, but he only nods slightly, encouraging me. Reluctantly, I tell the council about finding Buck and how the incident fits into General Torres' plans for revolution.

"We knew Torres was gathering soldiers," my mother says when I'm done, "and we guessed why. But we hoped it would pass us by."

"I knew all along this day would come," Nochalo says, making a fist. "I knew they would never let us be." Nochalo has been with us for over ten years now. He was *Netdahe*, and rode with my uncle, Golthlay on their endless war against the white man, but a bullet tore up his knee and left him unable to ride. Golthlay left him here to live with us. He is a bitter, angry man.

"What is your opinion on this alliance with the ranchers?" Dee-O-Det asks me.

I start to say I don't know, then realize that people expect more from me than that. I exchange a look with Tom, wishing I could pass this question to him. He shakes his head slightly as if he knows what I'm thinking.

"I don't like Buck and he hates Apaches," I say. "I can't speak for any of the other ranchers. But if Torres comes for us, we'll need allies."

Nochalo's face twists up like he bit into something sour and he bangs his fist on his chest. "We are Apaches. We don't need allies. I say let them come. We will see how they like the taste of our bullets."

No one responds to him. They're all still looking at me.

"If we can ally with the ranchers," I say, "I think we should."

Tom shifts in his seat and my mother looks at him. "You have something to add, Taglito?" she asks.

"If you want, I'll go talk to the ranchers and arrange a meeting. I know a few of them. I think they'll listen to me. I think even Buck Green will come around in time. He's stubborn and ornery, but he's no fool. The ranchers are even more vulnerable than you are."

My mother exchanges a look with Dee-O-Det before answering. "Once again you show yourself a friend of the Apache. I thank you for your offer."

Dee-O-Det turns to me. "What about the Yaquis?" he asks me.

"What I want to do is attack them," I say. "They have taken Torres' side and tried to start a war between us and the ranchers."

"That is your counsel, then?" Dee-O-Det asks, his gaze very sharp. For some reason I feel like his question is some kind of test. He is probing to see what kind of answer I will give.

I take a deep breath and shake my head. "No. Torres is our main enemy here. We can't lose sight of that. We can't weaken ourselves by fighting the Yaquis too or we'll have no chance against Torres."

"Ignore the Yaquis at your peril," Nochalo warns grimly. "They are ever treacherous."

Dee-O-Det is still staring at me, waiting. I feel other eyes on me as well. How did I get myself into this? "Is Kelzel still their leader?" Dee-O-Det nods. I was afraid of that. I was hoping Kelzel was dead. That man is far too smart. Ruthless too. I fear him. But I also respect him. He is the kind of leader for his people that Cochise was for ours.

"Kelzel is smart enough to know that Torres will turn on him eventually, once he's gotten rid of all his other enemies."

"Then why is Kelzel helping him?" Dee-O-Det asks me.

"He's playing a waiting game. He's going to sit on the fence and wait for his best opportunity. Once he sees who is going to win, then he'll act."

"So what should we do?" the old shaman asks.

I sigh. Why did I know it was going to come to this? "I should go talk to him." When I say it like that, it sounds so easy. The truth is that Kelzel's men will gun me down before I get within a mile of their village.

"What will you say to him? Why would he help us? A chief's first job is to provide for his people," Dee-O-Det says, still looking intently at me, as if his words have more meaning than he is letting on.

"I don't know," I admit. I wish my head wasn't pounding so much. It would be easier to think. "Hopefully I'll think of something."

"We will need more guns and ammunition," my mother says. "Much of what we have is old. Will the ranchers help us with that?" she asks Tom.

"They're not worth much as allies if they don't," Tom replies.

The meeting breaks up soon after that and while I'm walking away Mother calls to me to wait. She comes up beside me, takes my arm and briefly lays her head against my shoulder. "It is good to have you back, my son."

I'm not sure how to answer. Mostly because I'm not sure I'm really glad to be back. No matter how you cut it, things look pretty desperate for my people. The storekeeper in Bisbee said Torres has fifteen hundred men. Even if every rancher in the area joins our cause and we are somehow able to get the Yaquis on our side, we're still going to be outnumbered ten to one. Those are terrible odds. Probably we're doomed to lose.

I don't see any good way out of this.

"Come," she says, guiding me away from the cluster of wikiups and fire pits that is the *rancheria* and toward a footpath. The path leads up to a somewhat higher level of about fifty or sixty acres where the clan grows its crops.

"We planted more potatoes this year than ever before," Mother says when we get up there. We stop and survey the fields. Green shoots dot a sizable area. A handful of people are working in the fields. "Over there we planted corn, and down there are beans. We also put in peppers and at the far end there are tomatoes and squash."

I look the fields over, impressed in spite of myself. "The fields look bigger than I remember."

"Because they are bigger. We have not been idle while you were gone."

I try to ignore the subtle barb in her words and turn the conversation. "Is the mine still producing?"

One of the many benefits of Pa-Gotzin-Kay is a small vein of gold ore high up on the back side of the shelf. We had never done much more than scratch a few flakes and nuggets out of it until some years back when something unexpected happened.

One day one of the men guarding the entrance to the stronghold showed up with a prisoner. It was a white man in his thirties, with shaggy brown hair and a beard. His clothing was dirty and torn. He had a wound in his shoulder and he was limping badly. At the time none of us spoke English and he spoke no Apache, but we were able to talk to him in Spanish.

When questioned, the man said his name was Jim Ticer. He said some bandits tried to rob him and he barely got away with his life. He was trying to find a place to hide when he stumbled on our hideout. Deciding that he did not pose a threat, my mother allowed him to stay with us while he recovered his strength.

Later we learned that Ticer had been in the army, stationed at Ft. Huachuca in Arizona. He got a furlough and went to Tucson where he won some money gambling and then went on a long drunk. When he sobered up, ten days had passed and he was a deserter and a wanted man, so he fled to Mexico.

When he was healthy enough to leave, Ticer instead asked if he could stay. Most of the council was opposed to that, but my mother spoke up and said Pa-Gotzin-Kay was a refuge for those who wanted it and we should give the man a chance.

Ticer turned out to be a lot of help in the fields, but it was when he found out we had a gold mine that he really showed his worth. He taught us how to properly dig out the vein and smelt the ore. The gold allowed us to buy supplies in town.

It was Ticer's idea to teach us how to speak English and at my mother's urging the council decided that all children should learn, along with any adults who wanted to try.

"The mine still produces," she replies, "though we do not work it like we should since Ticer died two winters ago." She turns to face me. "But I did not bring you here to talk about fields or mines. If you remember, last time you were here I told you I needed to talk to you about something."

For some reason I immediately feel uneasy. "I should—" I begin, but she cuts me off.

"It is time to accept your duty," she says. "It is time to be the chief your people need."

20

“*What*?” I’m stunned, not sure I heard what I think I heard. I open my mouth and all that comes out again is “*What*?”

“You heard me,” my mother says calmly. “I want you to take over as chief.”

“Chief? I can’t be chief!” My voice cracks a little. I hate it. It makes me sound like a little kid.

“Don’t be so dramatic. You sound like your father. He was very dramatic too. Everything was the end of the world for him.”

“Why?” Oh no, did I just *whine*?

“Because your people need you.”

“I can’t be chief. I don’t *want* to be chief.”

She pats my arm again. “This isn’t about what you want, Ace. This is about what your people need.”

I shake my head. I’m finding it hard to breathe. I want to run. “No. I’d be a terrible chief. The worst.”

“Take it easy,” she says. “You’re getting all worked up. You look like a colt about to stick his tail in the air and run for the hills.”

“No, I don’t.” Okay, even I heard how childish that sounded.

“Yes, you do. It’s something else you get from your father. He never could stand the slightest bit of responsibility either. At the first sign of it he’d run.”

She’s right about my father. My earliest memories are of him being gone. When I was five or six he showed up out of the blue at Pa-Gotzin-Kay, looking ragged and a whole lot worse for wear. He stayed for months, healing up, and even behaved a lot like a father, teaching me a few things about his life, which was mostly gambling.

But one day he simply left without a word and I didn’t see him again for years. When he came back it was the same pattern, only that time he was wounded. He wouldn’t say who shot him, or why, only something vague about a card game that went wrong. That time around he taught me most of his card tricks, how to deal an ace at any time, how to set up a mark, and so on. But it wasn’t so much that he taught them to me because he wanted me to know. It was more that he was bored and I was the only one who cared enough to listen to what he had to say. I think he was also worried about getting rusty. I know he often said, "In this business one slip of the finger can get you killed. If that ace falls out at the wrong time, you better be ready to run."

"I'm not like him," I say firmly. "I'm nothing like him."

"Then you'll do it?" she asks me, a small smile on her face.

For a moment I can only gape at her. I can't believe how neatly she trapped me. She knows how much I don't want to be like my father. She brought him up deliberately. But I'm not finished yet. I've got some more cards to play.

"I've been gone too long. There's no way the clan will accept me as chief."

"You think I haven't already spoken to the council about it? We talked this morning before you showed up. They like the idea."

I'm starting to understand how a rabbit feels when the snare closes on his leg. The more I struggle the tighter the noose gets. "Why would the council…?"

"Everyone knows the story of how you got the black pearls. They are all very impressed."

"But I only told a few people," I say weakly. "It was only last night. How…?"

"Oh, Ace, you've been gone too long. You forgot how quickly stories spread here."

"There has to be someone better for the job. What about Chee? Or Hi-okee?" Now I'm grabbing at straws. Anything to slow this thing down.

"Chee and Hi-okee are good men. Chee's in charge of the crops and you can see how well they're doing. Hi-okee is responsible for the sentries and no one has gotten near Pa-Gotzin-Kay without them seeing. But neither of them has the experience you do. Cochise's blood runs in your veins, my son. You are a born warrior and war is coming. Who better to lead us?"

I rub my forehead. My head is exploding. "You planned this, didn't you?"

She smiles. "As soon as Dee-O-Det told me you were coming. Your place is here, Ace. Your people need you."

"I need time to think about this."

"Take all the time you want," she says. "But make it quick. Events are moving fast."

She walks away. I whistle for Coyote, saddle him up and ride. At first I have no destination. I only want to be moving. I think better when I'm moving. Things become clearer.

What I really want to do is just ride on out of here. Keep going and don't stop until I'm in Oregon or somewhere far away. I've always wanted to go to Oregon. I hear good things about it.

But I know I can't do that. I can't leave my people when they need me. I'm not my father.

But being *chief*? That's a lifetime commitment. I'm not ready for that at all.

When I come out of my thoughts I realize that Coyote and I are on the trail that leads up off the back side of the shelf Pa-Gotzin-Kay sits on. The trail takes us up to a high ridge that overlooks the *rancheria*. I can see the wikiups down below me, the neat lines of the fields, people moving here and there. It all looks so small from here. But I know that close up it's anything but small.

I turn my gaze further out. From here I have a commanding view of the countryside. I can see the village of Basaranca, off on the other side of Nacozari Canyon.

I can also see something else, something I didn't expect.

Coming up the canyon is a large number of people, hundreds of them.

They're heading right for Pa-Gotzin-Kay.

21

When I get back to the *rancheria*, Alchise is just arriving at a dead run. He runs up to me and says breathlessly, "People coming."

"I saw. How many are there? How well-armed are they?" I'm already counting out how many braves we have available to us to fight and thinking about where I want to place them to do the most damage.

He gets a strange look on his face. "Close to three hundred…but they're not armed. Or only a few of them are. Ace, they aren't soldiers. They're Indians."

"What?" I say, his words surprising me. "Are you sure?"

I realize immediately that was a dumb thing to say. Alchise has always been a serious, careful person. He would never say something unless he was sure.

My mother and Tom come up then. Tom is belting on his pistol. "What's going on?" my mother asks.

"We have three hundred Indians heading our way," I reply.

"What tribe?"

I look at Alchise. He shakes his head. "I thought it important to get you the news as fast as I could."

"They're not armed," I tell my mother. "So they're not here to attack us. I'm going down to talk to them."

"I'll come with you," Tom says. "Let me get my horse."

In a few minutes we're heading down the trail that leads off the north end of the shelf, accompanied by Alchise, Boa Juan, Kersus and Deya.

We get to the bottom of the trail and find Hi-okee and Chatto squatting behind some boulders, their rifles trained on a large group of people who are standing there on the sand, waiting.

I motion for them to lower their guns and ride forward. Tom follows. The rest I motion to stay where they are. Any worries I had about these newcomers disappeared as soon as I saw them. I don't see anything about these people that looks dangerous. What I see instead are people who are tired and run down. People who are on their last legs.

Most of them are women, children and old people. They're dressed in rags and they're painfully thin. Many aren't wearing shoes. There are only a few men of fighting age in the whole group. They have no horses or even donkeys. Up at the front I see two men with rifles, but the rifles are old, black powder. I doubt they still fire. Standing out in front of the group is their chief, an old man holding a white flag. He is watching us calmly, his face impassive.

We dismount when we get close. I don't want to loom over the old man and make him look up at us. Clearly he, like all his people, has been through a lot. His buckskin pants are in tatters and he has no shirt. I can count his ribs. But his back is straight and he gazes at me proudly.

"I am Chief Jemez," he says in Spanish, "*cacique* of the Tarahumara tribe."

"I am Ace…" My words trail off. I realize how close I came to saying chief next. "We are of the Chiricahua Apaches."

"I know," he says. "We have heard of your people. It is why we have come here."

That surprises me. Tom and I exchange looks.

"We have come to you for help," Jemez continues. He winces slightly as he says the words, as if they are painful for him to say. Strangely, I feel like I understand. To be chief, responsible for all these people, and to fall so low that your only choice is to approach strangers and hope they will help you…

I wouldn't wish that on anyone.

"We lived peacefully in Temosachic on the lands granted us by our treaty with the government," Jemez says. "Several months ago Torres' soldiers came and attacked us. We were given no chance to surrender. We could not fight back. Our weapons were taken from us when we signed the treaty. Many of my people were killed. The one who was chief before me went under a white flag to speak with Torres, but he was shot. We fled into the mountains, but the soldiers follow us and give us no peace."

He stretches his hands out, palms up. "We are beaten. We are starving. We have heard of the refuge called Pa-Gotzin-Kay. We have nowhere else to run to."

I look his people over. Those of us in Pa-Gotzin-Kay number less than a hundred. To add three hundred to our number seems impossible. How will we feed them all? What if the soldiers who are following them come after us?

But my whole life I have heard my mother speak of Pa-Gotzin-Kay not just as an Apache refuge, but a refuge for all who flee the world. It was why we welcomed Jim Ticer among us. And I know there is only one reply I can make.

"Welcome to Pa-Gotzin-Kay."

I climb back on Coyote. The Tarahumaras file by and start up the trail to the stronghold. Up close they're even more ragged looking. I see a few spears and some knives. One man has a machete. A number of them are sick. One man is coughing so much he's having trouble walking. They look dead on their feet, like people who've been running so long they've forgotten everything else.

But despite all that they move surprisingly quickly up the steep trail. It's impressive, to say the least. I'm not sure I could keep up with them. One old woman is balancing a large, cloth-wrapped bundle on top of her head, but she's skipping over the rocky trail like a mountain goat. Behind her is a little boy probably about three years old, clinging to the tattered edge of her dress. He's following along with no problem, no complaining or asking to be carried.

After all of them have passed by Hi-okee rides over next to me. There's a dark look on his face. "What is it?" I ask him, though I already know. I feel the same.

"This angers me. Soldiers chasing women and children." He draws out his rifle. "I want them to know what it feels like."

"They're going to be coming this way," Tom says. "We'll have to deal with them one way or the other."

"What are we going to do?" Hi-okee asks.

"We'll go after them," I say. We could wait here for them. I doubt there are enough of them to seriously threaten Pa-Gotzin-Kay. But I'm angry too. I don't want to hide in our fortress. I want to take the fight to them.

Hi-okee gives a savage smile at my words.

"When we get to the *rancheria*, gather everyone who can fight," I tell Hi-okee. "We leave in an hour."

At the *rancheria* I see that my mother has been busy. People are scurrying everywhere. The long plank tables have been set up. Huge pots of beans and potatoes are cooking. Two steers have been slaughtered and slabs of meat are hanging over cook fires. In the middle of it all is my mother, giving orders.

Tom rides off to gather his gear. I walk over to my mother. "Can we feed this many people?" I ask her.

"We'll find a way," she replies. A woman hurries up and she tells her to gather all the extra clothing she can find and to get out the bolts of cloth as well. Then she glances at me.

"Soldiers?" she asks.

"They were attacked without warning. They've been running for a long time. They heard about us. They have nowhere else to go."

She nods and I can tell that she will make this work. Somehow. Whatever it takes.

"There's room for them at the north end of the shelf. It's late, but I think not too late to get some more crops in. We can help them build wikiups. It's good you brought those supplies, but we're going to need more."

"I'll send someone as soon as I get back," I say.

"You're going after the soldiers." It's not a question. I nod. "You'll be outnumbered."

"I'll think of something."

She smiles at me. "I know you will. You have your grandfather's blood. Your father's too."

"Not much good his does me," I say, referring to my father.

"More than you think," she replies. "Sometimes the gambler is the safest bet."

I'm not sure what she means by that, but I don't have time to stand around and talk. Those soldiers are getting closer every minute and I want to meet them on ground I choose. In my mind I'm already going over the terrain to the south of here—the direction the Tarahumaras came from—thinking about different places to set an ambush.

"There is much to do," she says. She squeezes my arm and walks away, heading for where the Tarahumaras are standing in a tight group, looking about them with wide eyes. She goes up to Chief Jemez and begins talking to him earnestly.

Nochalo comes limping up to me then. He's carrying an ancient cap-and-ball pistol that's about as long as his forearm. His face is streaked with ashes and he has a water skin slung around his neck. "I'm ready," he announces.

I look him over. He's bent with age. He's weaving slightly. "Ready for what?"

He glares at me. "To come with you. What else?"

I can think of a dozen reasons why that would be a bad idea and that's overlooking the fact that his bad knee won't let him ride a horse very far. But I can also see that if I tell him that he's going to blow up. I don't need any new enemies and I don't want him back here angry and causing problems.

"I need you here," I say.

"For what?" he sneers. "To help with the cooking?"

"To defend the clan." He starts to reply, but I cut him off. "If we fail, the soldiers will come here. The stronghold must be defended."

He weighs this, shifting his weight as if his knee is hurting him. Then he nods curtly.

"Can I trust you to organize the defense?" I ask him.

He jerks his head. I'll take that as a yes. But I decide to leave Chee behind as well, to keep an eye on things.

22

Before we leave I talk with Chief Jemez to find out a few things like how many soldiers were chasing them and how well they were armed. I also learn that the Tarahumaras spent the last two days in Nacozari canyon, which means the soldiers are no doubt in that canyon as well.

All told there are twenty of us, the youngest only about fifteen, the oldest showing more gray in his hair than black. We can't ride right up the bottom of the canyon itself. I don't want to round a corner and run headlong into a force that outnumbers us almost ten to one. We can't ride along the top of the canyon either. It would be much too easy for the soldiers to see us silhouetted on the skyline. I don't want them to have any warning we're coming.

What we end up doing is skirting along the side of the next canyon over from Nacozari. The only trails are game trails and the going is slow. Making it even slower is that periodically I call a halt and walk up to the top of the ridge to scan the bottom of the canyon with my binoculars.

I don't spot the soldiers until late afternoon. I call Tom and Hi-okee to come join me. I hand the binoculars to Tom and point. He looks for a minute, then passes the glasses to Hi-okee.

"Not moving very fast, are they?" he says.

Hi-okee grunts. "They are sloppy. No scouts out. No organization." He hands the glasses back to me and gives me a grin. "If all of Torres' army is this bad, we'll have no trouble at all."

"Probably not," Tom says. "Why send good soldiers to chase a bunch of unarmed, starving Indians? My guess is these are the bottom of the barrel. They're not bothering to scout because they think they have nothing to fear." He looks at me. "How do you want to do this?"

"I don't know yet."

"They are poor soldiers," he says, "but there's a lot more of them than there are of us. This could get ugly fast."

"You have any suggestions?"

"Find a good spot where we can shoot at them, but they can't shoot at us. Try to hit them hard enough that they break. Have an escape route ready if it goes against us."

It's solid advice. I go back to studying the soldiers. All of them are on foot except four, who are probably officers. The officers are wearing uniforms, with knee-high black boots and buttoned up blue jackets with gold braid on the shoulders. Broad, white leather straps crisscross their chests.

The soldiers themselves look to be mostly conscripted peasants. They're wearing sombreros and white cotton shirts and pants. Many have serapes flung over their shoulders. Their weapons look old and of poor quality. They are plodding along with their heads down, their shoulders sagging.

The bottom of the canyon is narrow and tangled with piles of boulders that have slid down the steep sides. There's a small stream that winds through the rocks, only a few inches deep at best.

I look at the sun. There's still an hour of daylight left up here, but down in the canyon the shadows are already taking over. They're going to be thinking about making camp soon. Problem is, there's no place to really set up camp, the canyon bottom is so choked with boulders.

But up ahead of them about a half mile there's a place where the canyon opens up. The sides aren't nearly as steep. There's a pretty good-sized flat, open area. The stream pools up there too, along the base of a low rock ledge.

Just past that spot the canyon makes a sharp turn to the right. On the outside of the turn is a tall cliff, a couple hundred feet high.

I start to get an idea.

"What if we don't have to fight at all?" I say.

Tom looks at me like I might have hit my head. "Sounds good to me. You have a plan, or is it wishful thinking?"

"I have a plan," I say. "Sort of. Let's go rejoin the others and I'll tell you."

I tell the others my plan and smiles light up on their faces. If there's anything better than beating an enemy outright, it's tricking him into beating himself. I look at Boa Juan when I'm finished.

"Can you still do that howl of yours?"

He nods, grinning. "Want to hear it?"

"No. It gives me the chills. But you'll get your chance later."

Sure enough, the soldiers camp in the wide spot. I use the remaining daylight to send men to gather a few things we'll need. Some chunks of wood from the stump of the big, dead juniper we passed. A discarded rack of deer antlers. We'll need some tree limbs too, but we can get those down in the bottom of the canyon. Once we have everything, we backtrack until we find a game trail leading down into Nacozari canyon, a couple of miles downstream from the soldiers' camp. We settle down to wait.

Shortly after dark we mount up and ride to the base of the high cliff. I dismount. "Start getting everything ready," I tell them. "I'm going over and have a look at the camp. I don't want any surprises."

Wearing my moccasins, I sneak toward the soldiers' camp. There's only one sentry in the bottom of the canyon and he's sitting with his back up against a boulder. His rifle is on the sand next to him and he's singing softly, some song about a woman who loves an outlaw.

It's easy to slip by him. I could be banging a drum and he wouldn't notice me. It makes me feel even better about the chances of my plan working.

As I near the camp I hear a commotion and I duck behind some low trees and crouch down. I listen for a minute and soon realize that whatever has them all riled up has nothing to do with me or my men. I creep forward slowly until I get to a spot where I can peek out from between two bushes and see what's going on.

There are a half dozen campfires, soldiers clustered around them eating. Piles of gear here and there show where they've laid out their bedrolls. Four horses and a couple of mules are hobbled by the pool. A couple of soldiers are down by the pool, splashing water on themselves.

The commotion is by the biggest fire, a couple dozen paces from where I'm hidden. The four officers are standing by the fire. As I watch, a sentry comes walking up, dragging someone who is struggling behind him.

The sentry gets to the fire and throws the person down on the ground in front of the officers. One of the officers, the highest-ranking one it looks like, bends over and grabs the person by his collar, yanking him to his feet. For the first time I get a good look at him and I can see it's a boy who looks to be about twelve. His face is dirty and his eyes are wide with fear in the firelight.

"What are you doing here?" the officer snaps, shaking the boy roughly. "Spying on us, are you?"

"No, *señor*!" the boy cries. "Not spying. I was gathering seeds. *Mire*!" And the boy holds out a cloth bag to show the officer.

The officer snarls and slaps the bag out of the boy's hand. "You lie! You know what happens to spies, don't you?" He draws a knife from his belt and holds it up before the boy's terrified eyes. It's really more of a short sword than a knife, easily two feet long. "I'll cut you so your own mother won't recognize you."

"No, no!" the boy cries. "I swear!"

The officer slaps him, knocking him to the ground. Then he bends over and jerks the boy to his feet once again. He presses the knife underneath the boy's eye. "How about I cut your eye out first, eh? Then you will tell me the truth."

The boy is crying hard, tears and snot running down his face. The officer is a squat, powerfully-built man, broad shoulders thick with muscle and a large gut that is not all fat. A scar runs across one side of his mouth, pulling his lips down in a permanent snarl. One of his teeth winks gold in the firelight.

"Stop crying or I will give you a reason to cry," the officer barks, pressing in with the knife so that a spot of blood appears.

I draw one of my Colts. It will ruin the plan, but I'm not going to sit here and watch him cut this boy. I'll shoot him first.

One of the other officers speaks up. "*Mi teniente*, please. He is only a boy."

The lieutenant whirls on him. "What do you know? He's old enough to point a gun, isn't he?"

"But he doesn't have a gun," the officer says. He's a young man, easily fifteen years younger than the lieutenant, with only a faint wisp of a mustache. He is taller than the lieutenant, and the sleeves of his coat and pant legs are too short for his limbs. "He is only a peasant boy, I think."

"That is because you are an idiot," the lieutenant snaps. He shakes the boy again. "How many are with you? Where are they?" He looks up then, straight at the spot where I'm hiding. For a moment I'm sure he sees me and my finger tightens on the trigger. Before I run, I'm shooting him.

The moment passes and he looks down at the boy again. "We could hang you by your heels over a fire," he says. "Once your brains start to cook you'll talk."

The boy goes pale. He tries to respond, but he can't get any words out past his terror.

I think I'll be doing the world a favor by shooting this man.

The other officers look green at the threat. The young one who spoke before speaks up again. "*Teniente*, please. You cannot do such a thing."

The lieutenant whirls on him. "And who will stop me?" He points the knife at him. "You?"

"The men," the young officer says. "They will desert if you do this."

"Bah! Peasant trash," the lieutenant snarls. He shoves the boy so he falls down. "Weaklings, all of you. If our glorious General Torres is to rise to power it will not be because of worthless vermin like you. I see now why the Colonel sent me to lead you on this mission. Without me you would doubtless stumble off a cliff and the Indians would get away."

He turns back to the boy. "If anything happens, if we are attacked, I will make sure you die first." He waves the knife before the boy's eyes. "Understand?"

Then he stands. "Tie him up. Make sure he cannot escape." The sentry who brought the boy in hastens to obey, the whites of his eyes showing.

I slip back into the shadows and return to my men.

The moon has risen by the time I get back to them. Tom takes one look at me and says, "Complications?"

"You can barely see me. What makes you say that?"

He shrugs. "Something in the way you move I guess." I tell him what I saw. He swears. "Every army has men like him. The uniform is an excuse for their brutality."

I turn to the men. They all heard what I said. They're waiting expectantly.

"Remember, when we go in, shoot in the air unless they shoot back."

"But not the lieutenant, right?" Hi-okee says grimly.

"Right," I say.

23

We wait until after midnight before we move. By then the soldiers' camp is quiet. While the rest of the men handle the final preparations, I head back toward the camp. I have a couple more things I want to take care of.

The sentry is asleep. Snoring loudly in fact. I stand over him for a moment, looking down at him. He is only a farmer. Probably he had no choice but to join Torres' army.

If this works, will he rejoin Torres, or will he slip away to whatever village he came from?

I take his rifle and his pistol. He grunts and rolls onto his side.

I head into the camp. I pick my way around sleeping soldiers. The fires have mostly burned down, but there's enough light to see pretty well. I don't see anyone still awake.

But the boy is. He's lying on his side, bound hand and foot, tied to a bush. His eyes track me as I make my way toward him.

It takes only moments to cut him free. He opens his mouth, but I shake my head and put a finger to my lips. Then I pick him up and carry him from the camp. When we're away I stop and set him down.

"Run home," I whisper. He nods and takes off running. I head back toward my men.

It's time to see if my plan will actually work.

Near the base of the tall cliff the men have built a large pile of dry wood, mostly little stuff, grasses, twigs and small branches. It was easy to find the wood. There's lots of it in the bottom of the canyon, washed down by the floods from high in the mountains and wedged into cracks in the rocks. It's piled loosely so when we light it, it will burn fast. At the base are pieces of dried juniper stump, which we chopped into small pieces. The pieces should hold a lot the tree's oil in them. Which means when we light them, they'll go up fast and burn like they were soaked in kerosene.

While I was gone Hi-okee has tied the deer antlers on top of his head. "How does it look?" he whispers.

"Terrifying," I say. He chuckles.

I go over to the pile of firewood and take out some matches. We set the fire up behind a pile of rocks and driftwood so it can't be seen directly from the soldiers' camp. "Ready?" I strike a match and hold it to a clump of dried grass down at the base of the pile.

The grass flares up and pretty quick the flames spread throughout the pile. No sounds come from the soldiers' camp. Even if a sentry was looking this way he might not realize what he was seeing at first.

"Do it," I tell Boa Juan.

Boa Juan tilts his head back and from his mouth comes just about the eeriest, most terrifying howl ever heard. It sounds like some demon climbed up from the pits of hell and is looking for a meal.

At the same time, Hi-okee and Chatto—who are between the fire and the cliff face—start to dance. It's not really a dance, more of a crazy wild flailing of arms and legs. They add their own wails to the sound Boa Juan is making.

Because of where everything is located, the dancers can't be seen from the soldiers' camp at all.

But their shadows can.

The fire casts their shadows huge, fifty, sixty feet tall, on the cliff behind them. The shadows look like terrible monsters, the kind people tell their children about to make them behave. They play across the cliff face like something out of a bad dream.

I hear sounds from the soldiers' camp. They're waking up, looking around blearily, wondering what's going on. It's time for the next step.

Everyone pulls a burning branch out of the fire and runs and jumps on their horses.

We all give our best war cries and charge the soldier's camp, howling every step of the way, shooting into the air and waving the burning branches.

The soldiers, still trying to wake up and understand what is happening, look up to see giant, monstrous shadows thrown up against the canyon wall. Then, moments later, here comes a band of fiery demons, howling crazily and shooting.

It works about like I expected it to.

The soldiers panic. With wild yelps of terror they spring up from their beds and flee. Barefoot, hatless, no thought but escape. It's a stampede, plain and simple.

Shouts come from the officers, telling the soldiers to hold their ground. The soldiers completely ignore them. All they want to do is escape.

And then something unexpected happens. In front of me a figure rises up from the ground, something in his hand. It's the sentry I disarmed earlier.

Except that it looks like I didn't.

In his hand is another pistol, a pistol that I missed. He points it at Boa Juan, who's riding to my left. Flame blossoms from the barrel of the gun and Boa Juan jerks to the side.

Then Coyote strikes the sentry with his shoulder and the man goes down. We thunder on by and there's no time for anything but what's in front of us.

We charge into the soldiers' camp, the mass of panicked soldiers fleeing madly before us. Through the melee I see the lieutenant, his knife in one hand, a pistol in the other.

Him I'm shooting.

He stares right at me and his eyes narrow down. I draw a bead on him, but before I can fire the swarm of soldiers reaches him, and I can't see him anymore. By the time they pass, he's gone.

In a minute the camp is empty. We chase them for a ways further. As we head back to their camp I'm looking for Boa Juan. I have to know if he's okay. Around me men are talking and laughing, but I can't hear them. All my thoughts are on Boa Juan. How did I miss the sentry's other gun?

Then I hear his voice. "Did you see how they ran?" Boa Juan yells. "Like rabbits!"

"Are you hit?" I ask, riding over near him.

He puts his hand to his ear and it comes away bloody. "What?" he yells, laughing. "I can't hear you. I lost part of my ear!"

The sentry is nowhere to be found. He must have run off. I post a man to keep watch and make sure none of the soldiers double back, and then we proceed to pack up everything they left behind. There's a lot of it too, clothes, weapons, ammunition, food. The horses and mules bolted, but it's no trouble to find them.

Loaded down with all the soldiers' supplies, we head on back to Pa-Gotzin-Kay.

24

"I have to say this, Ace," Tom says, dropping down beside me. I'm leaning up against a juniper tree sharpening my Bowie knife. It's the middle of the next morning. "Things happen around you. Never a dull moment." He closes his eyes, sighs and leans up against the tree also. "I'm too old for all this excitement."

I don't reply and after a minute of sitting there in silence he chuckles and says, "That was surely something to see though. They took off running like their asses were on fire, didn't they? Some of them are probably still running."

I try to laugh a little too, but not much comes out. I'm still wound a bit tight, I guess. It was on the ride home that it hit me. Kind of like a fever or something. All of a sudden I was shaking and my heart was pounding. I couldn't make sense of it.

It wasn't until we got back here and I was trying to sleep that I realized what it was. I think it finally hit me that my plan to run off the soldiers could have completely blown up in my face. I could have gotten men who were following me, men I've known my whole life, killed. Boa Juan nearly was killed because of a mistake I made.

I'm used to crazy plans. What I'm not used to is the thought that other people could be killed if they don't work. Usually it's only me who's at risk.

Tom opens his eyes and looks at me. "What's eating you?"

"I don't think I like this chief business," I say. "I make a mistake and people die."

"Huh." Tom leans his head back against the tree. The silence returns. Finally, Tom says, "Did you know I was in the army?" I shake my head. "Way back before I ever met your grandfather. I served two hitches, made it up to sergeant. I served under a lot of bad officers, fools who couldn't find their heads in a hole in the ground. Men died who didn't have to on account of some of those fools. There was this one lieutenant though. Sharp kid. Knew what he was doing, knew how to listen to his sergeant—which was me. The kind of officer who was going places.

"One day he led us into an ambush. There was no way to know. Wasn't anyone who could've steered us around it. Hell, I sure didn't see it." Tom's face darkens at the memory. "A lot of men died that day. It was rough." He scrubs at his face and sighs again. "After that the lieutenant quit. Resigned his commission and walked away. Said he wouldn't ever be responsible for men dying again."

Tom finishes his story and we sit there for a minute. He closes his eyes again. Then I say, "So? Is that it?"

"Yep."

"Is that supposed to make me feel better?"

He opens one eye and looks at me. "Nope."

"Then what was the point?"

"Sometimes you do everything right and people die anyway. That's all there is to it."

I think on this for a minute. "Tom?" He grunts. "Next time you think I need some cheering up?"

"Yeah?"

"Don't."

I get up and walk away. I need to be alone. I need to think without anyone bothering me. I whistle up Coyote and saddle him. For once he gives me no trouble. Seems like he wants to move too.

As we start for one of the trails leading down from the stronghold, Chee sees me and calls out. I reluctantly rein Coyote to a halt.

"I heard it went well," he says.

"This time."

He looks puzzled. "What do you mean by that?"

"Maybe next time it won't. Maybe next time everyone dies."

He raises an eyebrow. "Why are you worrying about tomorrow?"

"Because I don't know what will happen next time."

"And worrying will make it not happen?"

I make a frustrated sound. "You don't understand."

He shakes his head. "I think *you* don't understand. You've been living too long with the white man, maybe. Tomorrow comes when it comes. Enjoy today while you can."

"I'll keep that in mind," I say irritably, snapping the reins so Coyote starts moving again.

"Where are you going?" Chee calls after me.

"I don't know," I say over my shoulder. "I'm going to take a look around."

I ride down the steep trail and then pretty much let Coyote have his head. I don't care where we go. I simply want to be moving. Things make more sense when I'm moving. I want things to make sense again.

When I come out of my fog a few hours later and look around, I realize we're on the trail to Basaranca. Basaranca is the nearest village. It's a pretty small place, maybe a few hundred people. Sleepy. Real quiet. I remember that Hi-okee told me Nakai lives there now, married to a Mexican woman. It would be good to see Nakai again. Meet his wife. See his babies. I hope he's got a good life.

Right then and there I decide to ride on into Basaranca. I'm not just going visiting, I tell myself. Nakai may have some information about what's happening in the area. If he doesn't, maybe Gutierrez will. Gutierrez is a doctor in the town. He's made the trip out to Pa-Gotzin-Kay a few times, when we had people too sick or injured to be moved. Last I heard the people of Basaranca elected him mayor. If anyone has news about Torres, he will.

It's late afternoon when I ride into Basaranca. The village sits on a flat plain, the nearest hills a mile or two away. It's good to see the familiar, whitewashed adobe buildings. The old Catholic church sits beside the road leading into the village, a leftover from the Spanish days, still as imposing as ever with its bell tower topped by a metal cross and tall, arched doorways. Off on the far side of the village is a new building with a high wall around it. I wonder what it's for. I'll have to ask while I'm here.

As I pass by the church I look for the black-frocked priest. He's usually somewhere about the grounds, sweeping off the front steps or scratching in his patchy garden, but today I see no sign of him. Weeds have grown up around the front door of the church and a large chunk of adobe has fallen out of the wall and not been fixed.

Coyote and I ride down the main street. Well, the only street, really. Basaranca is a hot, dusty little place, with a handful of drooping trees, chickens scratching in the street, pigs grunting and rooting around in the dirt. Most of the homes are simple one-room adobe with flat roofs and ramadas out front, although there's a couple of larger ones built around courtyards, with protective walls and rusted iron gates.

I pass by a man wearing a large sombrero and leading a donkey. He's wearing sandals, white cotton pants and a white shirt, and has a large bandanna tied around his neck. "*Buenas tardes,*" I say. He looks up at me and I'm surprised to see fear on his face. He opens his mouth and for a moment I think he is going to say something, but then he lowers his head, tugs on the donkey's lead rope, and hurries on by.

A child runs toward me, chasing a chicken. When he sees me he skids to a stop and runs the other way, abandoning his chase. A dog barks at me from the shade of a ramada, but then, as if the act of barking is too much effort, flops back down on his side and goes back to sleep. An old woman sweeping the dirt in front of her house looks up, sees me, and hurries inside, slamming the door behind her.

That's odd. The people here have always been friendly. I wonder if they are having trouble with bandits again. Years ago bandits took over this town. We helped drive them off, but maybe they've returned.

I stop in front of Basaranca's lone cantina. Like everything else, it's made of adobe, but the whitewash is long gone and the walls haven't been patched in a while. It's slowly slumping back into the soil where it came from.

I loop Coyote's reins around the hitching rail, push through the batwing doors, and go inside. There's no windows and the place is dim even though it's bright and sunny outside. The bar is a rough wooden plank laid across two barrels. The floor is dirt. A lizard runs up the wall. The only person in the place is the bartender.

I walk up to the bar and order a tequila. When I do, the bartender, a little man with a pot belly and big, sad eyes, kind of freezes. His eyes dart around the room, landing anywhere but on me. He swallows visibly. Then he nods, picks up a clay jug and pours me a shot. His hand is shaking, and he spills some of the tequila.

"What's wrong?" I ask him.

He wipes sweat from his face with a filthy bar rag. "Nothing," he mumbles. "Is all good."

"Then how come everyone looks like a mouse waiting for the cat to return?"

He shrugs.

"What's that new building on the far side of town?"

He says something so quietly I can't hear it.

"Say again?"

"I want no trouble. You want no trouble. There is no charge for the tequila. Only go, and quickly."

"But I only just got here. And your tequila is so good." Which it isn't. It tastes like someone soaked a dead bat in turpentine. I eye the clay jug. That might actually be true.

He sees something over my shoulder and his eyes bulge. "I warned you…"

I turn to see someone push his way through the doors. For a moment the man stands there, silhouetted against the bright light outside. His face is in shadow and I can't see who he is, though there seems to be something familiar about him.

Then he walks into the room and all at once I know who it is.

I should've taken the bartender's advice. I should've left when I had the chance.

25

It's the lieutenant. On his right hip, close to his hand, is the giant knife I saw earlier. On his left, the butt facing forward, is his pistol. It's clear which weapon he prefers. I set my glass down and shift my duster slightly so I can get at my pistols.

He walks in like he owns the place, all swagger and arrogance. I really wish I would have shot him when I had the chance. A man like him is nothing but trouble.

He walks to the bar and looks me over. I meet his gaze. Something flickers in his eyes, some hint of recognition. I move my hand closer to my gun.

"Do I know you?" he asks. His gold tooth glints when he talks.

"We've never met." I'm glad now I kept my hat on, hiding my hair. When we attacked the soldiers' camp my hair was down.

"Sure?"

"Believe me, there's no way I'd forget a face like that," I reply. "Woof."

He tenses and his lower jaw juts out. I half expect him to swing at me. "Do you think you are funny?"

I shrug. "Some of my friends think so. What do you think?"

He leans in closer. His breath smells like rotted onions. "I think you ask for trouble."

"Is no trouble here, Lieutenant Guzmán," the bartender says. "Please?"

Guzmán's eyes flick to the bartender. "Tequila," he growls. "And not the donkey piss you serve everyone else. The good stuff."

The bartender scurries through a doorway at the back of the room. Lieutenant Guzmán's eyes slide back to me. "I know you from somewhere. It will come to me."

"Don't think too hard," I say. "You don't want to pull anything."

His nostrils flare. The scar on his face gets darker. Oh, boy. That made him angry. Why did I say that?

Through tight lips he says, "You are beginning to anger me. You'll be sorry."

"I was sorry the moment I met you," I say and wince inwardly. That wasn't smart. Why do I keep baiting him like this? The man is nothing but trouble. Nothing good can come of this. Tom's right. I *do* bring trouble on myself. But I really can't stand this man. I hate what he did to that boy in the canyon. I hate how afraid the bartender is of him. I *want* a reason to shoot him.

And if he goes for that overgrown knife of his, I *will* shoot him.

He smiles. There's something that looks like part of a gecko—but that I really hope is gristle from whatever he ate for lunch—stuck in his teeth. "I could stomp you. I'd like that."

"You could try." I watch his eyes. They'll tell me a heartbeat before he acts.

He starts to respond, but suddenly there is a commotion out in the street, men yelling, the sound of a whip cracking. The bartender has come back into the room and he freezes, the bottle of tequila in his hand.

I go to the batwing doors and look out. There's a man down on his hands and knees in the middle of the street. His sombrero has come off and is lying in the dust beside him. He is dressed like a peasant.

Two men on horses are circling him. They are both wearing soldier uniforms. One has a whip and as I watch he strikes the peasant with it. The peasant cries out in pain and blood shows through his thin shirt.

The peasant gets to his feet, holding his arms over his head. The other soldier shakes out a loop in his lariat, twirls it around his head a couple of times, and throws the loop over the peasant's head. He jerks the rope tight and the peasant stumbles toward him, nearly losing his balance. For the first time I get a good look at the peasant's face and what I see shocks me. I'd know that face anywhere.

It's Nakai.

The whip cracks again and Nakai staggers, his hand going to his bloody cheek.

I drop my hand to my gun and push the door open—

The sound of a knife being drawn from its sheath turns me around. Lieutenant Guzmán is only two steps behind me. I'm not sure how he got that close without me hearing him. That terrible long pig sticker is in his hand.

"This is not your business," he says.

I could probably draw and shoot him before he could stab me. But he's close, so maybe not. And what are the chances he'll stab me even if I shoot him? Men like him sometimes need a few bullets before they go down. The knife looks wicked sharp.

I glance back out the door. I don't care how big his knife is. If the soldiers start to drag Nakai, I'm going to do something. Even if it means I get my guts spilled all over the floor. I'm not going to stand here and let my friend be dragged to his death.

The soldier holding the rope jerks on it. He points down the street. Nakai starts that way at a trot. The other soldier cracks his whip and Nakai runs faster. It looks like they're heading for that new building on the far side of the village.

I turn back to face Guzmán. "What did he do?" I ask.

"Lazy," he sneers. "Like all the peasants. They don't work unless you whip them."

"He works for you? Doing what?"

He waves the knife at me. "What is it to you?"

For once I do the smart thing and back down. "Nothing. I don't care."

Slowly he slides the knife back into its sheath. "Smarter than you look, then. Get out of town. If I see you again, I'll arrest you. You won't like what happens next." He throws his shoulder into me as he pushes past and leaves the cantina.

I go over and drop a peso on the bar. "What's in that building?" I ask.

There's sweat running down the bartender's forehead. He shakes his head. I drop another peso on the bar. Still he shakes his head.

"Where's the mayor? Gutierrez?"

He swallows heavily. "They shoot him."

He won't say any more. I leave the cantina and stand out front for a minute, thinking. Gutierrez is dead. The villagers are being forced to work for the soldiers. Something is going on in that new building and I'm not leaving until I find out what.

And I have to make sure Nakai is okay. Maybe I can convince him to leave Basaranca and come back to the stronghold.

The smart thing to do would be to ride out of town right now. Maybe come back during the night and have a look around.

But I haven't gotten where I am by doing the smart thing, have I?

I get on Coyote and ride in the direction they took Nakai. In the middle of the village is the *zocalo*, the town square. There's a tree in the middle and a couple of stumps for sitting on in its shade. Buildings front the square on all four sides. One of them is the jail. I ride up and take a peek through the window of the lone cell. I don't see anyone inside, so I guess they didn't take Nakai there.

Opposite the jail is a two-story building. Unlike most of the buildings in town, this one isn't made of adobe, but wood. There's a wide porch running along the whole front of the building, the posts supporting a balcony on the upper floor. The building is painted red and there are curtains in the windows. An outside staircase leads up to the second floor. A half dozen horses are tied up at a hitching rail outside. Two men flank the front door, both holding shotguns. They give me a hard look as I ride by. I touch the brim of my hat and nod to them. My guess is whoever is in charge here is headquartered there.

I follow the street to the new building. As I get closer I see that the two mounted soldiers and Nakai are out front. One of them is pointing at Nakai and saying something. After a moment Nakai lowers his head and nods. The soldier holding the lariat gives him some slack and Nakai takes the loop off from around his neck.

The soldiers ride away, laughing over something one of them has said. Nakai trudges toward the closed gate, which is made of wood and is as tall as the wall itself, close to ten feet.

I come trotting up and catch Nakai before he reaches the gate.

"Nakai," I call out in a low voice.

He turns and for a second his eyes show no recognition. But then he recognizes me and his eyes widen. "No, Ace. You must go. Quickly, before it is too late."

"Come with me."

He shakes his head. "I can't. My wife and children. If I run, they will kill them."

"We'll take them too."

"No. It's too dangerous. The soldiers are watching. They watch all the families. No one can leave. We must work in the factory. Now go, please, before they catch you."

"What are you making in there?"

His eyes dart around and he licks cracked lips. Up close I can see how exhausted he is. He's skinny and his face is darkened with what looks like soot.

"They make—"

Before he can finish, the gates swing open and I find myself staring down the barrels of a half dozen rifles.

26

With the men holding the rifles is the lieutenant. He smiles and flashes his gold tooth. "Not so smart after all," he says. "I'm glad."

Slowly I raise my hands.

The lieutenant's smile fades. "Giving up so easily? You disappoint me." He gestures with one thick hand. "Drop your guns."

I throw my Colts in the dirt and follow them with the Winchester. Once they're on the ground, soldiers hustle forward and jerk me out of the saddle. Manacles are clamped on my wrists.

I feel the presence of someone new and look up as Nakai sucks in a breath of fear. He's not the only one. Even the soldiers are afraid, hastily moving out of the way and shooting sideways looks at the man who is emerging from the open gates. Someone murmurs, "*El Colonel*."

The first thing I notice is his hat. It's not just any hat. It's huge, far too big for how small the man is. It's made of black felt and encrusted with gold braid. A long feather sticks out of it. I've seen a picture of a hat like that before, on a French king named Napoleon. It looked ridiculous on Napoleon, and it looks ridiculous on the Colonel.

The Colonel is wearing white pants tucked into shiny, knee-high black boots. His jacket is dark blue, covered with heavy braids on the shoulders and medals on one side of his chest. The jacket is cut strangely, the tail very long, while the front is cut very high, almost to his chest. He carries a cane with a silver head.

His eyes flick away from me for a moment, land on Nakai, then go back to me. "Get that man back to work," he says, jerking his chin toward Nakai. "I want him on night shift for the next week too. That will teach him to shirk his duties." One of the soldiers shoves Nakai, who stumbles and then hurries through the gates, looking over his shoulder at me as he goes.

The Colonel walks up to me. He's shorter than I am, only coming up to my shoulder. His features are very fine, almost childlike. He has no facial hair at all. He cocks his head to the side, studying me.

"What do we have here?" he says in an oddly high voice.

"Take your hat off when the Colonel speaks to you," Guzmán growls. One thick hand sweeps up and knocks my hat off. My long hair comes spilling out then and all at once Guzmán remembers me.

"*You*!" he hisses, drawing his long, evil knife.

I think he's going to gut me right there, and I'm already tensing to bring my hands up to try and can catch the blade with the chain holding my wrists together when the Colonel holds up one small, almost dainty hand.

"*Teniente*," he says.

His nostrils flaring with each breath, Guzmán lowers the knife and takes a half step back. "Let me kill him, Colonel. It is no trouble."

"You'll kill no one without my permission," Colonel says. "And I am not giving it at this time."

Guzmán subsides, but he's not happy about it. He looks like an enraged bull, a heartbeat from lowering his head and charging.

"Do you know this man from somewhere?" the Colonel asks.

Guzmán glowers at me. I can see that he doesn't want to answer. Probably still feels a little humiliated by what we did to him. So I decide to help him out.

"The last time I saw your lieutenant, Colonel, he and his men were running like the Devil was after them."

Guzmán's eyes go red and for a moment I'm sure I've pushed him too far and I wonder at myself. Do I really want him to cut me down right here and now? Have I lost my mind? But the Colonel speaks up again and saves my hide.

"Is this true?" he asks.

Guzmán swallows. He's so angry he's trembling. "It was the damned superstitious peasants."

"Interesting," the Colonel says, looking at me with new interest. "You must be a very clever fellow."

"Sometimes," I say. I consider my current difficulty and add, "Other times, not so much."

The Colonel is still studying me. "You are an Apache, unless I am mistaken." He turns his head and glances toward the mountains, then turns his gaze back to me. "You are from the stronghold, I surmise. You have come to see what we are doing down here, no?"

"I was in the area. I thought I'd come by and introduce myself."

"Very well. You are here. Who are you?"

"The name's Ace," I say. "I'd shake your hand, but…" I hold up the manacles. "Now it's your turn. Who are you?"

I feel the soldiers holding me stiffen. They are in disbelief that anyone would use such a tone with the Colonel. Guzmán steps forward and puts his hand on his knife once again.

"Now, Colonel?"

The Colonel gives the tiniest shake of his head. His eyes still locked on mine, the Colonel says, "Perhaps I have been rude. You are a guest here after all. It is only normal to wish to know who I am.

"I am Colonel Batista."

I'm stunned. I've heard this name, though there is another he is better known by.

"You're *El Carnicero*?" I say disbelievingly. "You're the Butcher?"

He inclines his head slightly. "I have been called that, it is true."

"You slaughtered an entire village."

"It was unfortunate. They were being most uncooperative."

"Unfortunate? You killed women, babies. You killed *everyone*."

He is unperturbed. "Sometimes examples must be made."

"That's what that was to you? An example?"

"And a most effective one, you must admit. My name has spread far and wide. Now when I enter a village, the peasants are most cooperative."

The fact that the man known as the Butcher is here, this close to Pa-Gotzin-Kay, is a staggering one. Things are worse than I thought. I have to get away and warn my clan. We have to act.

"Well, now that we've been introduced, I'll be moving along," I say. "If you could get these off?" I hold up my manacles again.

El Carnicero makes a sound and shakes his head. "You've come all this way for information, but you don't really know anything yet. Wouldn't you like to know what's going on here before you leave?"

"You're busy. I don't want to take up any more of your time."

"No, no. It's quite all right. I have plenty of time. What would you like to know first?"

I point to the building behind him. "What are you making in there?"

He gives a sly little smile. "It's a factory. We're making gunpowder. Lots of it. You want to know what it's for?"

No. I don't. But I nod.

He leans forward and in a whisper says, "We're going to blow up Pa-Gotzin-Kay."

27

His words hit me like a hammer. But I try not to let it show on my face.

"Bold words," I reply. "But empty. You'd never get close enough to use it."

"You don't think so? Ah, but you say that because you do not yet have enough information. This is why you cannot leave yet. You don't know enough. Shall I tell you more?"

The smile on his face reminds me of a little kid with a new toy that he's very proud of. I'm starting to think he's crazy. I glance at Guzmán. His eyes are all lit up. He's enjoying this too.

"The fact is that we don't have to get close to destroy your sad little village," El Carnicero says. "We only have to get within cannon range."

Now I feel better. I'm picturing those terrible steep trails up the side of the canyon as I say, "There's no chance of that. You'll never get cannons up the trail. We'll cut you to pieces."

He wags a finger at me. "Again you suffer from a lack of knowledge. Allow me to enlighten you. You are thinking of the old-fashioned cannons, big, ugly, cumbersome things. But we don't use those anymore. We have new cannons, much smaller and lighter, but with greater range. And we won't bring them up the trails. No, there is a certain flat-topped peak not too far from your village. From there it will be no trouble to smash your stick huts to splinters."

I know what peak he's talking about. From there he would have a clean field of fire at the *rancheria*. "But now you've told me too much," I say. "If I put men on top of that peak, you'll never get cannons up there."

He puts both hands on the head of his cane and giggles, his body shaking. It's kind of eerie to see. When the giggles die down he says, "But if you put too many men over there, you leave yourself open to an assault up the trails. You don't have the manpower necessary to guard two spots properly." Another little giggle squeaks out.

"We'll see about that," I say. I try to sound confident, but in truth I feel sick. If we had enough guns to properly arm the

Tarahumaras we might be able to hold both spots, but we don't. Now, more than ever, we need that alliance with the ranchers and the guns they can provide. All we need is some more time.

Which I don't know if we have.

I need to get out of here and warn my people. Which might be a little problem, seeing as how I am handcuffed and surrounded by people who want to kill me.

"Yes, we *will* see about that," he continues. "Very soon now. The truth is, I wasn't sure I would get the chance. Had the General's ploy worked and war broken out between you and the *Americano* ranchers, we wouldn't have needed the cannons to destroy you. Which would have been a shame, really. I'm quite eager to see what our new cannons can really do."

"You're *loco*," I say.

Another little giggle squeaks out of him. That sound is really starting to get to me.

"Perhaps you will change your tune when you see my new cannons in person. Would you like that?"

I pretend to consider this. "I guess so. It looks like I have a few minutes to spare."

"Perfect," he says. He turns to Lieutenant Guzmán. "Let us give our guest a demonstration. Have one of the new cannons brought out."

Guzmán barks an order and two soldiers dash back into the factory.

The Colonel looks at me, a twinkle in his eye. "I think you will enjoy this. The new cannons are much more accurate than the old ones. Boom!" He giggles again. There's definitely something wrong with this man.

"Bring my carriage as well. I believe I know where we will test the cannon." He looks at Coyote and wrinkles his nose. "Take our guest's *horse* away. He will ride with me."

A soldier leaves to fetch the carriage. Another soldier reaches for Coyote's reins. Coyote lays his ears back and bites the man on the shoulder. Actually, he does more than bite. He picks the man up and shakes him like a dog shaking a rat.

The soldier howls and flails wildly at Coyote, but it does no good. He's as helpless as a rag doll.

From the corner of my eye I see Guzmán draw his knife and step forward.

"Go!" I yell at Coyote. "Get out of here!"

Coyote doesn't hesitate. He drops the soldier, who crumples in a heap, and takes off at a dead gallop. In a couple of seconds he has disappeared around the corner of the gunpowder factory.

Guzmán sheaths the knife and looks at me. "I'm going to kill your horse, I promise you."

"You can try, but Coyote is too smart for you by far."

The carriage and the cannon show up. We climb into the carriage and head through the village. I wonder briefly what the Colonel is planning on demonstrating his cannon on, but mostly I spend my time trying to figure out how I'm going to escape. As we roll down the street the thought comes to me that if I dive off this carriage and cut between those buildings, I might be able to stay free long enough to whistle for Coyote.

But it's really not much of a plan, and before I get to try it Guzmán, who is sitting in the seat behind me, leans forward and says in my ear, "Yes, please do." From the corner of my eye I see the tip of his knife inscribing small circles in the air.

"You should keep your dog on a shorter leash," I tell the Colonel. His reply is another giggle.

We roll all the way through Basaranca and out the other side. Suddenly I realize what the Colonel's target is going to be.

"The church?" I say. Even knowing the Colonel is *loco* I have trouble believing it. I know how much store people set by their churches. Would he really blow up a church just to demonstrate his cannon to me?

"Yes! The church!" The Colonel claps his hands. He's so excited he can hardly sit still. "It is very old and not in such good shape. It will fall down anyway. I am only speeding things along."

The carriage comes to a stop and we dismount. Soldiers begin to set up the cannon. While they're doing so, the priest emerges from the church. He's holding a broom in his hand. He looks curiously at us. It takes a moment before he realizes what's going on. He cries out and starts running toward us, shaking the broom over his head.

The powder is tamped down and a soldier rolls in a cannonball. He steps back and nods to the Colonel. The Colonel looks at me.

"Now you will see." He turns to the soldier standing at the rear of the cannon. "Fire!"

A match is lit and held to the fuse. The priest, almost to us now, suddenly realizes that he's about to get blasted into tiny pieces. He flings himself to the ground, a fraction of a second before the cannon goes off.

A boom and a whistling sound.

The cannonball strikes the church dead on, beside the front door. Debris flies into the air. As the smoke and the dust dissipate I can see that there's a gaping hole in the front wall now.

The Colonel laughs and jumps up and down. "Do it again! Do it again!" he hollers.

The next cannonball takes out part of the bell tower.

The Colonel is breathless with glee. "Imagine what that will do to your stronghold," he says.

I am. I can see the wikiups exploding into splinters, everyone I know being torn to shreds. My muscles tighten. It's all I can do not to fling myself at him, to try and kill him before they kill me.

"I'll stop you," I say though gritted teeth.

The Colonel goes still suddenly, his laughter dissipating. "Grow up. There is nothing you can do. In two days we will destroy your village. Then we will move against the ranchers and any others who think they will stand in General Torres' way."

Guzmán gestures at me. "Can I kill him now?"

"Not yet. He amuses me. Lock him up. We can always shoot him in the morning."

28

They put me in jail and leave a soldier with sleepy eyes to guard me. Through the barred window I can see the *zocalo*. The Colonel and several of his officers enter the two-story building across the square. The *zocalo* is quiet, only a few soldiers on guard duty. An older woman appears, carrying a sack of something. She keeps her head down and hurries across the square. The sun goes down.

Coyote comes trotting into the square. He spots me and trots over.

"I thought I told you to get out of here," I say.

He whickers softly and sticks his nose between the bars. I swat him on the nose.

"I'm serious, Coyote. The lieutenant has it in for you. You need to leave before it's too late."

Coyote stomps his foot and lays his ears back. He's telling me what he thinks of Guzmán.

I look past him and see that one of the soldiers is heading into the two-story building at a run. Two others have picked up lariats. I don't like where this is going.

"Why do you have to be so stubborn?" I ask Coyote. "Just get out of here before it's too late. If you want to be useful, go back to the stronghold and lead them back here to me."

Coyote tosses his head and doesn't budge. I don't know why I bother. He never listens to me. Fool horse does what he wants.

I see Guzmán come out of the two-story building. He's also carrying a lariat. I start to feel a little desperate. The last thing I want is for that monster to get his hands on Coyote.

I lunge at the bars and take a hard swipe at his nose, thinking if I hit him hard enough he'll get mad and take off. But instead he jerks his head back and I miss completely. He gives me a triumphant look.

Three different soldiers with lariats, Guzmán among them, are creeping up on Coyote from different directions, loops at the ready. Guzmán has a wicked smile on his face. Three other soldiers are trailing them. Guzmán gives me a look and his smile widens.

"Dammit, Coyote!" I yell. "Get out of here!"

Instead of leaving, Coyote tosses a look over his shoulder. When he turns back to me there's a wicked glint in his eye and all of a sudden I feel better. He's seen them. He knows what they're trying to do.

"I hope you know what you're doing," I say softly.

Guzmán starts twirling his rope. A moment later the loop sails through the air and settles around Coyote's neck. Coyote takes a little side jump.

Another loop settles around his neck. Snorting, Coyote backs up and right then a third loop settles around his neck. The soldiers are calling to each other excitedly. The three who were trailing behind run to grab onto the ropes and help hold.

Coyote rears up on his hind legs and paws at the air. The soldiers whoop it up. A couple of others gather to watch. There's movement at the curtains of the windows on the upper floor of the two-story building.

Coyote rears again and then runs sideways a few steps. The soldiers dig in their heels and he drags them for a few feet before heading back the other way. Once again he hits the ends of the ropes and once again he drags the men a few feet before he changes direction. His movements get steadily more frantic. He's snorting and rolling his eyes.

Guzmán calls one of the watching soldiers out to help. Once the man takes hold of the rope, Guzmán lets go and draws his knife. He looks at me.

"I told you I would kill your horse!" he calls.

There are cheers from the soldiers and smiles all around. They think they've caught this wild, crazy horse. I have to admit, I think they do too. I grip the window bars tightly, helpless to do anything.

All of us are about to find out how wrong we are.

In the beginning, the men on the ropes were spread out. Which is the way you want to do it if you've roped a large, powerful animal and are trying to keep him from getting away. With everyone spread out and pulling from different sides, the trapped horse can't bolt in any direction. It's what experienced cowboys would do, although experienced cowboys wouldn't have roped from on foot. They would have gotten on their horses first.

But in his fighting and pulling at the ropes, Coyote has maneuvered around to where all the men on the ropes are now bunched up pretty tightly.

And all at once I know what he's going to do.

Suddenly Coyote stops pulling away—

And charges the men.

They gape at him, too dumbfounded at first to react. And by the time they do, it's too late.

Coyote hits them like a runaway train. Soldiers go flying everywhere. Being off to the side a little, Guzmán avoids the impact, though one of the flying soldiers hits him and knocks him to the ground.

"Okay, Coyote," I say quietly. "You made your point. Time to go before someone starts shooting."

But Coyote isn't done yet.

He spins around and charges them again. One of the soldiers staggers to his feet and tries to run. Coyote hits him with his shoulder. The man goes flying and crashes into the wall of one of the buildings fronting the square.

The other soldiers flee in every direction, except for one who is somehow still holding onto his rope. Coyote turns on him and the man's eyes get very big. Strangled sounds come from his throat, but he doesn't move.

Coyote actually stalks him. At least, that's what it looks like. One slow step after another, eyes fixed on the man the whole time. When Coyote is about ten feet away his lips pull back from his teeth, and he snorts.

The soldier breaks. He hollers, drops the rope and runs. Coyote rears up and whinnies triumphantly.

But then I see something that makes my blood run cold.

Guzmán is sneaking up behind Coyote, the terrible long knife ready in his hand.

"Coyote, behind you!" I yell.

Coyote looks at me, his head tilted to one side, his ears forward.

Guzmán is close. He raises the blade. I'm desperate, yelling like crazy. He's going to hamstring my brother. Time seems to slow down.

Almost casually Coyote shifts his weight to his front quarters. Both hind legs lash out simultaneously.

He catches Guzmán square in the stomach with both hooves.

The air whooshes out of Guzmán and he's lifted clear off the ground and thrown backwards, landing in a horse trough between two of the buildings.

I take a deep breath. That was way too close.

"Now would you just get out of here," I call.

Coyote kicks up his heels a couple of times and trots away, the three ropes trailing behind him.

I turn around and see my jailer standing there at the bars openmouthed. "That's some horse, señor," he says.

Yes, he is.

29

I feel better, knowing that Coyote got away unharmed. Now it's time to think about myself. I haven't forgotten the fact that if I don't find a way to escape, come morning I'll be standing up against an adobe wall in a hail of bullets.

My jailer goes back and sits down on his stool. He's a heavyset man, the buttons of his shirt straining to hold his belly in, and the stool creaks loudly when he sits on it. He leans up against the wall and folds his arms over his stomach. Right away his eyelids begin to droop.

I try the bars in the window. There's no movement. The adobe is solid. Where's Blake when I need bars ripped out?

I shake the cell door. It feels solid too. My jailer doesn't open his eyes. His chest is starting to rise and fall with the regular cadence of a sleeping person. Has he already fallen asleep?

He doesn't look like much. If I could lure him over to the cell I could probably disable him, get the keys off him or something. I don't see the keys on him anywhere and the little room is empty except for the stool. Maybe I could take his gun? But it doesn't look like he has one of those either.

Still, I have to try. There has to be some way out of here.

"Hey!" I call to the jailer. "Hey, wake up!"

I have to yell a few times, but finally one eye opens and fixes on me. The rest of him doesn't move.

"I have to go," I say, wincing and holding my stomach like it hurts me. I squeeze my knees together and bend over a bit. "I don't think I can hold it much longer. I think I ate something bad."

"No." The eye closes.

"Come on!" I cry. "You don't want me to crap on the floor, do you? Think how that will smell."

This time the eye doesn't open and the answer is the same. "No."

"At least bring me something to go in."

"No."

"All right. Then I'm going right here, on the floor and you know what?" I wait, but the eye doesn't open. Maybe he doesn't care what. “They’re going to blame you. You’re probably going to have to clean it up. How do you like that?”

“No.”

I swear at him for a while, but that doesn’t do any good either. I slump down in the corner. Of course there’s no bed or anything in the cell. Now that I stopped hollering my jailer is snoring loudly. I’m glad I didn’t interrupt his siesta.

This is looking bad. No one but Nakai knows where I am. I hope he stays out of it. I wouldn’t want his wife or children getting killed because of my stupidity. I should have left when I had a chance.

I lean back against the wall and tilt my hat down over my eyes. I might as well get some shuteye. Maybe I’ll wake up with some brilliant idea.

When I wake up it’s late. I sit there in darkness, wondering what woke me. Then I hear a soft whicker and see Coyote’s head at the window. I get up and walk over to him.

“Thought I told you to get out of here,” I say softly. He whickers again, then stamps his foot impatiently. It’s like he’s wondering what I’m doing standing around wasting time.

“I’d like to leave,” I tell him. “But there’s the matter of these bars.” I grip them and shake them to show him they aren’t moving.

Coyote tosses his head and stamps his foot again. Though I can only dimly see him in the moonlight, I can tell he’s irritated just by his posture. He makes a whuffing sound and rears up a little.

I think he’s trying to tell me something. But what?

Then I realize what it is and I immediately feel like the dumbest person on earth.

Hanging around Coyote’s neck are three lariats. How did I not think of that earlier?

“I think we know now who’s the brains of this outfit,” I whisper to Coyote. “And it’s not me.”

He twitches his ears toward me and comes closer. I reach out and grab the ropes. “Give me a second,” I say. I twist them together and run them around two of the bars and tie them off. I figure I need at least two of the bars out in order to fit through.

I pat Coyote on the neck. “Don’t hurt yourself, okay? Maybe pull gently at first to see—”

But I don't get to finish. Coyote bolts. When he hits the end of the ropes, there's a cracking, crunching sound and the bars fly out of the wall like nothing.

Okay, then.

I look over my shoulder, wondering if my jailer is about to raise the alarm.

He's still sleeping peacefully. I wouldn't want to be him in the morning.

I crawl out the window, pull the ropes off of Coyote and mount up. He gives me a sideways look. I'm pretty sure he's mocking me. Or maybe he's reminding him that I owe him yet again.

I start to ride out of the plaza, then pause. No one's shouting or shooting at me. It looks like I have a bit of time. I'd like to try and recover my guns, but I've got no idea where the soldiers put them, so looking for them is probably a bad idea.

My eyes fall on the Colonel's fancy, two-story building on the far side of the *zocalo*.

And I get an idea.

Spaced along the front of the building's porch are four large wooden beams. They're pretty thick, probably because they're holding the whole thing up. So, if something were to happen to those beams, I'd guess the Colonel would fall right out of bed.

I ride off down a side street. I saw a stable over here somewhere. A minute later I find it, a single corral with a small barn beside it. There's a dozen horses and mules in the corral. The mules are stronger, but I choose the horses. Horses panic easily. I need that for what I have in mind.

I rummage around in the small barn and find what I'm looking for. A kerosene lamp. I have some matches in my pocket.

I rope three of the wilder looking horses and lead them out of the corral. Three should be enough. While I'm at it I drive the rest of the horses and mules out and they scatter in the darkness. No doubt the soldiers have more horses somewhere, but losing these should slow down my pursuers a bit.

I take the three horses back to the *zocalo* and tie each one to a post. I sit there on Coyote and look up at the darkened second floor of the building. Somewhere up there the Colonel is sound asleep in bed. Maybe I'm lucky and Guzmán is in one of the other rooms.

"This is for you, Colonel," I say.

I light the lantern. Then I throw it on the ground at the feet of the horses, so the glass smashes. Kerosene spills everywhere and sudden flames spring up from the ground. At the same moment I let out my most bloodcurdling yell and wave my hat wildly.

The horses do exactly what horses always do when confronted with something scary and unexpected: they bolt.

They hit the ends of those ropes at almost the same time. There's a loud crack and the support posts rip out of the building. The horses charge away into the night, the posts dragging behind them.

The building sags forward, but the remaining post holds and it doesn't fall.

That's disappointing. I thought that would work.

Lights come on upstairs. A man emerges from one of the upstairs doors and comes out onto the balcony, holding a lantern.

It's my lucky day.

"Hey, Guzmán!" I call.

He snarls and runs to the railing, holding the lantern up to see better.

His bulk is just enough to tip the balance.

The remaining post cracks loudly. The whole building wobbles for a moment while Guzmán waves his arms, trying to catch his balance.

Then the whole thing collapses.

30

Dawn is breaking when I ride into the *rancheria*. Tom is standing by the horse trough, stripped to the waist, trimming his beard. He looks at me, squinting against the morning sun.

"Where have you been?"

I rein Coyote to a stop and grin at him. "Here and there."

"You look awful cheerful," he says.

He's right. I *am* cheerful. I'm still concerned about the cannons, but not that concerned. I don't know what we're going to do about them yet, but I have a strong feeling I'll think of something.

He looks me over. "Lost your guns I see." He puts his shirt back on. "I guess you found yourself some more trouble, didn't you?"

"More like trouble found me."

He grunts. "It's always that way with you, isn't it? You ride along, minding your own business, and trouble just jumps out at you."

"Something like that."

"You gonna tell me what happened?"

I give him a brief rundown, and when I'm done he shakes his head. "Don't that beat all," he says. "You and trouble are like flies and horseshit, you know that?" He scratches his jaw. "Seems that's what you needed, though. You're in a sight better mood than you were when you left here yesterday."

I consider this and then nod. It felt good, being out on my own again, only myself to worry about.

"Well, let's get the council together and figure out what to do about those cannons," Tom says. He gives me a sidelong look. "Unless you're planning on running off by yourself and taking care of it?"

I kind of shrug and he shakes his head irritably. "Dammit, Ace. Is that what you're planning on doing?"

"Not exactly."

Tom sighs. "I'm too old for this."

I tell the council what I learned. There are worried looks all around. “It’s not that bad,” I say. “They’re not moving until tomorrow. That still gives us tonight to do something.”

“Tell us, Ace,” Tom says. He still sounds grumpy. “Tell us what damn fool idea you’ve come up with. I can’t wait to hear it.”

“It’s simple,” I reply. “Rather than wait here and try to defend two places at once, we go right at them.”

“What are you saying?” Dee-O-Det asks.

“We blow up the gunpowder factory.” I look around at them with a smile on my face. My head really does feel a lot clearer today.

“You make it sound awful easy,” Tom says. “Didn’t you say there’s a wall around the place? And soldiers inside guarding it?”

I nod.

“You said the peasants are being forced to work in the factory. Nakai too. Will you blow them up as well?” Chee asks, frowning. I’m not surprised to hear Chee ask that. Even when we were little, there was always a gentle side to Chee that none of the rest of us had. Probably that’s why he’s in charge of the crops.

“We’ll get them out first,” I say.

“And the soldiers are going to stand around and let them leave without saying anything?” Tom says, crossing his arms over his chest.

“The soldiers will already be taken care of by then.”

People exchange frowns then, wondering what I’m talking about.

“Out with it already,” Tom grouses. “We ain’t got all day.”

I look at Hi-okee. “Think you can trap a skunk in the next few hours?”

Now everyone really looks bewildered. “A skunk?” Hi-okee says. “Why do you want a skunk?”

“I’ll tell you why.” Quickly I outline my plan. By the time I’m done Hi-okee has a huge grin on his face. Chee looks thoughtful. The elders are muttering to each other. My mother looks worried. Dee-O-Det is cackling under his breath.

But Tom looks even angrier.

“This is just what I was talking about, Ace. It’s a crazy, irresponsible plan. You’re hung out there on your own most of the time. If something goes wrong, no one can help you.”

"What if nothing goes wrong?" I tell him lightly. I know I'm egging him on, but I can't help it. I think this plan will work. Best of all, I'm the only one who's really risking anything by it. If it fails, it all falls on me.

"I think the sensible thing to do is to attack in force. Come over the walls from several different points at once. Shoot the soldiers guarding it, blow the place and get the hell out."

"If we do that, people will die," I say, my smile disappearing. "In the dark, with an unknown number of guards around? We might even end up shooting each other. My plan is better."

Tom grumbles and gives me a sour look, but he doesn't argue anymore. The elders discuss it a little more, and a few minutes later it's a done deal.

We're going with my plan.

"Go get me that skunk," I tell Hi-okee.

31

We start out midafternoon. Tom, Hi-okee, Alchise, Boa Juan, Kersus, Chatto, Deya and a half dozen other braves accompany me. In a bag, hanging from my saddle, is a skunk, securely bound with his tail down so he can't spray his scent around. Before we left, Dee-O-Det burned some crumbled herbs he'd mixed up and blew the smoke in the skunk's face.

"That will keep him quiet for a few hours at least," the old shaman said. It seems to be working. The skunk is quiet. He's going to be mad when he wakes up though.

The whole ride Tom won't talk to me. He's still sore about my plan. The most I get out of him is grumbling under his breath. I hear words like "reckless" and "straight up foolhardy" but that's it.

We stop about a quarter of a mile from Basaranca. Darkness has just fallen. "Wait here," I tell them. "When you hear the signal, move in fast."

I dismount and pat Coyote on the neck. "Stay close," I tell him. "I'll probably have to leave in a hurry." Coyote twitches his ears. "No, you're not going to have to rescue me again. I'm not helpless, you know." His answer is a bite on my shoulder, but it doesn't hurt all that much. It's his way of being friendly, I think. Coyote doesn't do friendly too well.

I slip off into the darkness, carrying the bag with the skunk in it. Back at the stronghold I picked up a couple of pistols to replace the ones I lost, but I leave them hanging from my saddle. I'm not going to be able to carry them with me for what I have planned. I should be able to conceal that okay.

I go quietly, eyes open, but it turns out I don't need to worry. There aren't any soldiers on sentry duty that I can find. The Colonel must be expecting us to be spending our time digging in for the attack. He probably figures he outnumbers us by so much that we'd never dare to attack him. I wish I could see his face when he finds out how wrong he is.

Hi-okee told me where Nakai's house is and I make my way there. I hope he's home and not working in the factory. A lot of this plan depends on it. I remember hearing the Colonel tell his men to put Nakai on the night shift as punishment. Last night when

I was in jail at one point I heard a bell ring over at the factory. I think that was the signal for the men working the night shift to show up. If I've calculated right, that bell should be ringing here in the next hour or so.

I get up close to Nakai's home and settle in behind a bush. It's a one-room adobe hut like the others around it. There's a faint light in the hut's only window, which I hope is Nakai getting ready to go to work. I give a hoot owl call and then wait.

A few seconds later I hear a return call. Nakai slips out through the window and pads over to where I'm hunkered down.

"I need your clothes."

He tilts his head to the side, looking at me curiously. "Ace? What are you doing here? Why do you want my clothes?"

"I'm going to blow up the factory."

He starts shaking his head. "No, no. There are too many soldiers. They'll shoot you."

"Not if I can help it."

Nakai sniffs the air. "What stinks?"

I point to the sack lying on the ground. It's moving a little. Mister skunk is walking up. "It's my dinner, but I'm not planning on eating it."

"That's good. Do I want to know why that is your dinner?"

"If this goes well, you'll find out later. We're running out of time. I need your clothes."

"Again, why?"

"You're not going to work tonight. I am. As you."

"I hope you know what you're doing."

"Me too."

He starts shedding. I change into his clothes. "When you go back in, toss out your sombrero," I tell him.

"I was wondering how you were going to hide your hair."

"Was it worth it? Cutting yours off?"

"I don't want to talk about it."

He turns to go, but I stop him. "Get your family ready. After we take out the factory, you need to be ready to run."

"I told Hi-okee already. My wife doesn't want to—"

"She won't have to. We'll find somewhere else for you. We're making an alliance with the American ranchers in the area. Maybe one of them will take you on. Either way, it won't be safe for you around here anymore."

He goes back inside and tosses out the sombrero. About then I hear the bell clang and I start down the street toward the factory. It's hard to do, but I resist the urge to look around or try to stay hidden. I walk in the middle of the street like I'm supposed to be there. I walk slowly, my head down, trying to look like a beaten man going to do something he doesn't want to do.

Around me other men are emerging from their homes, all heading the same way. A few muttered greetings are exchanged.

There's a line of men waiting outside the gates. I take my spot at the end of it. Two lanterns hang on iron hooks on the wall. A handful of soldiers are working the gates, carbines slung over their shoulders, a couple smoking cigarettes. They don't even look at me. They don't look at any of us. And why should they? They know we don't have any weapons. They know we won't risk getting our families killed. There's nothing to see but beaten-down peasants.

Even knowing that I still feel naked. I wish I had at least one of my guns. But I can't risk the chance they'll search me and find the gun. I could probably shoot some of them before they realize what is happening, but I wouldn't be able to get them all, and some of these workers would surely get shot. No innocent people are dying tonight if I can help it.

The gates open and the workers who are getting off shuffle out. The line I'm in starts to move forward. My heart sinks a little when I realize that the soldiers guarding the gates are searching each man as he enters. I can feel the skunk moving in the sack.

Not yet, I tell him silently. Only a little longer.

The line moves forward and then it's my turn. A soldier holds up a lantern while another pats me down. Neither of them bother to look at my face. I feel a bit of relief. I guess to them all peasants look the same anyway.

The soldier finishes patting me down and pokes the sack. "What's in there?"

"*Mi comida*," I tell him. My food.

"Open it up. Let me see."

I freeze. If he sees the skunk, well, let's just say that will pose questions I can't really answer. I note the revolver on his hip, picture myself grabbing it, shoving him into the other guard…

I hold up the sack and open it a crack.

He gets a whiff and takes a step back, his face twisting up. His puts his hand over his nose. "*Dios mío*," he says. "What's in there? Is that a dead skunk? Are you eating a skunk?"

"Times are hard," I say.

"Filthy peasant," he says, and shoves me. "Get that thing away from me."

I walk through the gates and into the factory compound. To my right is a small hut up against the wall. The door is open and inside I can see a table with several chairs around it. There are cards on the table, a loaf of bread, and a bottle of liquor. That's interesting.

I follow the rest of the workers across open ground to the factory building itself. The building is pretty large. It's made of adobe bricks and has a tile roof. Looks like they don't want anything that burns too easily near all that gunpowder.

We file through the door and go inside. We walk down a short hallway past a couple of closed doors and then into a large, open room. There are barrels and kegs stacked against the walls. In the middle of the room are a couple of long tables. On the tables are various sacks. Some are labeled sulfur, others saltpeter. There are large bowls on the tables and wooden implements for grinding up and mixing the ingredients. There are two wheelbarrows, one filled with sacks of charcoal, the other empty. Lanterns hang from the ceiling on chains, providing light. A guard sits on a chair over against the wall, looking bored.

From the look of things, I'd say they're making gunpowder for more than just the cannons here. I'd say this is where the gunpowder for all the ammunition for the army is produced as well. Blowing this place up will put a serious crimp in Torres' plans.

The workers set their meal sacks down in a pile by the wall, trudge over to the tables and take their places. I follow, one eye on the guard as I go. He doesn't even look up. And why should he? Any attacks, if they come, would surely come from outside. There's nothing to fear from the peasants doing the work.

I stand at one of the tables, wondering what to do. One of the workers gets the empty wheelbarrow and on a whim I follow him, hoping the guard won't notice and say something.

We go into one of the other rooms. He stops the wheelbarrow next to a big stack of large sacks filled with charcoal. "Grab the other end," he says, taking hold of one of the sacks.

When I do, he actually looks at me for the first time. He does a double take. "Who are you?"

"Shh," I say, looking over at the door.

"What are you doing here?" His voice has risen a little and he backs away, looking alarmed.

"I'm a friend. I'm here to help you." I hold my hands up to show that I'm harmless. I hope I don't have to knock him out or anything.

He looks over his shoulder as if gauging the distance to the door. I take off my hat so my hair falls down. When I do, his expression changes.

"You're one of the Apaches from up in the mountains." I nod. "What took you so long?"

32

Now I'm the one who's surprised. "What?"

He looks angry. "We sent someone out to you weeks ago, asking for help. You sure took your time. What, you couldn't find your horses?"

"No one ever showed up at the stronghold," I say. "We only found out about this yesterday."

"Oh." He looks like he only half believes me. "I guess they caught Carlos then. Or he took off. He has family in Chihuahua. I bet that's it. He was always a *gusano*." He walks back over to me. "Do you have a gun for me too? I want to shoot a couple of them, the one in there especially," he says, pointing toward the main room. "I hate him. He stole my food yesterday."

"I don't even have a gun for me."

"What kind of rescue is this? You can't do anything without a gun." He looks offended.

"Don't you think shooting a gun in a gunpowder factory would be a bad idea?"

"Not if you don't miss. Where's the rest of them?"

"It's only me in here."

"By yourself, without a gun, you'll take down a half dozen soldiers?"

"Well, I have my lunch."

His lip curls. "What kind of rescue is this?"

I'm beginning to think I don't like this man. "I have a plan."

"Sure you do. What is it?"

"Just keep your mouth shut and do what I tell you."

"As long as it doesn't include getting shot."

"Shut up already, would you?" I say irritably. "We need to get back out there before the guard gets suspicious."

He mutters a few things, but helps me load the charcoal onto the wheelbarrow. We go back to the main room.

"That took you long enough," the soldier growls. He's got one of the peasant's food sacks on his lap and is eating the food out of it. "If you people worked any slower, you'd be going backwards."

I walk over to him, holding my stomach. "Please. I need to go. My stomach…"

His face wrinkles up. “It’s the shit you peasants eat,” he says, stuffing the rest of the food back in the sack and tossing the sack on the floor. “It’s not fit for animals.”

He starts to say something else, but I’m tired of listening to him. I hit him. Right in the pit of his stomach.

The air goes out of him and his eyes go wide with surprise right before he folds up and topples off the chair.

I roll him onto his back. He’s still moaning softly. Not a lot of fight in this one. “You can live through this if you want. How does that sound to you?”

He nods.

“Good. Don’t give me any trouble and I’ll let you go when this is over. You understand?”

He nods again.

I take off my bandanna and gag him with it. I pull off his belt, roll him over, and bind his hands behind his back. I wish he had a gun, but apparently I’m not the only one who had the idea that guns and gunpowder factories don’t mix. I turn to face the peasants, who are all frozen in place, staring at me with big eyes.

“No, no!” one of them cries. He’s an older man, his hair mostly gray. “What have you done? You’re going to get us all killed!”

“Don’t worry, Juan,” the one I went to get the charcoal with says. “He has a plan. He doesn’t have a gun, or any help, but he has a plan.” Both times he says “plan” he kind of sneers.

“Who is he, Mateos?” one of the other peasants asks him.

I’m standing right here. He couldn’t ask me directly?

“He’s one of the Apaches from Pa-Gotzin-Kay. He’s here to rescue us.” This time Mateos sneers when he says “rescue”. I may tie him up and leave him here when I blow the place.

“I’m going to get you all out of here. All you need to do is exactly what I tell you.”

The old man is still shaking his head. “No. I’m not going. You don’t know what they’ll do to us.”

I’m done talking about this. “You can stay here if you want,” I say, “but in a few minutes this whole place is going to go up in one hell of an explosion. You might not want to be here when that happens.” The soldier looks at me with big eyes when I say this and muffled sounds come from him. “Don’t worry. I’ll give you a chance to run first.”

I don't look back when I head for the front door, but it sounds like all the peasants follow me. I snatch up the sack with the skunk in it. He's thrashing around in there, definitely awake now, and no doubt angrier than a…well, a skunk in a sack.

At the front door I stop and turn to the peasants. "Wait here. Run for the front gates when I tell you to."

"That's a brilliant plan," Mateos says. "I see why they chose you to rescue us."

Now I'm thinking about putting him in the sack with the skunk.

I open the door and peer out. There's no sign of movement. Voices come from the guard hut up by the gates. Good. I was hoping they would go back in there.

I hurry across the open area and press up against the side of the hut. The door is open and I can hear their words clearly.

"I still say you cheated," one man growls.

"That's what losers always say," another replies. "Why are you still talking about it?"

"Because I lost my boots! What am I going to wear now?"

"You can have my old boots."

"Your boots are full of holes!"

"It's not my boots that are full of holes, it's *your* boots." The speaker laughs and others join in. The one who lost swears loudly. "Avoid cactus. That's my advice."

"Horse shit too," someone else adds. More laughter.

I step into the doorway. One of the soldiers looks up and sees me. It's the same one who searched me. He's holding a boot in his hand that's mostly holes.

"What are you doing here?" he growls, starting to stand. The other four all turn to me. They don't look friendly.

"I decided to share my lunch with you," I say.

Their faces register confusion. I open the sack, slip off the thong I tied the skunk with, and toss the animal onto the middle of the table. Then I step back and slam the door.

Shouts and cries of alarm erupt almost immediately. Crashing noises as chairs are knocked over.

Then a sudden hissing noise.

Someone screams. "My eyes, my eyes!"

Running footsteps and someone hits the door and scrabbles madly at the knob. But I've got my foot wedged against it, holding it shut. I'm not letting them get off that easily. There's something about people who enslave other people that makes me angry.

Another hissing noise.

"Shoot it! Shoot the damned thing!"

"I can't see! Where is it!"

A gun goes off and there's a cry of pain. "You shot me in the leg!"

It's starting to smell pretty bad. I can only imagine what it's like inside the hut. I let the door go and step back.

It flies open and a soldier stumbles out. The stench hits me and it's even worse than I thought. The soldier is coughing and choking, his eyes squeezed shut, tears running down his face. It's easy to kick his feet out from under him. He goes down in a heap.

The second soldier comes out at a run. He trips over the first and sprawls on his face. He starts crawling away, gagging and retching.

The third soldier is screaming as he comes running out. It's the one who lost his boots. He's clawing at his eyes and he trips over the first soldier and then lies there moaning.

The fourth soldier comes out with his pistol drawn. "I'll kill you!" he shouts. "You're dead!" He fires two shots. But he's blinded by the skunk spray and the shots go wild. I kick the gun out of his hand. Another kick puts him down.

I peer inside. The last soldier is lying huddled up against the wall, holding his leg and whimpering.

Then the skunk stalks out.

"Sorry about that," I say. "You were a big help." He's not happy with me, but I don't think he's got any more juice so I'm safe for now.

There are shouts from the other side of the gates as the soldiers on duty out there respond to the noises they heard. Someone bangs on the gates and yells to open them. I hear running footsteps as other soldiers stationed at different places around the wall converge on the gates.

Which is exactly what I was hoping they would do.

Now they're all gathered in one spot. That makes them easy targets for my warriors. Any second now they will attack.

I get a new idea. A way to make the advantage even greater.

I duck into the guard hut. The skunk spray is more than a smell. It's a cloud. It's like being punched in the face. My eyes start burning instantly, and I feel a powerful urge to throw up.

I snatch up the kerosene lantern sitting on the table and run back outside, blinking hard. I throw the lantern over the gates. It lands and smashes open. Fuel spills and flames sprout up.

That should make it easier for my warriors to find their targets.

As if on cue, whoops come from the distance and gunfire erupts.

One of the soldiers is trying to stand up when I turn around. I kick him back down, then take his pistol and toss it off into the darkness. I quickly disarm the others as well, keeping one of the pistols for myself.

I run back to where the workers are still huddled at the factory door.

"Get out there to the gates. Once my men have driven off the soldiers, open the gates and run."

I run back inside the factory. The soldier I tied up is thrashing around, trying to get free. When he sees me, he freezes. I crouch down beside him and untie the gag, then shove it in my pocket.

"I'm going to blow this place up. Are you going to run? Or are you going to try and be a hero?"

"I'll run," he gasps. "I'll run so fast."

"I was hoping you'd say that." I untie his hands. He leaps up and takes off for the door without looking back. Smart man.

The gunfire outside is dying down. I need to hurry. Once my men clear out those soldiers, I'll only have a small window before more soldiers show up from the town's garrison. I don't want to be trapped in here.

I go to the stack of kegs against the wall and start knocking out bungs. Gunpowder spills out onto the floor. I pick a keg up and dump the gunpowder all over the stack. When it's empty I take another keg and back away, laying down a nice, fat line of gunpowder. That's my fuse. I'm going to light that and run like hell.

I pause, wondering how long I should make the fuse. How fast does gunpowder burn? I go ahead and make it longer. Better to be safe than sorry.

Once the fuse is laid out, I take down one of the kerosene lamps hanging over the table. I set it on the floor by the end of the fuse and pull out the bandanna I used to gag the soldier. I'll light the bandanna, lay it down on the gunpowder, and then run.

I drape the bandanna over the lamp chimney. While I'm waiting for it to light I take a moment to savor how well my plan worked. This'll show Tom not to doubt me.

Something hits me hard on the side of the head, and I'm knocked to the floor, lights flashing behind my eyes.

33

I shake my head to clear my vision and look up. I'm lying on my back, and there's someone standing over me. It takes me a second to bring my vision back into focus and realize who it is.

Shit.

This is bad. Really, really bad.

It Guzmán. He's holding that ridiculously large knife in one hand. I'm guessing he clocked me with the hilt. He has a big smile on his scarred face.

"I knew you would come back," he hisses. "I knew I would get another chance at you."

"What…where did you come from?" I was hoping something more clever would come out when I opened my mouth, but my brain is still rattled. I need to stall for time, get my thoughts back in order.

"Over the back wall," he says. "Too many bullets flying around the front gates." He cracks his neck and raises the knife. "I'm going to cut you in half. I'm going to cut you into little pieces."

"Which is it? In half, or little pieces?"

Okay, that was better. Things are starting to click back into place.

I remember suddenly that I have a gun. How did I forget that?

Slowly I reach for it…

It's not there. Did it fall out of my pants when he hit me?

"Not so tough without your gun, are you?" he hisses.

He slashes downward with the knife, the blade inscribing a wicked arc aimed at my crotch.

I roll to the side, and the knife hits the floor with a loud ringing sound, barely missing me.

I come out of the roll into a crouch. He recovers quickly and charges at me, his teeth bared, showing his long, yellow canines.

He swings the knife in a low swipe across my stomach that will spill my guts all over the floor if it lands. I jump backwards, but he's faster than I expected and the knife lays open the front of the shirt.

I look down at the cut. "That was my friend's shirt. Now I have to buy him a new one. He's going to be mad."

"Wait until he sees how much blood you get on it," he growls, and lunges at me again.

He stabs at me twice in rapid succession. It's all I can do to avoid them. I'm still unsteady, and I almost lose my footing after the second one.

I have no chance to counterattack either. Guzmán has fought with a knife before. Most people will put too much into a swing, and when they miss they leave themselves open. But his attacks are brutally efficient. Each miss flows right into the next attack.

He feints, then slashes. I spin, but the knife slice across my shoulder and blood flows down my arm. I resist the urge to clamp my hand over it. I can't allow myself to be distracted even for a moment.

"There is the first blood," he says triumphantly. "Soon there will be more. Much more."

He attacks again, the knife moving so fast it's practically a blur. I duck the first swing, land a punch with no real force behind it, then the second one scrapes across my ribcage. It's unbelievably painful.

"There is blood there too!" he crows. "What do you know?" He twirls the blade in his hand. "Shall we see where else we can find some?"

"You sure do flap your gums a lot, you know?" I say. "I have to admit, you've surprised me. I wouldn't have thought you could string all those words together at once. I guess you're not as dumb as you look."

I try to sound cocky, but in truth I'm starting to worry. If he doesn't make a mistake soon, I'm going to end up chopped up on the floor of a gunpowder factory. That's not really the happy ending I was hoping for.

He grins at me. "You think to anger me with your insults. Then maybe I will lose my head and charge you like the enraged *toro*, no?"

"The thought did cross my mind."

He spreads his thick arms wide. "But as you can see, I am not angry at all. In fact, I am having a marvelous time. Never have I felt so happy as now, when I am slowly cutting you into little pieces."

"So there's no point in saying anything about your mother, or about how bad your breath is?"

His answer is another flurry of attacks. I come through it mostly in one piece, though I am bleeding in two new spots at the end of it all.

I need a weapon in the worst way. My eyes flick across the floor, looking for the pistol I took from the soldier. He sees my eyes move and smiles again.

"If only you could get the *pistola*, eh?" He shakes his head. "Such a little thing, but it would help you so much." He lowers his shoulders as if catching his breath, but a split second later he lunges forward, trying to catch me off guard.

I slap the blade aside and manage to land another punch, but he moves just enough that the punch doesn't land solidly, and the knife flicks again before I can move away. Now my forearm is bleeding.

He really is cutting me into little pieces. Also, he's gradually backing me into a corner. I'm running out of room to move. The gunfire outside seems to have died down. Does that mean my men won? Will they come running in and shoot this guy for me?

"You seem to be taking this personally," I say.

"Oh, I am. It is all very personal."

"Was it something I said? Or do you always feel threatened by people who are, you know, better than you in everything?"

Now it seems I've finally gotten to him a little. His smile disappears and he glares at me. "You made me look foolish in front of the Colonel, who is a great man."

"Two things, Guzmán," I say, holding up two fingers. "First, the whole foolish thing? I think you did that all on your own. Two, the Colonel? Not a great man. Instead, I'd say he's a few cows short of a cattle drive, if you know what I mean."

His face darkens. "For that you will die even slower. And I will make it my life goal to hunt down your horse and kill him too."

"No chance of that last part," I reply. "Coyote is definitely too smart for you."

And that's when I remember something. Coyote kicked him in the stomach. That has to have left some kind of mark.

He grits his teeth and charges me again. He swings a vicious cut at my head. I duck and turn it into a roll, moving past him at an angle. He swivels and slashes at me again, barely missing.

I take off running for one of the tables in the middle of the room. He pounds after me.

I reach the table a step ahead of him and throw myself down in a slide, the knife hissing through the air where my head was an eyeblink later. I slide under the table, grab hold of the far leg as I go by it, and use the momentum to spin me around and pull me to my feet. I grab a handful of the sulfur from one of the bowls and fling it into his eyes.

But he turns his head as he slams up against the table and the sulfur misses his eyes.

I flip the table over on him. Bowls crash to the ground, but he jumps out of the way. However, that gives me the opening I need. I run and dive for the pistol. My hand closes around the comforting grip and I roll, bringing the weapon up as my free hand fans the hammer back—

But he's closer behind me than I thought, and I see the knife slashing down at me. The knife clangs off the pistol, knocking it out of my hand. It spins away across the floor.

I roll away as he swings again, and this time the knife draws a line of hot fire across my neck.

He smiles again, his good humor returning. "So close, that one. I think you are slowing down. Maybe the next one?"

I resist the urge to touch the cut on my throat. The tiniest bit more and I'd be bleeding out right now.

Standing there on the balls of my feet, bracing for his next attack, I hear an ominous crackling sound. I glance over and wince inwardly.

The bandanna I left lying across the lamp chimney? It caught fire while we were fighting. And now the fire has run down it to the gunpowder fuse.

He sees my look and grins hugely. "You're running out of time," he chortles.

"Don't you mean *we*?"

He shakes his thick head. Sweat flies from his face. "I don't care if I die. As long as you do too."

Really? "Now you're taking this too far. Being a little dramatic, aren't you?"

The smile he gives me is completely unhinged. From the feral light in his eyes I realize he's serious. This crazy asshole really doesn't care if he dies here.

"Why?" I ask.

"You made me a fool before the Colonel, who is a great man."

Yeah, you said that already.

"If I die here, he will see that I have killed you and he will respect me once again."

"Do you have any idea how *loco* that sounds?"

"Not to me." He gestures with the knife. "Surrender now. You have my word I won't kill you."

To my left, the gunpowder continues to crackle and spit and the flames move ever closer to the kegs. To my right is the hallway that leads to the front door and freedom. I glance that way, then reply.

"For some reason I don't trust you."

"I'll stop the boom," he says.

"Tempting offer, but I'll pass."

I glance again at the hallway, then turn and run the opposite way. It catches him off guard. He was expecting me to run for the front door. That gives me the head start I need.

I snatch up one of the powder kegs and spin, getting it up before me just as he stabs downward at my chest.

The blade sinks deep into the wood, deep enough that it binds. Only for a second, but it's all I need.

I twist the keg hard and he loses his grip on the knife. In the same motion I bring one end of the keg around and crack him hard in the jaw with it.

He staggers backwards. I drop the keg and kick him hard in the stomach, right about where Coyote kicked him. He groans and wraps his arms around himself.

I plant my feet and throw an uppercut, putting everything I have into the punch.

I hit him square under the chin, hard enough that it lifts him up on his toes.

He tips over backwards, out cold.

I stand there, breathing hard, bleeding just about everywhere. I glance at the gunpowder fuse and see that the flames are uncomfortably close to the stack of powder kegs.

I take off running. I hit the front door at full speed and then come skidding to a halt.

Now I know why no one came to help me.

Charging through the front gates are at least a dozen soldiers carrying rifles. Shots ring out and bullets smack around me.

I'm not getting out that way.

There's no going back inside, that's for sure. It's either go left or go right.

I go right. Bullets thud into the wall around me. Fortunately, none of them land.

But it's not really them I'm thinking about. It's that fuse. I can see it in my head. What is it, about two inches away now?

I round the factory. Against the back wall a couple of crates are stacked. That's all I need.

I scurry up the crates like a squirrel and leap for the top of the wall. A bullet snags in my shirt as more shots fly past.

I fling myself off the wall and while I'm still in midair the whole world suddenly turns to fire and light. The thick wall shields me from most of it, but still I feel it, like a giant fist smacking me out of the air.

I tumble head over heels and hit the ground hard.

Blackness takes me.

34

Next thing I know someone is patting my cheek and saying my name over and over. At least I think it's my name he's saying. The sound is muffled and seems to be coming from far away. Also, someone is loudly ringing a bell inside my head.

And I'm not entirely sure what my name is anymore. I'm not sure of much of anything. The pieces inside my head seem to have gotten scattered around, like someone smashed a clay pot.

I push the hand away. "Stop that."

"You're still in there, then?"

I know that voice. It's Tom. I thrash around a bit, trying to sit up. Hands help me up.

Now someone is patting me on the back. "Quit," I say irritably. "Why are you doing that?"

"I thought you were dead," someone says.

I search through the pieces and discover I know this voice too. It's Hi-okee.

"I'm not dead," I say.

"Looks like you came pretty close," Tom says. "Your shirt was still smoldering when we found you. And I think this sticky stuff all over you is blood. Your own blood."

More pieces fall into place. I remember Guzmán cutting me quite a few times. But I can't feel the cuts. Or I don't think so, anyway. It's hard to tell, what with my whole body feeling like a mountain fell on top of me.

"I'm all right." Now why did I say that? I feel everything but all right.

"You hear that?" Tom says. "He says he's all right. Good. We can all go home now. You want anything else before we go, Ace?"

"Not funny, Tom."

"No. It's not."

"Help me get on my horse. That's all."

Tom makes an irritated sound, but he and Hi-okee help me up. I see a horse looming up out of the darkness and I lean against it. I hear Coyote's whicker and he nudges me with his muzzle.

With a lot of help I make it into the saddle. I hear Hi-okee say, "You think we should tie him on?"

"No. I'm fine."

"There's your answer," Tom says. He sounds tired now. "Let's go home."

The ride is pretty awful. Every step sends shocks of pain through my whole body. I fade in and out of consciousness. More than once I come out of my daze to find myself slumped over the saddle horn, my face pressed into Coyote's mane.

I'm starting to really hate dynamite, gunpowder, things that explode in general.

At one point I sit up and realize that I can see the men around me. The sun is getting close to rising. Hi-okee is riding beside me.

"How are you doing?" he asks.

"Better." And I do feel better. I still hurt everywhere, but I think I'm going to make it. "The factory. It's gone, right?"

He flashes a ghost of his normal cocky smile. "Nothing but a hole in the ground. I'll say this, Ace. When you blow something up, you really blow something up."

I think about this for a moment. "The peasants got away?"

"All of them."

"I hope we got the cannons too."

"If they were anywhere behind that wall you did," he says.

"Then it was worth it."

He frowns a little. "Maybe next time some of us could help you."

I manage a smile. That hurts too. "Maybe."

We get to the stronghold an hour or so later. Tom won't talk to me the whole time. He seems angry.

When we ride into the *rancheria*, my mother comes running out. I climb stiffly down off Coyote and she wraps me up in a hug. "Oh, Ace," she says softly. "What did you do to yourself?"

"He tried his best to get himself killed, is what he did," Tom says. "Missed again."

I turn toward him. "I don't know why you're so angry. I got the factory, didn't I?"

"Yeah, and you almost got yourself at the same time."

"But I didn't. Isn't that what counts?"

"You want to know why I'm mad? I'm mad because you keep acting like you're the only one here who can do anything."

"I don't think that." But my words sound weak even to me.

"You sure act like it. When are you going to get that you're not in this alone? There's people here who can help you. Hell, some of them probably are fool enough to even care about you." And with that he stomps off, still muttering under his breath.

"He's right," my mother says.

"Not you too," I say.

"We're your clan, your family," she says. "We're all in this together."

"I never said you weren't." I'm starting to feel pretty angry myself. Why is she giving me a hard time? Shouldn't I be getting some kind of hero's welcome or something?

"You want to know how we've survived here at Pa-Gotzin-Kay all this time?" she asks.

"It's a natural fortress."

"No. That's not why. The reason we've survived this long is because we work together. That's where our strength comes from."

"Can we talk about this later? I really need to lie down," I grumble. What I want to do is mount up and ride away, but I know there's no way I can get back on Coyote right now.

"There is nothing more to talk about," she says. "I have said what needs saying." And I know she won't bring it up again, either. That's something I learned about my mother long ago. She doesn't nag. She says her mind once and that's it.

I stumble over to Coyote and start fumbling at the cinch. I gotta get his saddle off. He's going to end up with saddle sores.

Then Hi-okee is there, gently pushing me away. "Go lie down. I'll take care of this."

I think about resisting, then nod and walk away.

35

It's a few days since I blew up the gunpowder factory, and I'm sitting on a flat rock on the edge of an escarpment that overlooks Nacozari Canyon, thinking. I'm feeling a lot better. Some parts of me actually only hurt most of the time now instead of all of the time.

Tom is still mad at me. The day after I got back he rode off to talk to Buck about the alliance. When he got back I asked him how it went and he ignored me. Since then he spends most of his time working on our little gold mine. His anger confuses me. He seems to be angry because of how close I came to getting myself killed, but that makes no sense to me. Why should that bother him so much? I don't really even know him all that well. Sure, I saw him around a few times while growing up, but until I showed up at his ranch a few weeks ago I'd never spent much time talking to him. Why should he care so much?

It's my life. It's my business what I do with it.

At least that's what I keep telling myself. I don't understand why it doesn't make me feel any better.

Suddenly, out of nowhere, Dee-O-Det pops up. Right by my elbow. I'm so surprised I almost fall off my rock. The old shaman laughs.

"It's not funny," I say irritably, my heart beating too fast. "I hate when you sneak up on me like that." My people know how to move quietly, and I happen to think I'm pretty good at it myself, but I've never known anyone half as good as Dee-O-Det. The man is like a ghost.

"I know that," he says, patting me on the arm. He's grinning hugely. "But I wasn't really sneaking this time." He shakes his finger at me and puts on a stern face. "You weren't paying attention."

"I was thinking."

"And thinking very loudly. That's why you didn't hear me walk up."

I feel a little insulted. It's not like I was sitting here daydreaming. "I have a lot on my mind. You know, being chief and all." I know I haven't officially accepted the job, but still…

"Being chief is easy," he sniffs. He crouches and stares at me.

"No, it's not!" I snap at him. "It's hard."

"Yes," he agrees, nodding. He keeps staring at me with wide eyes, like I'm about to do something fascinating and he doesn't want to miss it.

"You think it's easy?" I say, my voice rising. "People will die if I make the wrong decision."

"People die even if you do not. It is the way of the world."

"That's not really helpful, you know."

"What would be helpful?"

"You know what would be helpful? If you found someone else to be chief. I don't want this job. I never wanted it." I don't say all that I want to say, about how most times I have no idea what I should do for myself. There's no way I can make decisions for the whole clan.

"I can't do that." He looks at me sadly. "It's your burden. You chose it. No one can take it away from you."

"That's ridiculous. I didn't choose to be chief. It was forced on me."

"Was it?" His eyes grow even wider, as if I said something really unexpected. "That's terrible. It really is. Poor Ace, shoved this way and that by larger forces."

"Did you come here just to make fun of me?"

"Of course not. I came to advise you. Because that is my burden. To advise the chief."

"So do it then. Advise me. Say something useful for once."

"Good. You are listening finally." He holds up his finger again. "I advise you that it is time to work on your stalking. It's been some time since our last lesson."

I groan inwardly. Dee-O-Det and his stalking lessons. I have always hated them. He's good at stalking, but terrible at stalking lessons. They're always full of things I don't understand.

"Maybe later. I'm busy right now."

"Ah, yes. Thinking. Thinking hard about important things. But we'll practice stalking anyway."

"Weren't you listening to what I just said?"

"Something about how sad you are to be chief?" he asks, crinkling his brow and scratching his chin. "And complaining that an old man snuck up on you without trying."

"I. Have. Important. Things. To. Do," I say the words slowly and with emphasis. How do I get through to this man?

"I. Know. That," he replies. "Stalking is not about the body, it's about—"

"I said I don't have time right now!" I yell.

Dee-O-Det stands up. I realize that I'm already standing. I don't remember standing up. He takes hold of my wrist. His grip is surprisingly strong. He stares into my eyes. "You're going to need this. Soon. Trust me."

Like that the anger runs out of me. I feel tired and vulnerable. "Okay." I force myself to relax. "Teach me."

"Better," he says, his wrinkled old features creasing in a big smile. He brushes past me and takes my seat on the rock. "Now, try to sneak up on me. I'll make it easy for you. I'll even close my eyes."

For a moment I only look down at him. I want to stomp off. I really don't have time for this. But I also know that once Dee-O-Det gets his mind set on something, he doesn't let up. Better to get this over with.

He closes his eyes and starts whistling. I walk off a hundred paces or so, then skirt around him to where I can approach him from behind his left shoulder. I'm not sure why I choose that angle exactly, only that I remember him telling me long ago that people are most vulnerable over their left shoulder.

"It's because death sits on the left shoulder," he told me at the time. "It is there, always waiting, always watching. Like animals we sense it there, and since we're frightened of it, we try to pretend it isn't there. That makes it a blind spot for us."

I take my time approaching him. The thing about stalking is, you get in a hurry and it won't work. Patience is the essence of stalking.

I use every skill I know as I approach him. Putting each foot down as if I was stepping on a bed of cactus thorns. I stay mostly to the rocks, avoiding twigs that could snap, or sand that could crunch underfoot.

Making it even easier is the whole time he whistles tunelessly. It's not a song that he's whistling. It's not melodic at all. It's an irritating sound, like a mosquito buzzing near your ear. I find it a little unsettling and it's harder to concentrate.

As I get near him I smile, pleased with myself. Whatever Dee-O-Det says, I'm good at this. After all, didn't I once sneak up on a grizzly bear? How many people could do that, huh?

I'm about to touch him on the shoulder when his arm raises and, without turning or opening his eyes, he taps me on the chest.

"You got lucky," I say, immediately irritated again.

His head swivels and he looks at me brightly. "You walk too angry. Angry is not quiet. Angry is loud." He scowls and pounds his fists on the rock, mimicking my footsteps. "Boom, boom, boom. At first I thought it was a herd of buffalo stampeding."

I throw myself down on the rock. "I don't walk angry."

He pats me on the back. "Your problem is you are too heavy."

I shoot him a sideways glance. "Are you saying I'm fat?"

"No. Heavy. It is not the same thing."

"Then I don't know what you're saying."

"You hold too tightly to the ground. Let go. You can't cling and stalk at the same time."

"You know that doesn't make any sense, right?"

"It makes more sense than stomping around all the time like you're mad at the earth. What did the earth ever do to you?"

I think of all the things I've been through in the past couple of years. One crisis after another. "Plenty," I say.

He chuckles and shakes his head. "No, you did those things to yourself. Now, try again, and this time don't be so heavy. Remember that you are spirit. Try to act like it at least a little."

"That's crazy. I'm not spirit. I'm a man."

"Sure you are. We all are. Everything is."

I slap my palm against the rock we're sitting on. "This, this right here? It's the real world. The spirit world is…" I wave my hand vaguely. "Out there somewhere?"

"Are you sure?"

"What? Of course I'm sure."

He shrugs. "Yet you are wrong. Your problem is you are only looking with your eyes. The eyes see only division and separation. There is no separation. Spirit and world blend seamlessly." He laces his fingers together. "All One."

I sigh. This stuff never makes any sense to me. "So how does this help me stalk again?"

"When you move, *know* that you are Spirit as much as Man. Float over the earth. Observe without touching."

"Float, huh?"

He nods.

I stand up wearily. "Okay, I'll float if that's what you want." I walk away grumbling under my breath. Dee-O-Det goes back to whistling.

And that's how I spend the most of the day. Sneaking up on Dee-O-Det over and over. We fall into a pattern. Every time he catches me easily. Every time I get angry and frustrated. Every time he tells me nonsense things about how my problem is I walk angry, that I won't let go and float.

It's a relief midafternoon when Deya comes running up. "We have a rider coming in. Looks like a cowboy."

Hopefully this is good news. Hopefully it means finally the ranchers are ready to talk about allying against Torres.

I look at Dee-O-Det, who's sitting there calmly, looking off into the distance as if he's forgotten anyone else is around.

"Sorry, but I guess we'll have to finish this later."

He looks at me. "Oh, we're done now. It probably won't help, but I did what I could." He stands up. "The rider brings news of a meeting with the ranchers. You will go to it. That is when you will need what I have taught you today."

"What does that mean? Are you saying that this meeting is a trick? Are they trying to lure us into an ambush?" I ask, alarmed. Dee-O-Det often seems crazy, but he has an uncanny way of being right about what is coming.

"No, no trick," he says, shaking his head. "Only you, stumbling around angrily again, making up things to run into." He pounds on the rock a few times and laughs.

36

A man is at the *rancheria* when we get there. From the way he sits the saddle and the hard-used leather chaps he wears, it's clear he is a cowboy. He is wearing a sweat-stained hat with a high crown and his mustache covers most of his leathery face.

"You Ace?" he says when Deya and I come walking up.

"That's me. Who are you?"

"Watkins. I'm from the Lazy R. I have a message for you." While he talks he has his hand near the stock of the rifle sticking up near his knee and his eyes are moving steadily, looking for threats. He's not feeling too comfortable being in the midst of a mess of Apaches. It probably doesn't help that Hi-okee and a couple of the other sentries are standing around holding rifles. They're not pointing at him, but the rifles aren't slung over their shoulders either.

"What is it?"

"There's going to be a meeting of all the ranchers in the area tomorrow at the Lazy R headquarters. They want you there."

I want this alliance, but I don't like the feeling that I'm being ordered around like I'm one of the hands. It makes me cranky. "That's short notice," I say. "I don't know if I can make it."

He looks surprised at that. While he's searching for something to say, Tom comes walking up. Watkins' eyes go to him gratefully. He's awful happy to see another white face here.

"That's a load of crap and you know it, Ace," Tom says. He goes up to the rider and holds out his hand. "Tom Jeffords. Pleased to meet you." Watkins shakes his hand and Tom says, "You're welcome to get down and sit a spell. We could rustle up some grub for you."

Watkins shakes his head. "I have to be getting back. Work to do."

"Well, we're much obliged for the invite, Watkins. Ace and I will be there."

Watkins gathers up his reins, but before he can leave I say, "What happened?" Watkins looks confused. "What made your boss change his mind?"

Watkins glances at Tom, looking for something. I can't tell what. Then he looks back at me.

"Soldiers came. Collecting taxes for General Torres. Only it ain't the normal time of year for taxes, and they wanted twice what it was last year."

"How do you like that?" I say to Tom. "Torres almost kills Buck and the man doesn't blink. But when he wants more money…"

"Play nice," he replies in Apache. "We need them."

"The meeting is for tomorrow afternoon," Watkins says, the words coming out in a rush. I think hearing Tom speak Apache spooked him. "There's a big feed planned. Barbecuing a pig. Roast chicken. Whiskey."

Tom's bearded face splits in a big grin. "That sounds right nice. I have a special fondness for barbecue pig." He rubs his stomach. "We'll be there with our eatin' bibs tied on."

After Watkins leaves, Tom turns to me. "It's been too long since I ate barbecued pig. Buck's from Texas. They know how to barbecue in Texas."

"What makes you think I'm taking you with me?" I ask him. Partly I'm joking, but partly I'm still a little upset about how Tom has been acting lately.

His smile goes away. "I should be there, Niño. Trust me on this."

"Why?"

Dee-O-Det comes up then. "When you parley with the white man, it is best to have one on your side. Tom will make sure it is fair."

At Dee-O-Det's words, a shadow passes over Tom's face. Very quick and gone. I'm not sure anyone but me saw it. I wonder at it.

"Perhaps you should bring your medicine man too," Dee-O-Det says.

He clearly heard that part about whisky. I can't let him go. Once he gets some whisky in him there's no telling what he'll do.

"I heard there has been an outbreak of fever in the Tarahumara children," I say. "Their shaman does not know what it is. I think he could use your help."

"Huh," Dee-O-Det says. "If you don't want me to go, all you have to do is say so. Am I a child to be tricked so easily?"

Tom and I leave the next morning. There was never any real chance I wouldn't take him with me. The ranchers will be more likely to trust me if he's there. And there's no one I'd rather have at my side if I'm going to have to meet with Buck and others like him.

It's only the two of us. I suggested bringing a half dozen of my braves, but Tom said that would send the wrong message. I'm not that happy about it, but I trust he knows what he's doing.

We haven't been riding long when out of the blue Tom says, "I know I've been a bit rough on you these past few days and…well, I'm sorry."

"It's nothing," I say.

"No, it's not nothing. I've been riding you and you deserve to know why."

I glance over at him. "So tell me."

"It's cause I feel responsible for you. I don't want anything to happen to you."

Now I'm confused. "Why would you feel responsible for me?"

He looks away. "I owe your mother that much. Hell, I owe all of you that much."

I'm getting more and more confused. "How do you owe us anything? No one has done as much for us as you have."

"Maybe I did too much," he says under his breath, still not looking at me.

I rein Coyote to a stop and after a moment Tom does as well. "Are you going to tell me what's going on?" I ask.

Tom's scowling. "Forget I said anything."

"Hell no. You started it, you finish it. We have lots of time. Spit it out."

"All right," he grumbles. "But let's keep moving while I do. I didn't eat anything yet today, and I think I can hear that barbecued pig calling me."

We start moving again. Tom shifts his hat, scratches his neck, looks around.

"I'm still waiting," I say.

"You…uh, you know the story about how I brokered the peace treaty between General Howard and your grandpa, don't you?"

"Of course I do. It's a legend." All of my people know of it.

The war had been going on for years. General Howard wanted to parley with Cochise, but after the Bascom affair, my grandfather no longer trusted the white man. And he had good reason not to. The Bascom affair started when Cochise was accused of kidnapping an eleven-year-old boy named Felix Ward, a boy who would later go by the name Mickey Free. Cochise knew the Pinal Indians had kidnapped the boy, not his people, but he also knew if he didn't meet with Lieutenant Bascom he would look guilty. He saw it as a chance to clear his people of guilt.

When he entered Bascom's camp, the lieutenant invited Cochise into his tent to have lunch and talk. But once in there, the lieutenant told Cochise that he was going to be held hostage until his people returned the boy. Cochise drew his knife and cut his way out of the tent and escaped. That triggered a renewal of the war.

In the midst of the war, one day this white man comes riding into Cochise's camp. Alone and unarmed. Most would probably have killed Tom outright, but Cochise was impressed by the man's bravery and welcomed him instead. The two became friends, a friendship that deepened to the point where they became blood brothers. With Tom acting as the go-between, Cochise and General Howard sat down and worked out the treaty that ended the war and gave the Chiricahua Apaches a large piece of their ancestral lands as a reservation.

"A legend," Tom says bitterly. "Is that what you call it?"

"What else would we call it?" I ask, surprised. "You ended the war. You got us our most sacred lands for our reservation."

"For what? A few years? And then they took it away from you and forced your tribe to move to the San Carlos reservation. My only consolation is that at least Cochise wasn't alive to see it happen. I could never have faced him after that."

"Wait. You blame *yourself* for what happened?"

"Who else should I blame?" he says gruffly.

"The US Government maybe? The miners who found silver on our land? The hotheads among our braves who decided to kill some settlers? It seems to me there's plenty of blame to go around."

In a low voice, Tom says, "I blame myself. Every single day. I talked your grandpa into meeting with Howard. Cochise was my blood brother and he trusted me. And I failed him. I've lived with that failure every day since then."

"You stopped a war," I reply. "A war we couldn't win. It's not your fault our lands got taken away."

"I shoulda known it would work out bad in the end. I saw it happen to other tribes. I shoulda known it would happen to you."

"That's not fair. You did the best you could."

He grunts. "Kind of you to say, Ace, even if it ain't true." He looks back at me. "That's why I'm here, you know. When I heard about the trouble brewing, I knew it was my chance to make up for what I did. It's not enough, but it's something. It's also why I've been riding you so hard. I can't let something bad happen to you. Your ma's been through so much in her life. I don't want her to go through that. And maybe in some small way I can pay back your grandpa too."

I don't know what to say. None of this makes sense to me. How could Tom feel bad about something other people did? But it seems to me there's no arguing him out of it.

"We are proud to call you our friend, Tom. No one outside the tribe has ever been such a friend to us. That will never change."

Tom shakes his head and swipes at his eyes quickly. "Goddamn it, Ace," he says, his voice thick. "Knock it off already." He leans over the side of his horse and blows his nose loudly.

"Anyway, now you know why I was bound and determined to go with you today. This time I'll make sure you're not being cheated. I swear it by all that is holy." He forces a smile. "And for the barbecued pig. I'm going for that too."

37

We drop down out of the mountains and move through an area of low, rocky, steep-sided hills. Organ pipe cactus and ocotillo abound. The morning is hot and we make good time. Around midday I spot the hill I've been looking for. It's more of a hump than a hill, all covered in rocks.

I point it out to Tom. "At the foot of that hill is a spring where we can water the horses."

The spring flows from the base of a massive cottonwood tree that looks as old as time. The water gathers in a wide, shallow, natural rock pool before spilling over the edge and dribbling away into the desert sand. Willows and lesser cottonwoods grow thick in the area and there's a thick band of reeds edging the pool itself.

While our horses drink I take my hat off and wipe the sweat from my forehead. It feels good in the shade of the trees. Summer is coming fast. We've made good time. It should only be a couple more hours to the Lazy R headquarters.

Suddenly the horses' heads come up, and they stare off across the pool, ears forward. Tom and I drop our hands to our guns. There's a rustling in the bushes. The bushes part and riders appear. Only two at first, then more and more until there's a couple dozen of them, their horses jostling each other in their eagerness to get to the water.

The men are bristling with pistols and rifles and knives. Gun belts and bandoliers bulging with cartridges hang from them. They're a hard looking bunch, a coldness in their expressions that says these are men who have killed before and will kill again. Something about them reminds me of the men who ride in the Rurales under Colonel Kosterlitzky, but these men have none of their discipline.

Tom and I exchange a look. Neither needs to say anything. These men are trouble any way you look at them. Our hands stay near our guns, but neither of us draws. We don't want to get into a shooting match, not with so many. There's still a chance we can walk away without trouble.

The man leading them is riding a dappled stallion with a black mane. His saddle is Mexican, elaborately-worked leather tooled in silver with a high saddle horn, but from his ten-gallon hat I'd guess he's a Texan. He's clean-shaven and his hair is freshly cut. He has piercing blue eyes, a hawk nose and a chin you could break rocks on. He's chewing on a matchstick as he sits casually on his horse, staring at us. All of his men—and they're clearly *his* men—are staring at us, but none of them speak. I get the feeling they know better than to speak before he does.

He takes out the matchstick. "No need to get your tails up, gents. We're here for water same as you." He's staring at me while he speaks, and I have the strangest feeling I've met him before, but I can't think where. "We can all relax."

Of course, no one actually relaxes, but no one starts shooting either. I call that pretty relaxing.

The man points his matchstick at me. "You Injun?"

"He's Mexican and he's with me," Tom says quickly. "I'm Tom Jeffords."

The leader glances at him and makes this little sound. "Heard of you. Heard you was an Injun lover."

Tom stiffens and I see the fingers on his gun hand curl slightly, but he doesn't take the bait. He simply stares coolly at the man. One thing about Tom, he's got sand.

"I also heard you got giant *cojones*." He turns to his men and holds his hands like he's gripping a watermelon. "Giant *cojones*! Did you men know this man rode alone into the camp of the baddest Apache war chief ever? I'm talking Cochise, here. And he went *unarmed*! How's that for *cojones*?"

The men look at us with new eyes. The leader turns back to Tom and sweeps his ten-gallon hat off with a flourish, bowing a bit in the saddle as he does so. "Well met, Tom. Well met."

And suddenly it clicks for me. I know who he is. I only saw him briefly and from a distance and the light was fading, but something about the way he holds himself gives him away.

It's Mustang Grey!

That makes the men with him the Scalphunters. I've encountered them before, while I was leading Victoria and Blake to the lost temple of Totec. These men make their living hunting down renegade Indians and turning their scalps into the Mexican government for bounty money. Word is they're not too particular whose scalp they take, so long as it looks Indian. They tried to scalp us. We killed a lot of them in return.

I go very cold inside but take care not to let it show. I press my knees into Coyote's sides and I feel his muscles tense in return. He knows we might have to leave very fast soon. He's ready. Making it look like I'm rolling my shoulders to loosen them up, I ease my duster back so I have a clean path to my shootin' irons.

Grey puts his hat back on and sticks the matchstick back in his mouth. He looks from one of us to the other. "We got no problems today here, do we?" he asks us.

Tom and I shake our heads. I can't believe this. Grey seems sincere. I think we're actually going to get out of here without shooting.

Tom gathers up his reins, then. "We'll be seeing you," he says.

But Grey is staring at me again. "I keep thinking I've met you somewhere," he says.

I shrug. "I've been around."

He nods like what I said suddenly makes the rest of the pieces of the puzzle fit. He points the matchstick at me.

"You're that gunslinger Ace!"

I almost, *almost* draw my guns then. Somehow I manage not to.

It's a good thing too. Because Grey isn't reaching for his gun. He's not shouting in rage or anything.

He's *smiling*.

"I've heard of you too," he says.

"What?" I say. I'm having a hard time believing we're still talking and not shooting. "What makes you say that?"

"Don't be modest. You're Ace Lone Wolf. I'm sure of it!"

"You're mistaken—" Tom starts, but Grey interrupts him.

"I know what I see," he says through gritted teeth. "And this is Ace Lone Wolf. The man who defeated the Hashknife Outfit singlehandedly. This man," he says loudly, turning again to his men, "Fought Wes Hardin and Killin' Jim in the street. Killed them both."

They all look at me in a new way. There's new respect there, but something else as well, and suddenly I understand what Tom meant that first morning when he said that wearing two guns marks a man as a gunslick and makes some men want to challenge him because of it. A few of the men facing me right now have an itch to measure themselves against me, to see if they're bad enough to bring me down. A man could make a name for himself that way.

"And if that isn't enough, Ace here was in the gunfight at the OK Corral," Grey continues. "Saved old Wyatt's bacon that day, he did." He turns back to me. "Word is they put you in the Yuma Prison, yet you ain't there right now, are you? How'd you get out?"

"Good behavior?" I say.

Grey throws his head back and laughs. "That's rich," he says, wiping his eyes. "Don't look so tense, Ace. You're kind of a hero, even if you are a half-breed." I notice a gap between his front teeth when he smiles. Why would I notice something like that right now?

"Any man who can escape from the government, well, he's a man to reckon with." He raises one eyebrow. "It's possible that if you were alone I'd consider finding out what the reward is on your head, Ace, but you being in such esteemed company and all…"

"You're saying you don't want us to shoot your gang to pieces," Tom says, surprising me. I glance at him. He's staring at Grey totally dead-faced and blank. He looked this way when Buck Green accused him of lying.

Grey winces. "Not how I'd put it, but still…" He tips his hat slightly.

"Hey, boss," someone calls from the back of Grey's gang. "You forgot something."

Grey turns, irritation on his face. "What?"

All the other Scalphunters are looking at the man who spoke. He's got stringy blond hair and a straw hat smashed almost flat on his head. His beard is as stringy as his hair, and he can't be more than nineteen years old.

"Ace also found the lost temple of Totec. You forgot to mention that."

"He…*what*?" Grey asks, and I know instantly we're in trouble.

"You didn't know that?" the blond man says.

Grey turns back to me. He's made the connection. His jaws are bunched up. His eyes are starting to turn red. "You're *him*!" he says.

And all hell breaks loose.

38

Everybody starts grabbing leather.

I draw one of my pistols, but with my other hand I grab the reins and jerk on them, thinking, like any normal person would, that now would be a good time to make tracks out of here.

Only one little problem.

Coyote has other ideas.

Instead of running away, my fool horse *charges*.

It surprises everyone. Hell, it surprises me. Grey and his men are still in the process of drawing their guns when Coyote leaps across the pool and barrels into their midst.

Several horses go down immediately, thrashing and squealing. The rest out and out panic, whinnying and fighting to get away from this crazed hellcat they thought was a horse until a second ago.

Coyote rears up on his hind legs and starts laying about him with his front hooves. He knocks a rider off his horse and clobbers another horse hard enough that the animal falls down.

I'm firing my gun, trying to do my part to help, but the whole thing is pure madness. Horses are screaming. Men are shouting. Bullets are flying. I don't know who I hit or if I hit. Mostly I want to make sure I don't lose my seat. A man could get stomped to death pretty quick down there on the ground.

Out of the melee looms Grey's face, lips pulled back from his teeth in a snarl. He fires at me, and the bullet whistles by my ear. I whip my pistol around and shoot back, but right then his horse staggers sideways and I miss too.

One of Grey's men swings a rifle at me like a club. It bangs off my shoulder but not hard enough to knock me out of my seat, and I swivel and shoot him in the chest. When I turn back around, I can't see Grey anymore.

All around me the Scalphunters are shouting and trying to get their mounts under control so they can get a clear shot at me, but the horses have different ideas.

They're getting the hell out of here.

It seems longer, but the whole thing probably only takes a few seconds from the time Coyote charges them until the battlefield is ours. Every horse that can still run is fleeing madly through the bushes and trees, riders hanging on for dear life. The horses that are down are thrashing and trying to get up. There's a couple of Scalphunters on the ground, moaning and trying to crawl away.

I pull on the reins. "Let's go, Coyote. Before they come back." For a moment Coyote refuses to move. He stands there with his head held high, like a conquering warrior.

"We don't want to be here when they return," I say.

He shakes his head and stomps one foot, then agrees to leave.

Tom is staring at us with wide eyes, his gun in one hand. "Wow." He shakes his head. "I just…wow."

"Follow me," I say. "I know a place we can hole up."

We race away from the spring. Years ago I discovered that there was a naturally defensible spot on top of the nearby hill and I head there now, Tom close behind. We crash through the rocks. The terrain is rough and it's slow going. The whole time I'm expecting to hear gunshots. We're awfully exposed up here on the side of this hill.

But no gunshots come and a minute later we make it to the top. There's an open area surrounded by boulders and piles of rocks, tall enough that the horses won't be exposed to gunfire. There's only one way in wide enough to get the horses through. We dismount, lead the horses in, and take up positions with our rifles.

I scan the desert. We've got a little elevation here, and I can see past the clump of trees and bushes that marks the spring. Grey and his men are out there milling about, getting themselves back in one piece. I could probably pick one of them off from here, but I'm still hoping that if we don't make any further fuss, Grey will take his men and leave.

Yeah, no way is that happening. Still, I can hope, can't I?

"You ever meet anyone who *didn't* want to shoot you?" Tom says.

I look at him. He's got that Henry rifle of his propped on top of one of the boulders. "What's that mean?"

"It means you make one hell of a lot of enemies."

"Not that many."

"Really? Because…let's see. There was the man you told me about who tried to feed you to the sharks. There's Buck Green. The lieutenant, Guzmán. And that's only in the last few weeks. There's also the Clantons and the James brothers, Jesse and Frank. And now these gentlemen. How do you do it? What's your secret?"

"You make it sound like I'm trying to make enemies."

"How else do you explain it?"

"I dunno. Bad luck?"

"Bad luck," he says skeptically. "You're going with that?"

"Maybe I have a way with people."

"I'll say. But it ain't the right kind of way."

"Is now really a good time for this?"

Tom checks his Henry. "Might be the only time we have left. What does this guy want with you? Why does he hate you so much?"

"I kind of killed a bunch of his men last year."

"I can see where that might rile a man." He peers down at the Scalphunters. Only a couple of them are still visible. The rest have taken cover in the trees. "Any particular reason why, or you just bad at making new friends?"

"Why what?" I'm watching the base of the hill, trying to figure out how they're going to attack. I don't really have time for this.

"Why you killed his men."

I shoot Tom an irritated look. "Are you taking Grey's side?"

"Nope. Only trying to understand what I'm about to get killed for."

"I had no choice. *We* had no choice. They were trying to kill us."

"Hmm," he says.

"What does that mean? What is 'hmm'?" I'm serious. I've heard so many people say that since I left the stronghold and went out into the world, but it's never really made sense to me.

"It means that. Just *hmm*."

"That's not an answer." I can see some shadows in under the trees. Probably they're massing for a charge. It's not going to end well for them. Our cover is good and the approach is rough.

"It's the only answer I got. Dammit, Ace, if you'd stop pissing everybody off, we'd be there by now. I'm missing barbecued pig!"

My stomach growls. I want barbecued pig too. Still, that doesn't make this my fault. "In case you were wondering, they were planning on scalping me and my friends and selling our scalps to the Mexican government." Well, mine anyway. I don't think Victoria's and Blake's scalps could have passed as Indian.

He ponders this for a moment. "So maybe that one really was bad luck. But it brings up another mistake you made."

"And what's that?"

"You shoulda killed him when you had the chance. Then we wouldn't be having this little problem."

I turn to him, forgetting all about Grey and his men for a moment. I'm a little heated. "When I had the *chance*?" I yell. "He and about a hundred of his men had us dead to rights, trapped in some old house. We barely escaped."

"A hundred? You expect me to believe he had a *hundred* men? Sounds like you're making excuses."

"Maybe not a hundred, but a lot. We were lucky to get out alive." I turn back to look at the trees again. "Since we have old Mustang Grey here where we want him now, why don't you show me what I did wrong? Here's your chance. Why don't you shoot him so we can go get our barbecued pig? Then everyone will be happy."

Tom shakes his head, then spits on the ground. "If I do that, how are you going to learn, Niño?"

Now I'm really starting to get mad. "Learn what?"

"About taking responsibility. You can't always run off and leave your duties behind. Your mother and I have—"

"You've been talking to my *mother*?" I'm starting to yell, I know, but I can't seem to help myself.

"Of course I have," he says.

"Why?"

"She's worried about you. And from what I've seen, she has every reason to."

"I don't think you should be talking to my mother."

"It's only to help you. This is all about you."

"That's funny," I say sarcastically, "because I thought it was about us not getting killed before we can stuff ourselves with barbecued pig."

"You're a stubborn one, ain't you, Ace?"

"Now I'm stubborn too?"

"Sometimes a gent has to admit what's right in front of his sniffer."

"And that would be?"

"That you keep running from things that you ought to be facing!" he snaps, a little red creeping from his beard into his cheeks. "Do I have to point out the signs to you or are you going to follow the trail on your own?"

Now that knocks me back on my haunches. I glare out at the open ground, hoping someone gives me something to shoot at soon. Why is it that everyone wants something from me? How is the clan my responsibility? I don't even live there anymore.

"Here they come," Tom says. He sounds like he's saying it's going to rain, he's so calm.

They burst out of the trees in a knot, riding hard up the slope, guns blazing.

It's almost too easy.

I could shoot a couple of the horses in the lead and they'd go down and snarl the whole mass. But I've never liked shooting horses. It's not their fault their owners are no-good, low-down snakes.

My first shot takes a man wearing an old Confederate army hat in the chest. He throws his arms up and goes over backwards. The horse right behind him swerves to try to miss him and runs into another horse, which then runs into another one.

That's the problem with being all bunched up like that. One problem ripples out and hits all of them.

Tom's first shot hits another Scalphunter right in the shoulder. The man turns from the impact and his gun goes off, shooting the man to his left out of his saddle.

Our next two shots take down two more Scalphunters. The charge wavers. A couple of riders peel off and some in the back sort of slow way down. I notice that Grey himself is one of them. I take a shot at him, but right then a rider veers between him and me and the bullet takes that man instead.

There's still a good dozen of them coming and they're shooting as fast as they can, but I can see hesitation there. They're used to running down scared, defenseless Indians and scalping them. They're not used to facing someone armed who knows how to fight back. This isn't nearly as easy as they thought it'd be.

Tom and I drop a couple more of them and then they give it up and turn tail and run.

39

"Made it through that one okay," Tom says. He starts reloading the Henry. "How long you figure before they try again?"

I look down the slope. I count five men down. "Probably not right away," I say.

"Think they'll leave now?"

I shake my head, remembering the last time I ran into this guy. "Grey's a stubborn one. He doesn't give up easy."

"I was afraid you'd say that. I guess we'll just have to convince him then," Tom says, levering a fresh round into the chamber. "You have any food in your saddlebags?"

"Nope. I thought we'd eat…you know."

"I was afraid you'd say that too. You got any good news?"

"At least it's not raining."

He gives me a sour look. "Are you trying to be funny?"

"It didn't work?"

A voice rings out down below. It's Grey.

"I've got you this time, Ace!" he shouts.

"You sure about that?" I yell back. "From where I'm sitting, we're winning."

"You won the first battle, but we'll win the war. We've got you surrounded. We'll starve you out if we have to!"

"Thirst will get us before hunger," Tom says under his breath. "I didn't get a chance to refill my canteen."

I didn't either. I also don't have a lot of ammo. But there's no point in bringing it up now.

"I tell you what, Grey," I yell down at him. "You leave now and I won't come out there and shoot you. How does that sound to you?"

Grey's response is to cuss up a blue streak. Not surprising, really. He's like all the other men out there I've met who fancy themselves bad *hombres*. He knows how to wave a gun around and terrorize people, but there's not a lot going on upstairs. Once you make them angry, they've got nothing but swear words. Grey isn't even good at it. All he's doing is repeating himself.

Once he tapers off, I yell again. "What was that, Grey? I think I missed something."

He sticks his head out from the trees and points at me. "You're going to die, you filthy, goddamned Injun! I'm gonna scalp you and cut your ears off and feed them to the hogs."

I shoot, and he drops out of sight. The echo dies away and I wait, hoping that I hit him. But then I hear his voice again.

"Shit, Ace, what'd you go and do that for? You just shot my cook, the only man in my whole outfit who can make a pot of beans without poisoning the lot of us." He sounds kind of sad now.

"Next time hold still and I'll make sure it's you!" I call back. "Take that as a friendly warning. Grab your poke and ride on out of here."

A barrage of lead is his answer. Tom and I hunker down and let it fly over our heads. When it stops again, I poke my head up. "You're wearing on my patience. Is that your final answer?"

More cursing follows, but this time Grey is smart enough to keep his head down.

I sit down and lean back against the rock. Tom sits down next to me. "I reckon they'll hit us about dark," he says. "What do you think?"

"I think you're right. Might as well get some rest." I take a sip out of my dwindling water. I'll be out by the end of the day. One way or another, this has to end tonight.

We're right. About the time it gets dark, they hit us again. This time they come on foot and attack us from every direction. Tom's on one side and I'm on the other, but there's no way we can cover every approach and they know it.

But we have a lot of rocks to hide behind, and we're ready for them.

Figures burst from the trees down below me and start running up the slope. I fire a couple of quick shots and hear a cry of pain. A second later I hear Tom's Henry barking behind me and a scream.

I drop down from my perch, take a few quick steps to my right and look out through the rocks to see a handful of men running up this side of the hill as well. I fire a couple of times, then move to another spot and shoot at the men I see there. Tom's doing the same.

We drop a few of them, but plenty of them still make it to the perimeter. I hear boots on rocks and turn to see a man silhouetted against the night sky. The Winchester's empty so I drop it and draw my pistols. The one in my right hand flashes and the man throws his arms up like he's having a hallelujah moment and topples over backwards.

Three men rise up on the rocks around Tom and he backs up, firing from the hip. He drops the first two and I shoot the next one a split second before he guns Tom down. The man crumples, his shot going wild.

The shooting gets hot and heavy for a while then, Grey's men appearing everywhere. Bullets whine by my head. A man appears in the gap in the rocks we used to get in here, and I spin and shoot him in the gut. He goes down and the man behind him trips over him. Which is lucky for him because then my next shot misses him.

I won't miss again.

Except when I pull the trigger again, nothing happens. I'm empty. I'm thumbing a shell into my pistol when the man jumps up. Hollering, he fires at me a couple of times. He should hit me, but he rushes his shots and they ping off the rocks instead.

I get a round loaded and bring my gun to bear on him, but he's he's too close to the horses. I don't want to hit them by accident.

He ducks behind Coyote. There's a couple of quick thumps and the man goes flying. He lies crumpled on the ground and doesn't move. I could have told him that was a bad idea.

Another man sticks his head up over the rocks. I fire and the head disappears.

Silence.

"Tom?" I say.

No answer.

"Tom!"

"No need to yell," he calls back, appearing out of the shadows. "I ain't deaf."

"You're okay."

"Of course I'm okay. No way varmints like these are killing me." He walks over to me, loading his pistol as he comes. "It ain't good, though," he says in a low voice. "I'm about spent. Six shots for the pistol, four for the Henry. What do you have?"

"About the same," I reply.

"We'll get some off of these bodies," he says, gesturing at the fallen men, "but I don't know if we'll survive another attack like that. We oughtta leave, you know."

"Sure. How about you dig us a tunnel?"

"I seem to have misplaced my shovel." I can see his teeth in the dimness as he smiles. "I guess we'll just have to stay and fight then. He's bound to run out of men sooner or later."

Grey calls out. "How's it going in there, boys? Did you stop any bullets?"

"Not a one," I call back. "I've never seen worse shooting in my life. Where'd you get these men, Grey?"

"I'm looking forward to your scalp, Ace, I really am. I think I'll keep that one, tie it to my saddle horn as a souvenir."

"Why don't you come up here yourself and take it," I yell. "Stop hiding behind your men and face me like a man." Who knows? Maybe I can shame him into fighting me one-on-one.

"And give you a chance to shoot me in the back? I don't think so," Grey calls. "But I know you fellers have to be running low on ammo. What're you down to, a dozen rounds or so? And water, how's that going? Getting thirsty yet?"

Tom and I trade looks. We finished our water around sundown. When that sun comes up tomorrow it's going to get unpleasant fast.

"I think all I need to do now is wait," Grey continues. "I'm holding all the cards."

He's quiet for a couple of minutes, then he starts up again. "It's funny we should run into you here. You know where we was headed when we ran into you?"

"I can't say I care," I reply.

"Sure you do. We were headed down to Chihuahua to join up with General Torres and his men. He promised me a hundred pesos for every dead Injun."

"And you should know that Torres is a liar and a cheat. You'll never see that money."

"That's where you're wrong. We're all going to be rich men. We're going to kill ever Injun in the north of Mexico. Probably even kill your mama while we're at it, Ace. How does that grab you?"

Now he's gone too far.

"You're right," I tell Tom. "I should have killed him when I had the chance. I won't make the same mistake again." I get my moccasins out of my saddle bags and start putting them on.

"What're you doing?" Tom asks.

"I'm going to go kill Mustang Grey."

40

I wait until well after midnight. The Scalphunters' camp is quiet by then, the fires burned down to coals. I shuck my hat and my duster.

"This is a terrible idea," Tom says.

"You said that already. About a hundred times."

"And I'll keep saying it because it's true. Grey's expecting you to try this. You won't get within twenty feet of him. He's holed up in those trees and there's all kinds of leaves and twigs under there. You're bound to make noise. His men are going to gun you down."

"Do you have any better ideas?"

That slows him down. He settles for glaring at me.

"Any ideas at all?"

"You know I don't," he grumbles.

"I can do this. Trust me."

He mutters something that might be agreement. The problem is, I'm not sure *I* trust me. I've spent the last few hours thinking about Dee-O-Det's words, about moving like a spirit.

I am spirit, I tell myself once again, hoping I'll believe it this time.

"At least take a gun," Tom whispers.

I don't bother to reply. We've already argued this too. I'm not wearing my gun belt because leather creaks. I'm not sticking a pistol in my pants because it might slip out at the wrong time. Lead isn't going to get me through this. It's either stealth or nothing.

"I've known donkeys that were less stubborn than you," Tom says.

I draw my Bowie knife out of its sheath on my gun belt. "I'm taking this," I say.

"Better than nothing, I guess," he replies. "I wish there was some wind at least. I've never seen a night so quiet."

"If you're trying to build my confidence, it's not working."

He waves me off. "Watch yourself out there. I'll be ready. If anything happens, I'll start shooting. Maybe I can distract a few of them."

"And maybe you'll shoot me by accident."

"Best if I don't," he replies.

I sneak out through one the gap in the rocks and freeze in a crouch, listening, watching, sniffing the air.

When I'm satisfied there's no one on the slope below me, I start for their camp. As I move, I repeat Dee-O-Det's words to myself. *I am spirit. I am spirit.* I sure hope I start believing it by the time I get to the bottom of the hill.

Near the base of the hill, in a darker patch of shadow by some rocks, I sense, rather than hear, movement. I freeze, staring at the spot, my knife at the ready.

A crunching of a bootheel and then another sound, the sound of someone scratching himself, followed by a soft sigh. I can't see the man, but I can see right where he is. I can smell him too, the reek of old sweat and tobacco. So at least one of Grey's men didn't fall asleep on watch.

I briefly consider taking him out, then discard the idea. I'm here for Grey. I don't want to get sidetracked. No matter how careful I am, there's always the chance that the man will cry out or manage to fire his gun. If that happens, I lose my chance. I won't get another one.

I come to the trees and slip into their shadow, where I pause. Like Tom said, it's going to be hard going here. Not only is it a lot darker under here, but the ground is littered with dead leaves and small twigs. It will be close to impossible to make it through here without making any sound, especially on a night so still, so quiet. A bird shifts its position on a branch overhead and it sounds incredibly loud. If I crack a twig, or rustle a leaf, someone's going to hear.

I wait and listen, hoping other sentries will reveal themselves. After a couple of minutes I hear a rustling sound off to the right. I look over there. A stray bit of starlight leaks through the foliage and glints off the barrel of a pistol.

Then off to the left I hear a new sound. Someone standing up. Whoever it is takes a couple of steps and then stops. He must be waking up someone to relieve him because I hear someone groan softly and roll over.

"Get up," the standing man whispers. My ears perk up. The voice belongs to Grey. "It's your watch."

The man on the ground sits up and mumbles something, too low for me to hear.

"I'm going to get some shuteye," Grey whispers. "You stay quiet and alert, you hear me?"

Another mumbled response.

"If you fall asleep, so help me God I will scalp you myself," Grey growls. He raises his voice slightly so the other sentry off to my right can hear him too. "That goes for you too, Lew. I mean it."

I wait there as the new man takes his position and gets himself settled. I hear Grey's footsteps as he goes to his bedroll and mark the spot. That makes things easier. At least I don't have to go looking around for him. Nice of him to help me out like that. I heft the Bowie knife, imagining sticking it in his gut.

The down side is that now I have to wait for Grey to fall asleep. But waiting is something I'm good at.

I let a half hour pass. The whole time I repeat Dee-O-Det's words to myself over and over. Strangely, it makes me feel different. I feel lighter somehow, like I'm barely touching the ground. It even seems like I can see better, outlines of things in the blackness that I couldn't see before.

At some point, without really making the decision to, I start to move. I don't try to push the gathered leaves and twigs aside to place my foot. If I do, it will make too much noise. So I don't try. I trust Dee-O-Det, trust what he taught me.

And it works. When I put my foot down I can feel the leaves and twigs through the sole of my moccasin, but they make no sound. Another step and still no sound. Then another, and another. I'm like a ghost. Touching nothing. Leaving no trace.

Ever so slowly I make my way through the center of the camp. There are only a few men sleeping here under the trees, which means that most of them are strung out in a perimeter around the little hill.

My path takes me right by one of the sentries. He's so close I could take his hat. Not that I'd want to. He smells worse than the other one. What is it about being a murderous villain that makes men forget how to clean themselves?

It takes a long time, but finally I get to where Grey is sleeping. He's a dark shape on the ground rolled up in a thin blanket, his hat over his eyes.

I crouch over him and raise the Bowie knife.

41

Dammit.

I can't do it.

No matter how I try, I just can't kill a defenseless man. I know I should. This man is the worst of the worst. He deserves to die. I'd be doing the world a favor by slitting his throat.

But it goes against the grain.

I can kill a man in a fight, but I can't kill him while he's asleep.

Now what?

There might still be a way out of this. What if I take him hostage and use him to get Tom and me out of here? Maybe I'll get lucky and he'll resist and I can kill him then.

I crouch by his head and place the blade against his throat.

His eyes fly open and he reaches for his gun.

So much for doing this quietly.

I lash out with the butt of the Bowie knife and crack him hard on the forehead. He sits up. When he does, I grab his hair and yank his head back, pressing the knife hard to his throat.

"One move and I'll cut your throat," I hiss in his ear.

The sentries are stirring. One of them, Lew I think, says in a loud whisper, "Hey, what's going on over there? You okay, boss?"

"This damn Injun's got a blade to my throat," Grey snaps. "Does that sound okay to you?"

"What?" Lew cries, scrambling to his feet

The other sentry makes a sound of surprise and says, "I was awake the whole time, I swear, Mustang. I don't know how he got by me."

"I do," Grey snarls. "He got by you because you're about as useful as tits on a bull. Both of you. When I get out of this I'm going to show you what happens to those who fail me."

The men who were sleeping are getting up now, and I hear a couple of sentries come running in, drawn by the commotion.

"You're a long ways from out of this," I tell Grey, standing and jerking him to his feet.

"Shit," he says, "you got nothing. You kill me, they'll kill you."

"But you'll be dead," I reply. "And I count that a win."

"You ain't gonna kill me."

"You sure about that?" I press the knife harder against his throat. It's sharp and I know he's bleeding now.

"Okay, okay, don't get so touchy," he says. "We can all ride away from this. That's what you want, isn't it? To ride away?"

What I want is to cut his throat. I haven't taken his gun yet. I want him to go for it. Then I get to kill him. I think he senses this because he's making no moves. I'd feel his muscles start to tense if he was about to do anything.

"You win," Grey says. "You got the drop on me, sure enough. I'll tell my men to back off, and you and your Indian-loving friend can ride away." He raises his voice. "All you men fall back. Let them go, you hear me?"

The men mutter their agreement, and I hear them moving away. From the hilltop Tom calls my name.

"It's okay, Tom!" I yell back. "Come on out and bring the horses." I shove Grey forward toward the hill. It's too dark and close under these trees. I can't tell who might be hiding where pointing a gun at me.

We emerge from the trees. Tom comes riding down the hill, Coyote following.

Tom looks down at Grey. "I thought you said you were going to kill him."

"He ain't got the spine for it," Grey says.

"Watch it," I warn him. I can see the blood running down his neck. If I push just a little harder I'll cut the artery for sure.

"I ain't watching nothing. You two ride on out of here and run as far and as fast as you can. But know this. There's nowhere far enough you can go. I'll hunt you to the ends of the earth and the last thing you see will be my gun pointing at your face."

"Shut up," I tell him.

"Or what? We already established that you're too noble to kill a defenseless man," he sneers.

"But I'm not," Tom says.

His pistol comes up and flame stabs from the end.

Grey crumples to the ground.

"I could not abide listening to that man say one more word," Tom says. He looks at me. "I reckon we should be going, don't you?"

I jump on Coyote and we hightail it out of there. A few shots ring out, but nothing gets close and none of them give chase. I've got a feeling Grey's men don't love him enough—or at all—to care about avenging him. Certainly not enough to risk getting shot over it.

We ride hard through the last hour or so of darkness, and when the sun comes up we pause by this little rocky knob, and Tom and I climb up it to sweep our backtrail with the binoculars.

"I don't see anything," Tom says, handing the glasses back to me.

"I'm sorry," I say. "I couldn't do it."

"Don't be sorry, Niño," he says. "You're not a killer. There's no shame in that."

"But you are?"

He shakes his head. "Naw, I'm not a killer either. I will shoot a man to save a friend's life, though." He gives me a bearded grin.

We walk down the hill and mount up. "You think they got any of that barbecued pig left?" Tom asks me. "I'm feeling a mite peckish."

42

We're still a couple of miles from the Lazy R ranch, riding down the road, when I see a flash of sunlight on metal on a low ridge to our right. Without pointing, I say, "There's someone up in those rocks."

Tom grins. "You only now noticing that?"

"You're telling me you already knew?"

"Saw him half an hour ago," he says.

"Sure you did." I glance up where I saw the flash, but I don't stare, instead sweeping my gaze across the spot so he won't know I'm looking at him. When I do I see the barrel of a rifle sticking out between two rocks. "What do you want to do?" I ask Tom.

"Keep on riding like you saw nothing."

"And just let him shoot us?"

"I'll lay you pesos to pig ears he's not going to shoot us. He's one of Buck's hands. He wants to make sure we're friendly, that's all."

"You'd bet a peso against a pig's ear?"

"It's a saying, Ace."

"A strange saying."

"They all are. Promise me you won't do anything rash like you normally do."

"I don't normally do rash things."

He chuckles. "I don't think you know what rash means then."

I don't. Not really. I mean, I know what a rash is. I knew a cowboy once who had a terrible rash all over his back. I have a feeling he isn't talking about that kind of rash.

"It means you are prone to hasty decisions," he says.

"I knew that. Still not true."

"Whatever you say," he says agreeably. "No sense in trying to ride a dead horse."

That one I'm pretty sure I know what it means, but I don't see how it fits here. I decide to leave it alone.

"Stop right there!" the man calls out.

We stop. "It's Tom Jeffords and Ace," Tom calls out. "We're here for the meeting."

"You're late! The meeting was yesterday."

Tom gives me a look. Clearly he still blames me for the whole Mustang Grey mess.

"We know that," Tom calls back. "We were unavoidably detained. But now we're here."

"You look familiar," the man says.

"Because I *am* familiar, gosh darn it!" Tom says, finally getting a little heated. "I was here only a few days ago meeting with Buck."

"I allow you don't look like any of Torres' men."

"Are we going to stand here and flap our gums all day?" Tom says.

The gun barrel rises. "Go on then. You know where the ranch house is, I expect."

"I expect it's at the other end of this road," Tom grumbles. He looks at me. "Hired for his guns, not his brains I guess."

We ride on down the road. I can feel that rifle barrel at my back, but nothing happens.

The road leads up and over a ridge. Off in the distance I can see a large building, looks like a church with a wall around it, but the road doesn't seem to be heading there. I point. "That's not the headquarters, is it?"

Tom shakes his head. "Some kind of ruined mission or something, from the old Spanish conquistador days. No one's lived there for a hundred years, so Buck says."

The road drops off the ridge. Down the other side is the headquarters.

"Remember what we talked about," Tom says. "Let me do the talking, okay? I don't need you puffing up like a bantam rooster and starting a gunfight or something."

"Puffing up like a what? What makes you think I'd do that?"

"Because I know you. You're a hothead."

"Only when there's good reason," I grumble.

"Which you always seem to find."

The ranch house sits in the bend of a wide, sandy creek, nestled between two long, black, volcanic ridges. Cottonwoods grow alongside the creek, which only has a trickle of water in it that disappears into the sand after fifty yards or so. A couple of willows shade the front yard. The house is neatly painted and there's curtains at the windows. A black buggy sits in the yard.

We ride across the yard, and Buck comes walking out of the house. He still has a bandage wrapped around his chest. He stands on the covered porch, hooks his thumbs in his belt and watches us approach. He doesn't holler a welcome or anything. He doesn't look happy.

We come to a stop and sit there on our horses staring at Buck while he stares at us. Buck speaks for the first time. "You're late. The meeting was yesterday."

"Yeah, I heard that," Tom replies.

"Thought maybe you weren't coming after all," Buck says, staring suspiciously at me.

"It got a little close," Tom agrees. "Mustang Grey and his men got in our way."

"You tangled with Mustang Grey and you're still alive?" Buck says, his eyes widening a bit. He's having to change his opinion of us. Then his eyes narrow back down in suspicion. "Grey rides with a tough crew and I don't see a scratch on either of you. How does that work?"

"I just have a way with people," I reply, ignoring Tom's warning look. "Everybody likes me. Once I explained things to Grey he let us go. Even gave us little presents, all tied up with bows."

Buck scowls darkly, and I give him my biggest smile. Something about Buck that gets my dander up. I can't help but needle him a little.

"The point is that we made it," Tom says. "And judging by the brands on the horses in your corral and that buggy there, the others are still here."

Buck nods. Still he stands at the top of the step, not calling us inside. He chews on his lip, thinking.

"Dammit, Buck. Are you going to invite us inside or not?" Tom snaps.

Buck squints at me. "Don't know how I feel about having an Apache in my house."

That's enough for me. I feel a strong urge to plant my fist in Buck's face. "I *know* how I feel about going into your house." I spit on the ground. "I'm leaving." I start to turn Coyote to leave, but Tom grabs my arm.

"Bad enough I have to handle one pigheaded fool," he says in a low voice. "Don't make it two."

He turns back to Buck. "We came all this way and we're coming inside," Tom says, dismounting. "Don't forget who saved your life after you got drygulched by those Yaquis."

"We still don't know if it was Yaquis or not. Coulda been someone else." Buck is looking belligerently at me. I wish he didn't have that bandage wrapped around him. I'd like to get down and pound some manners into him.

"Come on, Ace," Tom says and I get down. Tom walks up the steps and I follow. Buck reluctantly moves aside.

"We'd sure be obliged if you could rustle us up a couple of plates of grub, Buck," Tom says cheerfully, trying to smooth things over. "A mess of that barbecued pig would go down nice. You still have some, don't you? You didn't eat it all yesterday?"

"We still have some," Buck allows. He walks inside and we follow him.

I take off my hat and look around, my eyes adjusting to the room, which is dim after the bright sunlight outside. There's a stone fireplace and over it is mounted a stuffed bear head. On another wall is a stuffed elk head. They look at us with glass eyes. I look away. I don't know what it is, but I don't like those dead eyes looking at me. It makes me uncomfortable.

In the middle of the room is a long table with chairs drawn up around it. At first I think there's no one else in there, but then I realize there is a man sitting at the table. He's a little guy, with narrow shoulders and small hands. His hair is neatly trimmed and oiled down and he's wearing a fine brown suit with a string tie. On his lap he's holding a large leather case, both hands clasped on top.

"Marla!" Buck bellows. "Got a couple of mouths to feed! Fetch up some of that pig and beans!" To Tom he says, "I'll go roust the others. They're sleeping it off here and there." As he says this, the back door opens and a balding man with gray hair comes in. He looks to be in his sixties, but he's a long way from feeble. His back is straight and the severe look in his eyes says he doesn't have a lot of patience for foolishness.

Then the door to the kitchen opens and a long-nosed woman with her hair tied up in a bun comes into the room. She's wearing an apron and she's got a rolling pin in one hand, holding it like she wants to use it on someone.

"Buck Green!" she barks, loud enough that we all flinch. "What have I told you? I'm not one of your hands. If you want something from me you can come address me in a civil fashion. Don't go bellering at me like a mad bull or you'll be out on your ear with nothing to eat." She shakes the rolling pin at him while she talks.

To my surprise, Green doesn't respond by shouting back. His eyes drop and he lowers his head a little. He says something under his breath.

"What was that?" she asks, a hard glint in her eyes.

"Yes, dear," he says quietly.

She looks over at us and smiles. At both of us. If it bothers her having an Apache in her home, she doesn't show it. The smile does wonders for her. She doesn't look nearly so sharp anymore. I decide I like this woman.

"Welcome to our home, gentlemen," she says in a friendly tone. "I hope you won't judge our hospitality by Buck here."

"No, ma'am," Tom says, and I echo him.

"I'll whip the two of you up some food in no time. Would you like some eggs fried in butter with that?"

"I surely would," Tom says eagerly. He sounds like a puppy offered a treat. "Nothing could make me happier." She looks at me and I nod. She heads back into the kitchen.

Buck starts for the back door, but the old guy stops him. "They're coming. Just soaking their heads a bit is all. Some people can't handle their whisky."

He walks over and shakes Tom's hand. "I'm Wilson Task, owner of the Triple M ranch."

"I'm Tom—" Tom starts to say, but Wilson cuts him off.

"I know who you are, Tom Jeffords. Your reputation precedes you, sir. I'm glad to see you here on our side."

Wilson turns to me. He doesn't stick his hand out and neither do I. He looks me up and down. "It seems your reputation precedes you as well, Ace." His eyes bore into me.

I tense. It's generally not a good thing when someone knows who I am. The last I checked I was wanted in Texas, Colorado and the Arizona Territory. Maybe the New Mexico Territory too. I'm not sure.

"I heard you helped out Wyatt Earp with a little problem he had," he says at last. "A friend of Wyatt's is a friend of mine." He sticks out his hand and I shake it.

Buck goes to the sideboard and picks up a bottle sitting there. With his other hand he grabs a handful of glasses. He sets it all on the table, pours himself some whisky, then pushes the glasses around. He offers the bottle to the little guy with the greased-up hair. The little guy shakes his head, and Buck shrugs and pours himself a little more. Wilson sits down but doesn't reach for a glass.

Tom and I take seats. Tom pours himself some whisky, but I refuse. I still don't trust Buck Green and I want to keep my wits about me. My people have a long history of getting drunk around white men and having bad things happen.

The back door opens and three more men enter. They're all in their forties and fifties, all of them ranchers by the looks of them. Green introduces them to us. None of them do more than nod in my direction. Two of them I forget their names instantly, but the third I remember.

His name is Riggs. He has a patchy beard and a crooked nose. He's the only one who doesn't take off his hat when he comes inside. It's a big, black felt cowboy hat. He's got a thick neck and thick shoulders and he walks with his chin jutting out in front of him, like he wants to poke someone with it.

I instantly don't trust him. From the look on his face, he doesn't trust me either.

We all sit down around the table. "Now that everyone's here, we can finish our meeting," one of the newcomers says. He's the youngest of them. He's wearing a tan leather vest and his pistol is shiny and nickel-plated. His eyes are bloodshot, but he flashes a smile around the table at everyone.

"Damn straight," Riggs says. "I got work to get back to. I don't have time to waste waiting for people who don't show up when they say they will."

That gets my back up a little and I open my mouth to reply, but Tom kicks me under the table. Oh yeah. I seem to remember agreeing to let him do the talking and not acting like a rooster or something.

"The important thing is we're here now," Tom says smoothly. "You've all had time to talk. What's the consensus?"

"Ain't one," Riggs says. "Some want to ally with the Apaches. Others got more sense than that." It's clear from his tone which side he falls on.

"So that's it, then?" Tom asks. "You know Ace's people have been up there in those mountains for years not causing problems, but you still won't trust them?"

"An Apache is an Apache," Buck says. "Can't change that any more than a wolf can change into a dog."

"That's you speaking the language General Torres wants to hear," Tom says. "He wants you all divided, because then it's going to be easy to pick you off one by one."

"Now hold on," Wilson says. "He isn't speaking for all of us. Tony here," he gestures to the young man with the bright smile, "and Slaughter's man over there," he jabs a thumb at the little man with the slicked-back hair, "and I want an alliance."

"What about you, Horace?" Tom asks the other man who came in with Riggs. He's in his fifties, a dour man with rugged features and a battered old hat that's mostly holes.

"Ain't decided yet," he replies.

"It was the Apaches who blew up the gunpowder factory," Tom reminds them. "That has to count for something."

"My hat's off to you for that," Wilson says, nodding at me. "Tom says it was you who went in and did the deed. Almost got yourself blown up too."

"They were planning to bring cannons into the mountains and use them on women and children," I say.

"They would've used those cannons on you next," Tom says. "On any of you who didn't fall into line."

Marla brings two plates of food in then and sets them down in front of Tom and me. We thank her and she beams at us. She looks over the others at the table, does a quick head count and leaves, shaking her head.

"They'd have to get them in place first," Riggs growls.

"And because of Ace now Mustang Grey and his Scalphunters won't be joining Torres," Tom says.

Wilson sits forward, his eyes intense. “You saw those vermin? Where?”

“We ran across them a few miles back. There’s fewer of them now, and they’re missing a leader,” Tom replies.

“Hot damn!” Wilson says, clapping his hands together. “But that’s good news. I’ve been wanting to shoot and stuff that polecat for years.” Smiles and nods come from the other men, all except for Riggs and Buck, who are still scowling.

“As I said yesterday,” the little man with the slicked-back hair says suddenly, “my employer, John Slaughter, is fully prepared to enter into an alliance with the Apaches.”

Everyone turns and looks at him and he swallows nervously. I expect him to sink down in his chair, he seems so mouse-like, but with an effort he straightens and continues.

“I have here in this case something which will greatly aid us in our cause.” With an effort, he lifts the case and sets it on the table.

“I’ve been wondering what you had in there, Trevayne,” Wilson says.

“It’s not a Gatling gun, is it?” Buck asks, his ears perking up. “A Gatling gun would sure enough come in handy.”

“Unfortunately, no,” Trevayne replies. “But something perhaps even more useful.” He opens the case and we all crane our necks to see what he has in there.

I don’t know about the others, but I’m disappointed. It looks like some kind of folding metal stand, and there’s a round mirror that looks like it connects to the stand.

“A mirror?” Riggs scoffs. “What are we supposed to do with that? Blind the General’s soldiers?”

“That’s perfect,” Tom says, breaking into a grin. “Do you have a partner for that?”

“Out in the buggy,” Trevayne replies.

Tom rubs his hands together. “Things just got a lot easier.”

“Someone want to tell me what that thing is?” Buck says irritably.

“It’s a heliograph,” Tom says.

Buck scowls. “A what?”

“A heliograph. The army uses them for signaling,” Tom says.

“Mr. Slaughter thinks with one mounted on top of Sentinel Peak and the other up in the mountains by Pa-Gotzin-Kay we should have no problem staying in constant communication," Trevayne says. "He is also prepared to offer the use of two telescopes."

Wilson slaps the table loudly. "That's a damn fine idea."

"I still think a Gatling gun would have been better," Buck grumbles.

"Not so. What's the biggest problem this alliance has?" Tom asks.

"You mean, apart from the fact that it ain't a true alliance yet?" Buck asks.

"It's that we're too spread out," Tom continues. "It takes half a day at least to get anywhere. But with the heliograph, that all changes. All we have to do is mount them and keep them manned. When anybody has any trouble they flash the others and we know to come running."

"That's not a terrible idea," Buck allows grudgingly. Riggs still looks unconvinced.

"My employer hoped you would see it that way," Trevayne says.

"So, does that help any of you who're sitting on the fence still?" Wilson asks.

A couple of hours later we're leaving the Lazy R ranch. Tied to the back of my saddle is a heliograph and a small telescope.

"See, Ace," Tom says. "I told you if you just let me handle the talking everything would work out."

"I'm not sure why you needed me along at all."

"They needed to get a look at your face in person, see that you're not quite the bloodthirsty savage they thought you were."

"I don't think we convinced Buck or Riggs."

"Well, Buck is…Buck. He'll come around. I'm not sure I think much of Riggs myself. Something about that man that gets under my hide. Still, we don't need to like him. We just need to not be fighting with him."

43

"We need the Yaquis," my mother says.

We're sitting in the council circle. Tom and I just finished telling the council about the meeting with the ranchers. In the end all of them agreed to the alliance, even Buck and Riggs, though neither one looked too happy about it.

"I agree," Dee-O-Det says. "The cowboys will bring guns and bullets that we need, but the Yaquis are fierce fighters."

Both of them are looking at me. In fact, all of the council is looking at me. "Kelzel isn't going to ally with us," I say. "Torres gave the Yaquis their land back, remember?"

"He's going to betray them," my mother says. "You know this."

"The question is, does Kelzel?" I reply.

"Kelzel is wily," Dee-O-Det says. "He knows."

"Which is why you need to go talk to him," my mother says. "You can convince him to join us."

"Me? Really? Did you forget that the last time I ran across some Yaquis they staked me to an anthill and left me to die? They even stole my hat. There's still some hard feelings there."

My mother and Tom exchange looks. "Your son has a knack for making friends," Tom says. "I've tried talking to him about it, but you know how stubborn he is."

"You are the chief. Put it behind you for the good of your people," my mother says.

"You know, I never really agreed to be chief," I say.

"You don't need to," she says calmly. "It's who you are."

"Can we talk about this some other time?"

"If you wish," she says, her tone making it clear there's nothing left to talk about.

I try again to get them to see reason. "I can't exactly ride up to Kelzel and say, let's talk. They'll shoot me before I get a word out."

"You'll think of something," Dee-O-Det says confidently.

"Why don't you go talk to him?"

"I can't," he says. "I'm too old. And there's bad blood between me and Kelzel's medicine man."

"What? How? You've never even met him."

"Not in the sunlight world, no. But we have met in the spirit world. He envies my powers."

"You're making that up. You've never met in the spirit world."

"Don't talk about things you know nothing about," he says. "Leave the spirit world to the shamans. You worry about how to swing Kelzel to our side." He looks around at the rest of the council. "We are agreed then? Ace will go and parley with Kelzel?" Everyone nods. He looks back at me.

"Don't I get a vote in this? It seems like if I have to be chief I should get a vote."

"The council has made its decision," he says calmly. "You should have spoken up when you had the chance."

"But I did!"

"It's too late now. This meeting is over." Everyone starts getting up to leave.

"Sometimes I hate you," I say to Dee-O-Det.

"I am a rascal," he agrees.

"That's not the word I was thinking of."

"Don't upset yourself," my mother says, taking my arm and guiding me out of the council circle. "I wanted to tell you that your decision to take in the Tarahumaras was a wise one. They are settling in nicely and they have crops planted already. They will be valuable allies."

"But the real benefit is all the brides we will get in return," Dee-O-Det says with a leer.

That confuses me. "Brides?"

"Haven't you noticed that your braves spend most of their free time up at the Tarahumara camp these days?" my mother says.

"You should pay more attention," Dee-O-Det says. "You can't watch over your tribe if you're not watching."

"In case you hadn't noticed, I've been a little busy lately. You know, gunpowder factory, meeting with the ranchers, chasing off soldiers…"

Dee-O-Det waves off my words. "We'll have a wave of weddings soon." He rubs his gnarled old hands together and grins. "I like weddings."

"So you can get drunk and dance," I say. I know I sound petulant, but I'm irritated.

"People like my dancing." And Dee-O-Det does a little twirl right there. Tom laughs.

"Don't encourage him," I say to Tom.

"And what about you?" my mother says, taking my arm.

"What about me?"

"When are you going to go up to the Tarahumara camp and sniff around?"

"I'm not going to sniff around. I'm not a dog."

She chuckles. "All young men are dogs. That's why it's so important to get you settled down with a good woman." She looks into my eyes. "I've seen many of the maidens looking at you. I'm sure any of them would be happy to have you."

"I'm not looking for a maiden," I say crossly.

"It's not normal for a chief to be unmarried," Dee-O-Det says, holding up one finger. "It sets a bad example."

I can see they're not going to let up on me. I look to Tom for help, but he's got a huge grin on his face that says he's enjoying this. "Maybe this could all wait until after we finish with Torres," I say.

"All the good ones will be gone by then," my mother says, frowning. "Since you are so busy, maybe I should go talk to Chief Jemez and we could pick out a suitable bride for you."

"No!" I say, horrified. "Don't do that!"

"Don't be so dramatic. You'd still get a chance to meet her before the wedding."

"There's not going to be a wedding. I'm not getting married yet."

My mother looks at Tom. "You'll talk to him, won't you? He listens to you. I think you are kind of a father to him."

"I'll do what I can," Tom says. "But you know how stubborn he is."

"I hate when you talk about me like I'm not standing right here," I say.

"We only want what's best for you," she says.

I've had enough. I stomp off. Dee-O-Det laughs. Tom catches up to me.

"Don't start," I tell him. "I don't want to hear about brides."

"Later, then," he agrees. "What I want to talk about is Kelzel."

I rub my face. After all that talk of brides, Kelzel doesn't seem so scary anymore.

"How are you going to do it?" Tom asks. "How are you going to convince him to meet with you?"

"I don't know. You have any ideas?"

"Ride up waving a white flag?"

"I don't think Kelzel cares about white flags."

"I could go. He might talk to me."

"And he might skin you and turn your hide into a rug. A really ugly rug."

"We don't have a lot of time. If Torres is leaning on the ranchers, that means he's getting close to moving. If we can't get Kelzel on our side, we need to at least get him out of the picture. We don't want to be fighting him too."

"I know. Give me some time. I'll think of something."

44

I'm sitting up in the foothills of the Sierra Madres, looking at the countryside down below with my binoculars. A couple of miles out I can see the sun reflecting off the Rio Yaqui. On this side of the river is a village and a fair number of acres of land that's been planted with crops. That's where the Yaqui Indians live. Kelzel is there somewhere. All I have to do is find a way to get in and talk to him without getting killed.

Easy, right?

Except I've been sitting here for a few hours and I'm not any closer to coming up with an idea than I was when I got here. The village is out in the open so sneaking up on it is out of the question, especially because, if I know Kelzel, for every sentry I can see, there's sure to be two more I can't see. Going after dark won't help either.

I've even considered swimming down the river and getting in close that way, but I don't need Tom to tell me that's beyond foolhardy. Besides, I don't much like swimming. It wasn't something I got to practice a lot, growing up where I did.

I'm about to put the binoculars down when I notice movement off to the north of the village. I turn and focus on it. It's a lone Mexican soldier on a horse. He's carrying a square of white cloth tied to a stick, and he's heading for the village.

And like that I know how I'm going to get in. The soldier must be a messenger sent by Torres. All I have to do is intercept him and take his place. I trace his route and see that he's going to cross a shallow canyon about a mile from the village. If I hurry, I can beat him to the spot. Fortunately, he's moving pretty slowly. Probably not in a huge hurry to get there and I can't blame him. Kelzel's been a holy terror in this part of the world for a long time now.

I have to push it, but I get into the canyon ahead of him and settle back in the bushes. As he comes around the bend I nudge Coyote forward and we step out into the open. I've got the Winchester leveled at his chest. "That's far enough," I say in Spanish.

He jerks in surprise. His eyes fall on the rifle and he starts waving the white flag frantically. "Don't shoot! Don't shoot! Oh, please…" Then, to my dismay, he starts to cry.

Right away I feel uncomfortable. It's always bothered me when women cry. Shoot, all Victoria had to do was shed a couple of tears and I went all the way to the temple of Totec for her. But I've never really seen a man cry and I have to say, it makes me even more uncomfortable than when a woman does it.

"Stop that!" I say, probably a little louder than I meant to because he winces and practically falls of his horse.

"I'm sorry, I'm sorry," he blubbers. He starts blinking and trying to wipe away the tears, but all he's really doing is smearing them all over his face.

"Oh, I knew I'd never survive this duty," he moans. "I knew it the moment the captain picked me. I knew I'd get killed and scalped and tortured." A few more tears run down his face. "Would you at least let me say a last prayer before…" He swallows hard. "You know…"

"I'm not going to kill or torture you," I say, lowering the rifle.

"So it's scalping then?" he says. He's shaking so bad he can barely hold onto the flag. One hand goes to his head. "Will it…does it hurt terribly?"

"I don't know. I expect it does. But I'm not going to scalp you either." Personally, I've never understood the fascination some people have with scalping. The thought of scalping someone disgusts me. Why would anyone want to do that?

He brightens a little. "Then what are you going to do?"

"I'm going to take your clothes."

Now he looks confused. "My clothes? Why?"

It occurs to me that this is the second time recently that I've asked someone for their clothes. And if I go back a little bit further it's actually the third time I've done it. I hope this isn't going to turn into a regular thing. "Does it really matter?"

"Well…I just. When I go back and I don't have my clothes anymore someone is sure to ask me why. What do I say?"

"Would you rather I scalped you?"

"The clothes it is." He starts clawing at his shirt so frantically I'm afraid he's going to rip it, which won't help me at all.

"Slow down. You're going to bust all the buttons off."

"Sorry, I'm sorry." He starts fumbling at the buttons, but his hands are shaking so bad he's not getting anywhere with them.

I rub my eyes. I almost wish I would've shot him. "Stop. Stop!" He stops and looks at me with rabbit eyes. "Take a deep breath." He takes a little breath. "Deeper." He nods and tries, but when he does, he starts coughing.

"Enough," I say. "Get off your horse."

His eyes bug out. "You're going to shoot me now, aren't you?"

"I won't lie. It has crossed my mind. But no. Not yet, anyway. Get off your horse."

He dismounts and I put my rifle back in its scabbard and do the same. I walk over to him and he covers his face with his hands. "Relax. I'm just going to help you."

I start unbuttoning his shirt. I really can't believe I'm doing this. Geronimo never had to do anything like this I bet. The man quivers and shakes the whole time, but I manage all the buttons finally.

He shucks the shirt and stands there with his arms wrapped around himself shivering. "Is that it?" he asks.

I wish it was. But his pants match the shirt, all part of the uniform. Probably it wouldn't matter if I rode in wearing my own pants. Lots of Mexican soldiers have incomplete uniforms. But with Kelzel it's best to be careful.

I shake my head.

"The pants too?" he says.

"The pants too."

"Okay." He starts unbuckling his belt. "Only…"

"What?"

"Would you turn around?"

"Seriously?"

He nods.

My first thought is to pull a gun and force him to take the pants off anyway. But he's liable to panic if I do. Even worse, he might piss himself out of fear. I don't even want to think about that.

"All right. But don't try anything or I *will* scalp you."

He nods mutely. I turn away and cross my arms. When I turn back a minute later he's crouching behind a bush. The pants and shirt are lying on the ground.

"This is ridiculous," I say.

"That's it, right?" he replies. "You don't want my…do you?"

Ugh. No. A man will only go so far to avoid getting shot.

"But I do need your sombrero."

He gets a pained look on his face. "You would take a man's hat even?"

"Sorry. I have to." If I show up wearing my own hat it'll give me away for sure.

He tosses over his hat. I gather up his clothes. Briefly I consider taking his horse, but decide against it. If I need to leave in a hurry, I'll need Coyote.

"You can keep your horse," I tell him, "if you promise me you'll go back the way you came. *Pronto*. Understand?"

He nods vigorously. "Only…please…"

I turn back. "What is it now?"

"I can't go riding around with no pants on. What if someone sees me?"

"So what if someone does?"

"Please, señor."

I can't believe this. Now I really want to shoot him. "I agreed not to scalp you. Isn't that enough?"

"Please?" He gives me a big hangdog look.

Muttering to myself, I take off my pants. I'm way too nice. If Ike Clanton saw me now, or Frank James or Mustang Grey, any of those guys, they'd laugh so hard they wouldn't be able to stand.

I toss him the pants. "Thank you, thank you," he babbles.

"I don't want to hear about it. Get on your horse and get out of here before I change my mind about scalping you."

He nods and runs for his horse. Something occurs to me and I stop him.

"One more thing. What were you going to see Kelzel for?"

"To give him this," he says, rummaging in his saddle bags and pulling out a large envelope. I open it up. Inside is an official-looking document granting the Yaqui Indians their ancestral lands forever. Torres' signature is at the bottom.

He rides away. When he's out of sight I pull off my shirt and put his clothes on. I tuck my hair up under the sombrero and start for the Yaqui village.

I can't shake the feeling this is a terrible idea. I might make it in there, but I can't see how I'm going to make it out. This makes sneaking up on a grizzly bear seem like a smart thing to do in comparison. The smart thing to do would be to turn back right now and ride hard for the stronghold.

I take a deep breath and ride down the canyon. Here goes nothing.

45

I ride toward the village, holding the white flag up so it's easily seen. I try my best to look like a frightened soldier. The frightened part isn't all fake. If this goes bad I'm going to learn some new things about pain. Unless I get lucky and they kill me outright.

Two Yaqui braves come riding up, their rifles held in the crooks of their arms. In bad Spanish, one of them tells me to hand over my guns. I give him my rifle and then unbuckle my gun belt. When I hand it to him, I realize something.

I know this man.

He's a bit older than me, shorter and stockier. There's a large lump on the side of his nose that says it was badly broken and never set right. The lump is the giveaway. There's no way to not recognize him.

It's Yooko.

As in one of the men who staked me to an anthill and left me to die.

And stole my hat.

I tense and come close to grabbing for the pistol hidden under my shirt. If he recognizes me, this is going to get ugly fast.

But no recognition shows in those flat eyes. He takes my weapons with a grunt and jerks his head toward the village.

They flank me on the way into the village. I sneak a peek at Yooko. He's riding along staring at nothing. He doesn't seem the least bit interested in me. And why should he? To him I'm nothing but another Mexican soldier, some nameless peon.

I notice he still has the little bones tied in his long hair. I've never seen anyone do that, not even a Yaqui. Does he think it makes him look fierce? I think it makes him look silly.

He seems to feel me looking at him and his head turns. I quickly look away, slouching in the saddle and looking down.

"*Es un caballo muy feo*," he says in Spanish and the other brave laughs. It's an ugly horse. "Better to go on foot. Eat the horse and be done with it."

As always, Coyote seems to know when people are saying bad things about him. His ears twitch, and he turns his head toward Yooko.

But I'm ready for it and I pull his head back around. Now is definitely not the time, Coyote.

We ride into the village. Most of the homes are brush wikiups, though a few more permanent dwellings of stone and adobe are in the process of being built. There's even a pattern to the layout, with broad lanes left open as streets. It looks like Kelzel is planning for the future.

For the most part the people pay little attention to me, though the children stare and whisper to each other. This isn't the first time a Mexican soldier has showed up here then.

Near the center of the village we stop in front of a small adobe building with a thatch roof. Yooko gestures and tells me to go inside.

I walk through the door. It's dim inside, not much light filtering in through the two small windows. They're not really windows, more rifle slits. Kelzel isn't taking any chances. Someone could hold out here for a while.

Kelzel is sitting cross-legged on the floor. A woman sets a bowl of food in front of him, then leaves. He looks up at me.

I've never met the man before, only seen him from a distance, but I'd recognize him as Kelzel even if I hadn't ever laid eyes on him. He has a hawk-like nose and dark, piercing eyes. He's somewhere in his sixties, but age, rather than diminishing him, seems to have made him harder. As if the decades of wind and weather have scoured away all the soft parts and left only the leather and muscle behind.

He holds out his hand. I take out the envelope and hand it to him. He takes his time and studies the document intently. It doesn't surprise me that he can read. As a warrior and a leader, he would realize the importance of understanding his enemy's tools and weapons, so he could use them in defense of his people. It strikes me that this is a man who knows how to be a chief. There is about him an air of command, a calm, steady confidence in his own abilities. This is a man who had led his people through many years and many difficulties. I could learn a lot from him.

Looking down at him, I feel strangely diminished. Who am I to sneak in here like a thief, hiding behind a disguise? Now is my chance. He's not paying any attention to me. I could easily draw my hidden pistol now, but I don't. It feels wrong. It feels dishonorable.

He looks up after a few minutes and nods. "You can go now." He waves me off and goes back to his food. When I don't move he looks back up at me. "Why are you still here?" Unlike Yooko, his Spanish is very good.

"General Torres wants to know when you're going to carry through with your side of the agreement." The words kind of pour out, surprising me. I realize then that I really want to hear Kelzel's response. I'm having a hard time reconciling the man who would agree to ambush someone in order to start a war, with the man I see before me.

His eyes narrow. "I did what I said I would."

"The rancher lives. The Americans are talking to the Apaches instead of shooting at them."

"That's not my problem. Our agreement was that we would shoot the rancher and leave him on Apache lands."

"He didn't die."

He shrugs. "Not everyone dies when you think they will."

I really should pull my gun now, but I can't seem to help myself, and I keep going. "The General questions your commitment to the revolution."

"I have no commitment to the revolution." He taps the document. "This is all I wanted."

"The General would be a powerful friend to have, once he is president."

"And I would be a powerful enemy to have, if the General has second thoughts about our agreement," he says in a low, flat voice that makes the hair stand up on the back of my neck.

"That's it, then? You won't help anymore?" I wait, realizing that this answer is the one I most need to hear.

He gives me a calculating look. I'm suddenly sure he sees through my disguise. But that's ridiculous. If he knew who I really was, he would have done something by now.

"I will help by staying out of the fight. This and no more."

I reach into my shirt and pull my gun. He shows no surprise, no reaction at all. It makes no sense, but I have the feeling he expected this.

"I'm not a Mexican soldier," I say.

"I know. I knew the moment you walked in here."

"What? How?"

"You don't walk like one of them. You walk like a hunter."

I shake off his words. "So you say. But why should I believe you? You let me walk in here and get the drop on you."

"Did I?"

"Who's holding the gun?"

"For now," he says, staring into my eyes. His expression is utterly cold.

I feel a sudden chill. I realize I made a terrible, probably fatal, mistake. I underestimated this man and it will cost me. I have the gun. He's done nothing threatening. His rifle is across the room, out of his reach. I see no pistol on him. So why do I feel like the one in danger?

"You're an Apache. The one who calls himself Ace Lone Wolf." His lips twist slightly when he says Lone Wolf, as if he finds the words humorous.

"How did you know?" I ask him.

"A leader must know," he replies. "How else can he protect his people?"

"You put my people in danger. By rights I should kill you."

"But you won't," he says calmly.

I wave the pistol at him. Somehow it seems like no more than a child's toy now, something incapable of hurting this man. "You don't know that."

"I do. You came to talk. If you came to kill, you'd have come at night." He leans forward slightly. "I've been expecting you."

"I don't believe that. If you were, you'd never have let me walk in here armed."

"I wanted the measure of you."

"And?" I wait for his answer, not sure why it feels so important to me.

"I don't know yet."

"You're on the wrong side of this fight," I say.

"Am I? We have our land back. Torres has fifteen hundred men. He may be president soon."

"He'll turn on you. As soon as he doesn't need you anymore."

He shrugs. "Maybe." He sounds completely unconcerned, yet at the same time his concentration is as intense as the hawk watching its prey far below.

"Torres hates all Indians. You know this is true."

All of a sudden the door opens and Yooko steps into the room. He looks at the pistol in my hand, then at me. For a second there's nothing there, then his eyes light up with recognition. "It's *you*!" he snarls and draws the pistol tucked into his belt.

Kelzel holds up one hand. Instantly, Yooko freezes. "You know each other?" he says.

"Sort of. He staked me to an anthill."

He nods. "Yooko likes the old ways."

"And he stole my hat."

Kelzel frowns. "You've been around the whites too long. Who cares about a hat?"

"I do." My eyes flick to Yooko, then back to Kelzel. Even though Yooko is the one holding the gun, Kelzel is more dangerous by far. "Kosterlitzky didn't get you."

"It was close. He might have, but he wanted Ike Clanton more." Yooko's eyes go to his chief, and he says something in Yaqui. I don't speak the language, but I don't need to. He's asking Kelzel if he can kill me. My finger tightens on the trigger.

Kelzel shakes his head without looking at Yooko. Yooko scowls and his jaw bunches.

"Maybe if you said please," I say to him.

The look Yooko gives me is murderous. Probably I shouldn't egg him on, but on the other hand, why not? I made him look pretty foolish that night around the fire. On top of that, I snuck in here right under his nose. I don't guess I can make him want to kill me any more than he already does.

"Why are you here?" Kelzel asks me.

"Join us."

One eyebrow rises. "Us?"

"The ranchers and the Apaches."

"Torres has fifteen hundred men."

"I have the Tarahumara Indians. And through the ranchers, many guns."

"We have guns too."

"Good guns. Not the junk Ike and his kind sell you," I say, gesturing at the pistol Yooko holds, which looks pretty ancient and has rust on it. The rifle leaning against the wall hardly looks better. "How many of them even work?"

"We have good guns too."

"Torres would never allow that," I say.

"Torres knows less than he thinks he does. Things here are not as they seem."

"You have the good weapons hidden so he will underestimate you when the times comes," I say in sudden understanding. "You expect him to betray you."

"A snake always bites. Sooner or later. We watch always. I will know when Torres turns on us. He will find nothing here because we will already be in the mountains. My warriors and I will fall on him hard. He will pay for betraying me. He will pay with his life."

"You won't kill Torres in battle. He always leads from the rear."

"Who said we would kill him in battle? Why not kill him in bed?"

The way he says this, so calm and certain, makes me hope I never have this man as my enemy. Torres has no idea who he tangles with here.

"But still you ally with him."

"My people tire of fighting. Too many of our men are dead already. It is good to rest. And maybe Torres will be too busy elsewhere to think of us."

"So you won't join us."

"I have what I want. This is good land."

I gesture with the pistol. "So where does that leave us?"

He motions with his head toward Yooko. "He badly wants to kill you."

Now it's my turn to shrug. "He's not the only one. The line is kind of long actually."

"Do you want to kill me?" Kelzel asks, leaning forward and fixing me with his dark eyes.

I think about it for a moment. The Apaches and the Yaquis have been enemies for a long time. And he tried to start a war between us and the ranchers so Torres could slaughter us both. But the world has changed. Or my understanding of it has changed.

The picture is bigger than I first thought. I shake my head. "Not really, I guess."

"Why not?" He seems genuinely curious.

"What you do, you do for your people, as any chief would." The words cut into me for some reason. I wonder if my commitment to my people will ever be half of what this man's is.

"You would do the same?" he asks.

"I don't know. But I can't hate you for it."

"Then perhaps we are not enemies," he says, sitting back and putting his hands on his thighs.

"So I get to walk away?"

"That depends on you."

I make a quick decision and lower my gun. From the corner of my eye I see Yooko's glare. He wanted me to make a different choice.

"We will meet again, Chief Lone Wolf," Kelzel says.

I wonder about that, about the Lone Wolf part. Ever since I left the stronghold and went out into the world I've been telling people that was my name, but now I don't know. Is it really? Am I done running alone?

Kelzel glances at Yooko. The man lowers his pistol and steps back, but he's not happy about it.

"Next time you want to speak to me come openly," Kelzel says. "I was curious this time, but I am not always so. Mostly I believe it is better to shoot first."

"Send a man if you change your mind." I look at Yooko, who's still glaring at me from the doorway. "Not him."

46

"You're back," Tom says when I ride into the *rancheria*. "Did you kill anybody? Make any new enemies? Run into old ones?"

"No and no. Yes. I did run into an old enemy."

"Did he try to shoot you?"

"He wanted to, but Kelzel made him stop."

"So is he an ally now?"

"No. But neither will he help Torres again. He got what he wanted and now he's staying out of it."

"Do you trust Kelzel to do that?"

I don't have to think about my answer. "I do."

Tom's looking at me closely. "You respect that man, don't you?"

I nod. "He is a true chief."

"And a bad man to have as your enemy, from what I hear."

"That is also true."

"Well, you didn't get shot, and I don't see a pack of men chasing you with their guns out, so I think we have to count this one as a win," Tom says with a grin on his bearded face. "Don't you think?"

"Maybe." I'm not really listening. Ever since leaving Kelzel I can't stop thinking about what it means to be chief. Whether or not I have what it takes to be one. Too many questions crowding my head and not enough answers. I wish it would all go away. I wish I had something else to think about.

Hi-okee comes running down the hill, calling my name as he comes. He skids to a halt in front of me. At first he's so excited he can barely get the words out.

"Slow down, pardner," Tom says.

"A message," Hi-okee says finally. "On the…" He waves his hands, unable to come up with the word he needs.

"We got a message on the heliograph?" Tom asks.

Hi-okee nods. "It's an attack. Soldiers are headed for the Lazy R ranch. They need us there as fast as we can make it."

"Buckle up. Here it comes," Tom says.

"Gather every brave," I tell Hi-okee. "Send someone up to the Tarahumara camp and tell them we need every man who can ride and carry a gun." Hi-okee dashes off, shouting.

"You're not leaving anyone here to guard the *rancheria*?" Tom asks. "You're leaving them undefended?"

"They will have guns, the strength of this position. They can hold out."

Tom looks concerned, but doesn't argue with me. I kind of wish he would. Already I'm questioning my decision. Why does being chief have to be so hard?

An idea hits me.

I see Alchise hurrying by and call him over. "That dynamite we have for the mine?" I say to him. He nods. "Take two of the boys with you and place some at both trails leading into here. Give them matches and tell them that if enemies come while we are gone, they are to blow the trails." I look at Tom. "That will buy them some time." Tom nods in approval.

Tom goes to fetch his gear, and I hurry to find Mother and Dee-O-Det. They are talking in front of her wikiup. Quickly I tell them what's happening.

"I'll get my *hodenton* powder and bless you before you leave," Dee-O-Det says, heading for his wikiup.

My mother puts her hands on my shoulders and looks into my eyes. "Keep your head, Ace. It is still your best weapon." She gives me a quick hug, and then I go to gather my gear.

I stuff my saddlebags with ammunition and food. There isn't nearly as much ammunition as I'd like. If we have to fight for very long, we're going to run out. Fortunately, once we hook up with the ranchers, we should have all we need. Slaughter's man said they had recently brought in crates of ammunition from the US.

A few minutes later we ride out. The women and children watch us go silently, their faces brave. I look at them and feel the weight of responsibility threatening to crush me. How many husbands and fathers won't return? How will I face the survivors?

We ride hard, pushing our horses. We've been going for a few hours and we're riding up the bottom of a dry canyon when Tom rides up beside me. "I don't like this," he says. "Something smells."

"I don't like it either," I admit.

Tom turns in his saddle and calls back to Hi-okee. Hi-okee catches up to us. He's riding this little yellow mare that I haven't noticed before, one of the few horses as short as Coyote and with nearly the same coloring.

"You sure you got all of the message?" Tom asks him.

"I'm sure," he says.

"You responded, but they didn't answer?" Hi-okee nods.

Tom shakes his head. "Why? Why wouldn't they respond?"

"Maybe the soldiers were close and they had to run," Hi-okee says. "If Torres knows about the mirrors, he might have sent soldiers to take them."

Tom still looks troubled. "I hope that's it. When I was in the army I learned the hard way about the bad things that can happen when you go charging into a fight without knowing what's up ahead."

I notice some of the men nearby listening in, worried looks on their faces. "There's nothing to worry about," I say. "I'll send some scouts on ahead. We'll see what's going on before we ride into anything. Besides, the soldiers we're fighting are slow and stupid. There's no fight in them. Remember how easy it was to run off the ones who were chasing the Tarahumaras."

I see smiles on the faces of the nearby men and hear chuckles as they remember that night. Stories about what happened have been going around the *rancheria* non-stop since then. I only wish I felt as confident as I sound. The truth is I'm more worried than Tom is. My thoughts have been circling around and around the whole day, wondering if I've made the right decision, if we're riding into a trap. It's making me feel a little crazy.

The canyon we're in narrows. It's not very deep, but the walls are steep and rocky. Once we get through this stretch we'll turn east and leave the canyon for the final stretch to the Lazy R.

"You take point," I tell Hi-okee. "I'm going to round up some men to scout ahead."

Hi-okee nods and spurs his horse forward. I rein Coyote back and start looking for the men I want.

Then the shooting starts.

47

A whole barrage of shots ring out. I wheel Coyote around in time to see Hi-okee clutch his chest and fall from his horse. His horse staggers and falls to its knees.

Warriors yell and race for cover. Tom has his rifle out and is firing up the side of the canyon.

I drag my Winchester from its scabbard. There's movement up above, four men crouched behind some rocks, firing down at us. I start firing at the spot as fast as I can, not bothering to aim, simply wanting to stop the men from shooting any more. Meanwhile, others have drawn their rifles and started firing at the men as well.

The men on the side of the canyon fire a couple more shots, then they break cover and run. They're close to the top. Probably their horses are waiting on the other side out of sight. The canyon wall is rugged, no easy way up it. Once they make it over the top, they're gone.

I pull Coyote to a stop and raise my rifle to my shoulder. Slow my breathing and focus. They reach the top and dart over one by one. The last man is silhouetted against the sky just for a moment. Long enough for me to squeeze the trigger.

The shot goes off, the rifle recoils, and the man goes down.

I race over to where Hi-okee went down, dreading what I'm going to see. Tom is already kneeling over him when I get there. Chee is beside him. The others have taken up defensive positions and are scanning the canyon walls for other attackers.

I jump down. Hi-okee is lying on his back, his arms flung wide. There's a lot of blood. He's not moving. "Is he…?" I ask.

Tom presses his fingers to Hi-okee's neck. "He's not dead." He sounds surprised.

I rip open Hi-okee's shirt. There are four bullet holes in him, two high on his chest, one in his stomach and another low on his side. He's shot to doll rags, but I can see the slow rise and fall of his chest.

"I don't know how he's still alive," Tom says. "He shouldn't be."

"The nearest doctor is in Basaranca," Chee says.

"Go get him," I tell Chee.

"He's not going to live long enough for the doc to get here, Ace," Tom says gently.

"You don't know that!" I snap. I turn on Chee. "Why are you still here? Get the doctor!" I shout.

Chee whirls and runs for his horse. I turn to Alchise. "Bandage his wounds. Keep him alive until the doctor gets here." I grab the front of his shirt and jerk him close. "Do you understand me? Keep him *alive*."

I let him go and bend over Hi-okee, touch the side of his face. "I'll get the men who did this, brother. I promise you." His eyelids flutter, but I can't tell if he hears me.

Alchise crouches over the wounded man. I run for my horse. "The rest of you come with me," I order.

I jump onto Coyote's back, and we start up the rocky slope. I can hear the others clattering through the rocks behind me. The whole way I can see nothing but the image of Hi-okee lying there bleeding. It's my fault. Those bullets were meant for me. If I hadn't told him to take point, it would be me lying on the ground.

At the top I find the man I shot. He's lying in a large pool of blood and not moving. I don't recognize him. Down the other side of the hill, still tied to a palo verde tree, is his horse.

Tom is the next one over the top. I point to the dead man's horse. "Do you see that brand?" It's an R turned sideways. Buck Green's brand. "I told you we couldn't trust him," I snarl.

"Now hold on a second—" Tom starts.

"I don't want to hear it!" I yell. "Those bullets were meant for *me*. This ambush was to make sure I died. But Hi-okee was out front and riding a horse that looked like mine so they shot him instead."

Tom goes silent. Then he says, "I still don't—"

"I don't care," I say harshly. "I'm going to make him pay."

I kick Coyote in the ribs, and we follow the tracks left by the ambushers.

"If they ambushed us once, they may try it again," Tom warns me when he catches up after a minute.

He's right. There's too many places in these hills to set up an ambush. As much as I want to ride straight and hard for the Lazy R, I know I can't. I don't want to get any more of my men shot.

But being careful slows us down a lot. We have to stop frequently and check the terrain ahead, scanning it with our binoculars for signs of movement, looking for places where they could be hidden.

During one stop Tom puts his hand on my arm and says, "I know it's hard, Niño."

I turn on him, my fists clenched. "Do you? Because Hi-okee has been my friend ever since I can remember. You didn't even know him."

"I've lost good people too. Some died because I made the wrong decision. There's nothing harder. But you can't let it send you off half-cocked or you'll make more mistakes and lose other good people."

I stare at him for a moment, breathing hard. Then I jerk my arm away and spur Coyote onward.

By the time the sun starts its last drop for the horizon, we're still a mile or two from the Lazy R headquarters. I'm losing the light and the ambushers' tracks are getting harder to follow. The trail leads up the bottom of a wide, dry wash. The summer floods haven't come yet to sweep the sand clean, and the bottom of the wash is dimpled with thousands of tracks of cows, horses and wildlife. Soft sand is one of the hardest places to track in. I can do it, but it's going to slow us down even more, enough that we won't arrive until after dark at the headquarters, and I'm not willing to do that.

"Enough," I say. Tom has gotten off his horse and is crouched, squinting up the wash. "We know where they're going," I tell him. "There's no need to track them any longer."

Tom starts to say something, but I ignore him and ride off. I don't look back to see if he's coming or not. There comes a time when action is called for.

It's almost sunset when we reach the headquarters. There are a few horses in the corral, all of them looking like they've been ridden hard. There are a half dozen hands about. They look up in surprise as we come riding in, rifles out. They run into the bunkhouse or into the barn, whichever is closer. One man ducks behind an unhitched wagon sitting beside the ranch house.

I ride up to the ranch house. "Buck!" I yell. "Come out and face me!" I could get shot any second, but I'm past caring. There's something here that needs settling and high time I did so.

When the door doesn't open right away, I yell again. "Are you a coward, Buck? Afraid to face a man who can fight back?"

I can feel, rather than see, the gun barrels pointed at me from the bunkhouse and the barn. Any one of Buck's men could shoot me right now—hell, Buck could shoot me from the window—but I'm gambling they won't. I just called their leader a coward. There's nothing worse you can call a man in this world. If Buck doesn't come out and face me, he'll never command these men again. No cowboy will ride for a man they consider yellow. He has no choice but to face me.

A little voice in the back of my head is telling me I might be wrong, but I shut it down. The whole way here I've been thinking about Hi-okee. He's probably going to die because they thought he was me.

They thought he was *me*.

I can't let that pass.

The door opens, and Buck steps out onto the porch. I can see his wife's face over his shoulder, a white patch at the kitchen window.

"I knew you couldn't be trusted," he says. "Once a thievin', murderin' Injun, always one."

"You have a lot of room to talk," I say back, my voice low and deadly. "Since you just tried to drygulch me. Are you surprised to see it didn't work?"

His face twists and he points at me. "No one calls me that and lives," he says.

"And yet I just did."

He licks his lips and his eyes look over my shoulder at my men, spread out behind me, weapons ready. "You speak like a man who's got the drop on me. Are you going to give me a fair chance to defend myself or are you planning on shooting me down like a dog?"

"It's only what you deserve," I reply, "but I'm not like you. I don't shoot a man when he's helpless, so I'm going to give you more chance that you gave my friend."

"I never ambushed anyone," he says, "but I've no problem killing you."

I slide down off Coyote and flick my duster back to expose my pistols.

Buck comes down off the porch and circles to the side. He doesn't want any stray bullets going in through the window and hitting his wife. "You get down, Marla!" he calls. "Get on the floor!" Her face disappears from the window.

"You've had this coming for a long time," he says. "You need taking down and I'm the man to do it."

I flex my fingers and watch his eyes. When a man decides to go for his gun the decision shows in his eyes a split second before his hand moves. When I see that I'm going to kill him.

In the silence I can hear a rifle cock. I hear other things too, ordinary things. Horses in the corral fussing over hay. A dog whining under the porch. Chickens clucking in the henhouse.

Buck's eyes narrow down—

48

A heartbeat before I drag iron, there's the sound of pounding hooves and a man shouting.

"Stop it! Stop it, you damned fools!"

It's Tom, riding like his tail is on fire. He beelines straight for the two of us and pulls up sharp, raising a cloud of dust that hangs in the still air.

"It wasn't Buck, Ace," he says to me. "He's not the one who ambushed us."

"But the tracks—"

"To the devil with your tracks. You were in such a hotheaded rush, so sure you were right, that you didn't bother to follow the tracks. I did and they turned south after a bit. They weren't coming here."

"It still could've—"

"Stop talking until you're ready to say something with a lick of sense in it," he barks, glaring at me.

"Huh," Buck says. "I knew this Apache wasn't—"

"The same goes for you, you stubborn old varmint!" Tom snaps, wheeling on him. "If you hadn't been as red-eyed as an old rooster from the beginning it woulda never come to this."

Buck draws himself up. "You can't ride in here and talk to me like that."

"The hell I can't. I just did, didn't I? Now you boys put your hackles down before something happens we all regret." He glares from one of us to the other.

After a moment I gesture to my braves and they lower their weapons. Buck shrugs and jerks his head and his men do the same.

"If Buck didn't ambush us," I say. "Then who did?"

"Maybe you tripped over your diapers and shot yourselves," Buck responds.

Tom whirls on him. "Keep it up and I'll let him shoot you."

"He'd try," Buck grumbles.

"You haven't seen this man shoot. I have. Trust me. You won't win."

Tom turns back to me. "First sensible thing you've said all day, Ace. Obviously, someone sent that signal to lure you down here.

They must have stolen horses from the Lazy R and then skedaddled this way so you'd think Buck was behind it. They were counting on you both being such idiots that you'd start shooting at each other and save them a whole lot of trouble."

"That still doesn't tell us who did it," Buck says.

"It has to be one of the other ranchers. Who else knew our codes? Buck, you ranchers are switching off monitoring the heliograph. Whose turn was it today? If we figure that out, we've got our traitor."

Buck frowns. "I have to go check the list to be sure, but I think it was Riggs' turn today." His face darkens. "That skunk turned on his fellow ranchers. When I get my hands on him I'm going to..."

He keeps on in this vein, but I'm no longer listening. Coyote has his head up and is looking to the south, his ears perked forward. All at once I realize something.

This wasn't about getting me and Buck to shoot each other. That would've only been the gravy on the steak. This was always about getting our men all together in one place.

"It's a trap," I say.

Right then one of my braves shouts and points. We all turn. Coming over the ridge to the south is a long line of men on horseback. There must be a hundred of them at least. As they charge down the slope, they fire the first round. Puffs of smoke dot the air and bullets whine by. One of Buck's hands hollers and grabs his shoulder.

The range is too long for a good shot, but they're closing fast. I run to Coyote. I'm getting my men out of here. But Tom stops me.

"We have to stick together if we're going to have a chance. Buck's men need a minute to mount up. We have to give them that minute."

He's right. I pull my rifle from its scabbard and call out to my men to slow them down.

I lay my rifle across the saddle to steady it, take careful aim and squeeze the trigger. A rider in the front ranks throws up his arms and falls backward off his horse. Other shots ring out and other riders go down. Their riderless horses snarl the charge, slowing it somewhat.

I fire again and again. They're massed together enough that it's hard to miss even from this range. Nor, it seems, do they have much stomach for riding into gunfire. But, even though they've slowed quite a bit, they're still coming fast.

But it's enough. When I turn and look behind me I see that most of Buck's cowboys are mounted. Nothing like a little flying lead to put the hurry in a man. I climb on Coyote and ride over to Tom. "Which way?" I ask him.

"North," he says. "We have to join up with Slaughter. He's got the most hands and all the extra ammo and weapons."

That makes sense to me. I wave to my men and we gallop away from the ranch headquarters and head north. I hear Buck yelling to his men and they come hard on our heels.

This ridge to the north isn't as steep as the one to the south, so we make pretty good time climbing it. Bullets fall around us but, though a couple find targets, no one goes down. The horses are sweating and breathing hard by the time we gain the top of the hill.

That's when we get the second dose of bad news.

Off to the northeast another mass of soldiers is riding toward us, less than a mile out.

"Well don't that beat all," Buck grunts, riding up beside me and Tom. "I guess we're not going that way."

"West it is, then," I say.

"Uh…chief?" Deya says, pointing.

A third mass of soldiers is closing on us from that direction.

Buck swears. "Sumbitch. How'd they get that many men into place without us seeing them?"

"They must have moved in under cover of darkness," Tom says. "Torres planned this trap well. Suggestions?"

Looking around, my eyes fall on a building in the distance. "The old mission," I say. "We can hole up there."

The first group of soldiers is coming up behind us from the south. The second is closing in on us from the northeast. The third is coming from the west. The mission is somewhat northwest of us. If we're lucky, we just might get there before they cut us to pieces.

We take off running. To throw them off and gain a couple of precious minutes we first head north, like we're making a break for Slaughter's. But, once we're down off the top and out of sight of the three bands of soldiers, we veer left down a ravine.

A couple of minutes later the soldiers coming from the south crest the hill. They can now see where we're really headed, but that doesn't matter. It's the soldiers coming from the west we have to worry about. They're the ones who can cut us off.

We race along the bottom of the ravine. I keep looking up at the ridgeline, fearing I'm going to see a line of soldiers break over the top of it. If that happens we're doomed. But the minutes pass, and they don't appear.

"Turn right up ahead!" Buck yells. "There's a trail that will take us right by the mission."

In a cut on one side of the ravine lies the trail. We turn our horses up it and break out onto flat terrain again. We're on the home stretch. I can see the mission in the distance. I check over my shoulder to see how my men are doing. It's as I feared. Their horses have already been pushed hard and this last sprint is wearing them out. Most of them have fallen behind Buck's cowboys. I pull back on Coyote's reins to let them catch up to me. I'm not leaving anyone out here.

Suddenly shots ring out from the hillside above us to our left. One of my braves—I can't see who—cries out and barely manages to hang onto his saddle. I snap off a couple of quick shots at the oncoming soldiers and ride over next to him. It's Kasale.

"Hang on," I tell him. "We're almost there."

More shots and up ahead I see one of the cowboys go down.

There's a mesquite thicket we have to pass through, which gives us some cover, but also slows us down. When we break out of the thicket we're only a few hundred yards from the ruined mission. To the right I see a few dozen soldiers appear, racing to cut us off.

I veer toward them, firing the Winchester as fast as I can. I see a couple of them go down and the others slow their charge in confusion.

We race onward and there's the gateway in the mission wall, the ruined gates lying half across it. We thunder through the opening, lead spattering around us, dozens of men and horses desperate for the safety of those thick adobe walls.

49

"Get that opening barricaded!" Buck yells. Men run to the rusted remains of the mission's iron gates and prop them across the opening as best they can. It's better than nothing, but it won't hold up for long. We need something heavy to stack behind them. Outside, the first of our pursuers arrive. Gunfire erupts anew.

I cast around, looking for something else we can use. My eyes fall on the old church. There might be something in there. I call to a couple of my men to help me, and we run inside. It's dim and cool in there. Birds fly up from the altar and perch in the rafters. The last of the daylight comes in through broken stained glass windows. Most of the wooden pews are still in place. They look big enough for what we need.

We stagger out carrying a couple of the pews. They fit across the gateway almost like they were made to do so. Who knows? Maybe they were. Those old priests must have learned a few things about surviving out here on the frontier.

While we're getting the pews in place, other men are taking up positions on the mission's walls. They begin returning fire, and the first bands of soldiers wheel their horses and fall back, taking shelter behind the scattered trees dotting the landscape.

Now that the immediate danger has passed, I can take a moment to look around. What I see makes me feel better. The wall around the mission has crumbled in a few spots and in one place it's only waist-high, but for the most part it's intact and there are rifle slits in it so we can shoot at the soldiers without taking too much return fire.

If we lose the wall we can always fall back to the church. The lower windows are narrow enough that they could be defended as long as the doors can be held. There's a bell tower. We'll want to get some shooters up there. There are also other buildings inside the wall, living quarters and kitchens I guess, along with what looks like a stable.

There are fallen stones on the ground around the crumbled areas of the wall, and Buck puts some of his men to work stacking the stones in the openings as best they can. The horses are herded into a back corner of the mission and a temporary rope corral set up to keep them out of the way.

"I say we go up in the bell tower and get a look around," Tom says. "Get a better idea what we're facing."

Buck and I follow him into the church. Behind the altar we find a narrow doorway behind a crumbling curtain. Ancient wooden stairs lead upwards. They creak loudly as we make our way up, but we're careful to stay to the edges and none break. I look over the side as we near the top. It's a long, painful fall to the stone floor below.

The bell is rusted, the rope used to ring it rotted away to nothing. The floor of the bell tower is covered in bird droppings and a handful fly away at our approach, scolding us as they go. There are arched openings in all four directions. We're about fifty feet up, high enough to have a good view in all directions.

The view isn't pretty.

Tom whistles. Buck swears. I wish I was somewhere else.

"Damn," Buck says in a low voice. "Looks like every soldier in northern Mexico is out there."

He's probably not far off. There are only about two hundred mounted soldiers out there right now, but there's a whole lot more of them coming, converging on us from three directions. In the fading light I see three different bands. They'll be here in ten minutes or so. Beyond them are two more solid masses of soldiers on foot, marching our way.

"Think they'll attack tonight?" Buck says.

"If they do, we'll make them pay," Tom says. "This is a good, strong position we have here. The real question is, how long can we hold them off?"

"As long as our ammunition holds out," Buck says. "That's our biggest weakness right now. The walls are strong. We have enough men to man them. There's even a well in that back corner for water. But we plain old don't have enough bullets."

About then one of Buck's hands fires a couple of times, but the range is long and the light is bad and it doesn't look like he hits anything.

"Knock off the shooting, for Pete's sake!" Buck yells. He can really yell. "Save your ammunition! Don't shoot if you don't have to."

"We need reinforcements," Tom says. He looks at me. "What do you say? Once it gets dark, you or one of your men sneak out and hightail it to Slaughter's?"

"It shouldn't be a problem," I reply. My first thought is to say that I'll go, but a moment later I realize I can't do that. I'm the chief. I have to stay here. Deya or Boa Juan then.

"He'll want to steal a horse," Buck says. "It's a long ways to Slaughter's spread on foot. Might be our reinforcements would get here and find nothing to reinforce." He gives me a look I don't like. "That shouldn't be any trouble for an Apache."

I resist the urge to slug him. I don't need Tom to tell me the last thing we want to do is fight amongst ourselves. I can't stand Buck, but right now I need him and his men.

Tom peers out into the distance. "What are they doing out there?"

I move up beside him and look. In several different places I see small clouds of dust, all drawing closer to the mission. We stand there and stare and after a minute there's a couple of new ones. All at once I realize what we're seeing.

"Those are trees. That's what's raising the dust. They're dragging whole dead trees behind horses."

"What for?" Tom asks.

"Firewood," Buck says. "And more coming."

No one says anything then. We all know what this means. Torres' men know our only chance of surviving is if we get reinforcements. So they're planning on building fires in a ring all around the mission.

Sneaking out just got a whole lot harder. Maybe impossible.

The three of us look at each other, all of us thinking the same thing.

We're probably none of us going to survive this.

"I'm going to go talk to my men," Buck says. "They deserve to know what we're up against."

"I'm going to keep watch up here for a while longer," Tom says. "See if I can learn anything else that will help us."

I follow Buck down the stairs. The inside of the church is dark now. I'm glad of the darkness. It hides what I'm going through. I feel absolutely sick to my stomach.

This is my fault. Torres set a trap and I ran headlong into it. I've got no more sense than a baby calf. Everyone following me is going to be dead in a day or two. And after that our families. They'll be wide open, no one to protect them.

I shouldn't have come home. My people would be better off without me. What have I done?

Buck steps out of the church and pauses. He runs a hand over his face and takes a deep breath, then looks over at me. The light is fading, but I guess there's enough for him to see my expression because he takes one look at me and says, "You better put a different face on before you go talk to your men. If they see you like that..."

He turns and walks heavily away.

I stand there, unable at first to take a single step. I can't do this. My failure is crushing me. My mistakes parade in front of me, one after another.

I hear Buck calling his men together, and that's what finally goads me into action. If he can keep his chin up, then I can too.

I gather them over by the temporary horse pen. I don't sugarcoat it. I tell them straight up what's facing us. There's still enough light left for me to see them and what I see when I finish talking surprises me.

Not a one of them look like I feel. Not my own men and not the Tarahumaras. I see resignation there, but I see determination too. They're fighters, every one of them, and they're not going to give up.

Most importantly, on no one's face do I see blame.

They don't blame me.

And with that realization, something changes inside me. I realize that nothing that happened up to this point matters now. All that matters is what we do going forward. What *I* do.

These men are looking to me for leadership. I have to deliver.

I'm not going to fail them again.

50

We keep a close eye out all night, watching for an opportunity, an opening where someone can slip through the enemy lines and bring help, but the opportunity never comes. The fires burn brightly the entire night and the sentry lines between the fires are nearly a solid mass of soldiers, rotated every hour.

Shortly before the first light of dawn cracks the eastern sky, Boa Juan wakes me up.

"They're coming," he says.

I stand up from where I was leaning against the wall. Around me the other defenders are stirring. I hear a few low voices, but for the most part they're staying quiet. I send Boa Juan to get everyone in place and head for the front gates.

Buck is already there, peering out into the darkness. Tom joins us a moment later.

"They're getting ready," Buck says.

I peer through the gaps in the pews. The fires have died down mostly, but beyond them I can see moving figures here and there. It looks like soldiers lining up to attack.

"They'll hit us at first light," Buck says, cocking his rifle. He glances at me. "Your men in position?"

Streaks of light appear in the east and the desert begins to emerge from the gloom.

A bugle blows out in the darkness, followed closely by the sounds of running feet and hooves.

The mounted soldiers hit us first, a knot of them charging right at our makeshift barrier, guns blazing.

"Hold your fire!" Buck thunders. "Don't shoot until you have a sure target!"

The horses get closer. I hear a defender cry out in pain and someone loses his composure and shoots. But everyone else holds.

Closer.

We can see individual horses and riders now, dark shapes looming ever larger.

Closer.

"Now!" Buck yells.

All around me guns answer. Flames pierce the darkness.

Horses whinny and men scream. One side of the charge falters, but the rest comes on. The attackers are firing wildly. A bullet tugs at the collar of my duster and a man on the wall to my right grunts and topples backwards, his gun going off into the air.

I chamber another round and take my time lining up my next shot. A big man on a tall horse is bearing down on the gates, his reins in his teeth, firing pistols with both hands.

I hit him square in the chest. He jerks from the impact and falls backwards off his horse. Freed from its rider's control, the horse veers to the side and gets tangled up with two others. They both go down, riders sailing off over their heads and slamming into the barrier.

All at once the cavalry charge breaks. Those still alive swerve and dash away, leaving behind horses thrashing on the ground and broken soldiers.

But the charge served its purpose. It distracted us long enough for the infantry to get close. They're less than fifty yards away now, a solid mass of men running towards us, shouting and shooting. In the few endless moments we fought the cavalry, the light came and I can see other charges coming as well, heading for the weak points in our wall.

We fire into them as fast as we can, but there are far too many of them and not nearly enough of us. We can slow them, but we can't stop them.

They hit the barrier like a human flood. The iron gates groan as the barrier bulges inwards. A moment later it collapses and the flood sweeps into the mission.

My rifle is empty now, but there's no time to reload. Soldiers are pouring through the opening. I drop the rifle and draw my pistols, shooting the attackers point blank.

From the corner of my vision I can see Buck to my right. More bear than man, he's roaring and swinging his rifle like a club, dropping men left and right. To my left Tom is fighting like a man possessed, his knife in one hand and his pistol in the other.

The sheer mass of soldiers bears me backwards, one foot, then another. Buck and Tom are being forced backwards too. I feel pain in my shoulder, but it's distant, as if it happened to someone else.

We're forced back a couple more feet. The only reason we've held this long is that the gateway is a bottleneck. The charging soldiers can't bring their full force to bear on us. The debris choking the gate slows them as well. And we've been plain lucky.

But that's changing. Every step they push us back we have a wider arc to defend. We'll be swept away soon.

Yells come from behind us and more defenders join the fight. Deya steps up beside me and shoots a man in the face just as he points his pistol at me. On the other side of Buck a cowboy with a double-barreled shotgun opens up, the weapon tearing terrible holes through the attackers.

The fight seems to go out of all the soldiers at the same time. Suddenly the surge reverses itself and begins heading the other way. We hack at them as they flee and a few more fall to the ground, then the survivors make it back through the gates and start running back to the safety of their lines.

We survived to fight a little longer.

Next to me Tom is bent over, his hands on his knees, breathing hard.

"You okay?" I ask him.

He looks up at me. There's blood spattered all over his face, but he nods. Then his eyes go to my shoulder. "You took a bullet," he says.

I remember the pain in my shoulder then and look down at my right shoulder. Blood stains my duster. I move the jacket aside. It hurts bad, but it's only a crease.

I hear something I don't expect behind me and spin to see what it is.

It's Buck. He's holding his rifle in the air and he's laughing. Or something like laughing. It's a hair-raising sound, part howl, part laugh, part mad wolf.

"Come on back!" he bellows at the fleeing soldiers. "Come back and get some *more*!"

He turns to us. There's blood all over him. At least some of it has to be his, but he doesn't seem to notice it. His eyes are wild.

"That was something, wasn't it?" he says.

"You're bleeding," Tom tells him.

Buck looks down at himself. "So I am," he grunts, then looks back at us. "For a minute I thought we weren't going to hold them," he says. "It was close, closer than a barber's shave." He shakes his head and drops of blood fly from his bushy beard. "You gents can fight. I'll give you that."

He turns away, hollering to his men to get the barrier back in place. Tom and I help and when it's back up we lean against it, peering out at the enemy.

"I don't think we'll make it through another one of those," Tom says. "If they wouldn't have given up when they did…"

He doesn't have to finish his sentence. I know how close we came to being overrun. "Let's hope they don't try again right away," I say.

"Looks like someone new arrived during the night," Tom says, pointing.

Surrounded by a thick wedge of riders is a man in a uniform with about a mile of gold braid on it. He's got a looking glass and is studying us.

"General Torres himself," Tom says. "Where's my Henry? I'd like to see if I can put a hole in him." He starts poking around through fallen bodies looking for it. I pick up my rifle, wipe off some blood, and start loading it.

Like he knows what we're up to, Torres lowers the glass and rides away.

51

Once it's clear Torres isn't going to attack again right away we gather all the men in the courtyard. The good news is we only lost three men in the morning attack. The bad news is we're still outnumbered something like twenty-five-to-one and we're low on both food and ammunition. My men showed up pretty well prepared, but Buck's men have almost nothing. We divvy up what we have and pass it around.

"Eat up," Buck says loudly once it's all handed out. "There's no sense saving food for tomorrow. One way or another, this ends today."

Tom pulls Buck aside. "Did you have to say that?" he says irritably.

"Why not?" Buck replies. "It's the truth, ain't it? Everyone can see we don't have enough ammo. Pretending there is won't change anything."

Tom shakes his head. "It's bad for morale."

"It's dying that's bad for morale," Buck says.

Men take up their positions on the wall and we all settle in to wait. We can probably withstand one more concerted assault, but that's it. After that we'll be fighting with knives and teeth.

A few hours pass and nothing happens. Tom and I go up in the bell tower to get another look around. From there we can see that the soldiers aren't even in formation. They're sitting around or napping. There's a few cooking fires going.

Tom stares at them for a few minutes in silence and then says, "They're waiting for something."

"What? Reinforcements? Torres has more than enough men to wipe us out right now."

"That's true," Tom says. "But what's also true is he's trying to gather an army big enough to defeat Diaz. He doesn't want to waste any more men than he has to here." He slaps the wall. "We're burrowed in here like a tick on a mule. With enough ammo, we could put a lot of hurt on his little army before we go under."

"Except we don't have the ammo."

"Also true. But he doesn't know that." He starts rolling a cigarette. "He's waiting for something that will change the battle completely. Something to cancel out these walls. What could…" He trails off as something hits him. "Of course. What else could it be? Lord, but I'm dense sometimes."

"What? What is it?" I ask him.

"What's more powerful than stone walls?" he says.

I frown at him. "Cannons?" He nods. "But I took care of his cannons when I blew up the factory."

"Are you sure about that?"

"No."

"He might have had others anyway. Either way, I'd bet my last corn dodger that's what he's waiting for."

"What do we do?"

"There's nothing we can do. Except hunker down once the shelling starts and hope when it lets up there's enough of us left to give him something of a fight."

"You know, I've decided I don't much like war," I say.

"Can't say I have much use for it myself. Which is probably why I quit the army."

Somewhere around noon I see a plume of dust to the south, on the old washed-out road that leads to the mission. Tom and I stare at it as it slowly draws closer. Sure enough, it's a wagon with two cannons in it.

"Well, we might as well go down and tell everyone," Tom says, heading for the stairs.

Buck listens to the news with a dark look on his face. Then he goes and stands on the top step in front of the church and hollers for all the men to listen up. "They got cannons now," he says. "I don't need to tell you what that means."

"It means we're well and truly screwed," one of his men calls out. He's got a patchy black beard and a narrow face like you'd see on a starving dog. "We got no chance at all."

"Yeah, we do," another says. "We could surrender."

A few voices are raised in agreement with him, but Buck is already shaking his head. "You boys don't know Torres like I do. We bloodied his nose. Shot up a bunch of his men and made him look bad. He's a proud man. He won't stand for that. He's gonna make sure none of us leave here alive."

"You're just saying that so we stay and fight," the narrow-faced man says, "but I ain't about to die for your ranch. I didn't hire on for this. I say we surrender."

More voices are raised. None of them are Apache or Tarahumara. I don't need to say anything to them. They know as well as I do that Torres might let the cowboys leave, but he'll never let us out of here alive.

Buck shouts until they shut up enough to listen to him. "No one's forcing anyone to stay," he says. "You're right. This isn't your fight. Hell, maybe Torres is feeling generous today and he'll let you leave. If any of you want to lay down your guns and walk out of here, I won't stop you."

"Damn straight you won't," the narrow-faced man says.

Ten of them head for the gates. They spend a couple of minutes there arguing about who's got a shirt that's clean enough to serve as a white flag. What they come up with is a long way from white. In fact, it's a whole lot more like dirty brown than white. But they tie it to a stick and pull back the barricade enough so that they can squeeze on out.

"Leave your guns," Buck says.

"The hell I will," the narrow-faced man says.

Buck draws his pistol and points it at him. "If they let you live, they're going to take away your guns. At least this way we can put them to good use."

The narrow-faced man curses him for a bit, but then throws his pistol and rifle in the dirt. The others do the same. They start to work their way through the opening.

"Last chance," Buck tells them. "Stay here and you can at least go down fighting. You go out there and Torres will cut you down in cold blood. I guarantee it."

That changes a few minds and in the end only six of them stick with the plan. The narrow-faced man is the last one through the opening. He looks us all over. "You're all damned fools," he sneers. "Not a brain in the lot of you."

He leaves. I go to the barricade to watch what's coming. I have a gut feeling Buck is right.

The little band of men sticks close together. They make a big show of waving their sort-of-white flag over their heads. I hear the narrow-faced man call out that they want to surrender. There's no response from the watching soldiers.

Hesitantly, the men keep going. They're fifty yards from the mission, now a hundred, a hundred and fifty. They call over and over, but not once is there an answer. The soldiers stand there staring at them.

They're about fifty yards from the soldiers when suddenly a bugle blows a single note.

The whole front rank of soldiers raises their rifles. The men scatter and try to run, but it's too late. A few seconds later every one of them is dead.

"Damn," Buck says. "I was hoping they'd make it. I really was." He looks at Tom and me. "So, you figured out what your last words will be? Better practice them now. You're going to get to use them soon."

"I wish I had some whisky," Tom says.

Buck nods. "Not too bad. What about you, Ace?"

"I'm not planning on dying."

Buck flashes some teeth at me. "I like that even better. You got any ideas to back them up? Something you know that we don't?"

"Nope. Only that I'm not planning on dying. Not here. Not now." Strangely, saying it aloud like that makes it feel real to me. I feel the most positive I have all day.

"Fair enough."

He starts to turn away, but Tom says, "What about you? What do you have for last words?"

Buck thinks about it for a minute. "I don't know yet," he says. "I always thought last words were for another day. I never practiced any for today. I'll say this though." He looks square into my eyes, then sticks out his hand.

"I was wrong about you, Ace. You're a man to ride the river with."

I shake his hand. "Let's give them something to remember."

He walks away and Tom whistles softly. "Did I see what I think I saw?" He chuckles. "Truly it is a day for miracles. We may survive yet."

The cannons are rolled forward a few minutes later. We pull everyone off the wall. Nothing they can do up there but die. The cannons start firing. The balls hit the wall, and chunks of stone spray everywhere. The wall isn't going to hold up very long.

After about a half hour, the guns go silent. The smoke drifts away. What's left of our wall doesn't look pretty. Our barricade is completely destroyed, along with a whole section of wall about twenty yards wide. We'd need twice the men and a whole lot more ammunition to even have a chance of holding them off.

A bugle sounds and here they come. No cavalry this time, only infantry. They walk at first, then break into a run. I wonder if the man whose clothes I took is among them. I hope he deserted and went home.

I crouch down behind one of the piles of broken stone, Deya and Boa Juan flanking me. We exchange looks, but we don't say anything. There's nothing to say. We start firing at the same time.

We kill a whole lot more of them, but there's simply too many. We can't possibly stop them. Men go down around me. Deya reels backward suddenly, blood coming from his head. He gets back up again. There's blood all over his face, but he holds his rifle steady.

It's hard to see through the smoke from the gunpowder. The screams of men fill the air and the sound of gunfire is a constant thunder.

Somehow, unbelievably, we hold. The charge falters and then stops. Partly it's because there's nowhere really for them to go. The opening in the wall is choked with fallen soldiers, so many that those behind them have to climb up over them.

The soldiers fall back, but I hear officers shouting and I know the reprieve won't be long. I count five cowboys and three Tarahumaras down. Deya is wiping blood from his face. Boa Juan is reloading his rifle.

"How many rounds do you have left?" I ask him.

He pats his rifle. "These are the last." His grin is savage.

In the distance the bugles blow and the soldiers mass once again. We'll never survive this charge.

I hear Buck bellowing, "Fall back! Fall back to the church!"

Inside, we stack the remaining pews across the doorway. Men take up positions at the windows and poke gun barrels through the new barricade.

"Still got any rounds for that thing?" Tom asks me, pointing at my rifle.

"A dozen or so."

"I've got about the same for Betsy here," he says, patting his Henry.

"I didn't know you had a name for your gun."

"You never asked."

There's blood soaking through his shirt down low on his side. "Are you okay?" I ask him.

"Hell no," he says. "But it makes no difference."

"Would you two quit exchanging love letters already and get up in the tower?" Buck yells. "They're closing quick and you're missing shots."

We hurry up the stairs. I bring up the rear and I can see how Tom is lagging by the top. I take his arm and help him up the last few steps.

"Thanks," he says, and sags against the wall. "Not as young as I used to be. I'm getting old."

"No, you're not. You're Tom Jeffords. You'll live forever."

He shakes his head. "Too long for me." He looks out the window. "Here they come."

We pick our targets carefully, mindful of how low we are on ammunition. We drop one with every shot, but it makes no real difference. There's far too many of them. They boil into the courtyard in front of the church, shooting the whole time. Gunfire answers from the church, but it's sporadic. Pretty soon it will stop altogether.

Tom jerks back suddenly. I see a fresh wound high on his chest.

"Damn," he says. "That hurts a lot."

"Let me look at that."

He waves me off. "No. There's no point."

"Can you still shoot?"

"Probably. If I had any rounds left." He sits down and leans up against the wall.

I take aim at a soldier and squeeze the trigger. Nothing happens. "I guess I'm out too," I say.

There's a lull in the shooting. Probably everyone on our side is empty. The soldiers form up in the courtyard, getting ready to make the last charge, the one that will finish us off completely.

I sit down near Tom. He smiles. There's blood in the corner of his mouth. "Damn shame we don't have any whisky. It helps the pain, you know."

"So I've been told."

He pushes his hat back and rests his head against the wall. "It feels good to rest," he says. "Been tired for a long time."

He's right. It does feel good. I feel like I've been running my whole life. In the end, what was it for?

"It's been a pleasure knowing you," Tom says. His voice is very faint. There's a lot of blood. He's bleeding out. "You're a good man."

"I am honored to call you my friend," I say.

There's no answer. I look over and see that his eyes have closed. He looks peaceful. At least he won't have to suffer anymore.

I should be doing something. I should go downstairs and fight to the last. But what's the point? It won't change anything, except that a few more wives will lose their husbands and children their fathers. The war is over and we lost.

It's not dying myself so much that bothers me. I've danced on the edge of death for too long to have illusions about it. What's worst is knowing all my men will die too. I let them down. I should have made better decisions. I shouldn't have been so rash.

The gunfire starts up again.

Here it comes.

A moment later I realize something and open my eyes.

That gunfire didn't come from the courtyard down below.

I move over to the window and look out.

Out beyond Torres' men, riding in from the south, are two groups of mounted men. One group is wearing sombreros and black shirts. At their head is a man waving a sabre. The other group is made up of Indians, led by a man I recognize even from here.

It's Kosterlitzky and his Rurales, along with Kelzel and his Yaquis.

They fall on the Mexican soldiers from the rear. Torres' men crumble almost immediately. Men and officers begin fleeing in all directions.

The soldiers gathered in the courtyard look over their shoulders in surprise. Once they realize what is happening, they begin a mad scramble for the exit.

In a few minutes it's all over.

Sometimes miracles do happen.

52

Quickly, I strip off Tom's shirt and tear it up into strips, wrapping the strips tightly around the wound in his chest. The one in his side has mostly stopped bleeding. Then I pick him up and carry him gently down the stairs. In the church, I kick aside some scraps of wood and lay him down on the floor. He looks bad. The color has left his face, and he's barely breathing.

"Hold on," I tell him.

His eyes open and fix on me. "Did we win?"

"We did."

"Good." He sighs and closes his eyes.

I slap him gently on the cheek. "Hey, hey!"

His eyes open again, but they look distant, unfocused.

"You're not dying on me, are you?" I say.

His lips turn upwards slightly. "I was thinking about it."

"Stop it. You got no call dying now. Not after we won."

"Okay," he says, but the word is barely a whisper. I'm not even sure that's what he said.

Up at the front of the church Buck is hollering and laughing madly as he tosses aside the pews blocking the doors. "Hot damn, but that was close!" he yells.

I run over to the front doors. Buck sees my face and his smile leaves. He turns and looks back, sees Tom lying there.

"Oh, damn," he says softly.

Kosterlitzky and Kelzel are just riding into the courtyard, a handful of their men following them. I hurry outside and go up to Kosterlitzky.

"Do you have a doctor?" It's a long shot, but it's the only one Tom has. There's nothing more I can do for him.

"As it happens, I have in my company a man who was a doctor before he fell afoul of the law," Kosterlitzky says. He gestures and a man rides up beside him. He's wearing glasses and has a small, neatly-trimmed mustache.

"Go with him, Emilio," Kosterlitzky tells the man, who salutes and dismounts. He unties his saddle bags and follows me inside. We hurry over to where Tom is lying.

"Can you save him?" I ask him.

"I will do my best," he says. His Spanish is neat and precise. He opens his saddle bags and begins removing implements. "Get me some water and move these men back. They are blocking my light."

I send Boa Juan for water and yell at the men gathered around to move back. Emilio rinses his hands and instruments with what I think is alcohol and then unwraps the bandages. Tom doesn't move. The doctor probes the wound delicately.

"The bullet will have to come out," he says. He looks up at me. "Now you are blocking my light. Please move at once."

I back up. After a moment I realize I can't stand there and watch. It's killing me. I feel so helpless. I go to check on my men.

Deya is leaning against the wall. When I crouch by him he smiles at me. "We did it," he says.

"We did. How are you?"

He shifts and winces against the pain. "I'll live. I might want a couple of stitches when the doctor is finished, though."

Two of the Tarahumaras are dead, along with one Apache. Another dozen are wounded and one man got part of his foot shot off, but they all look like they'll survive.

Buck comes limping across the room. He has a bloody crease along the side of his face and there's blood on his leg. "I'm sorry about Tom. He's a good man."

"He's going to live," I say fiercely.

He nods. "Tough old buzzards like Tom don't die all that easy, I've found." He looks around the room. "Good of the cavalry to show up just in time, don't you think?"

"It was almost too late."

"That it was. I think we should speak to Kosterlitzky about his timing. Speaking of…" He gestures with his chin.

Kosterlitzky is making his way across the room to us. Kelzel is with him. Kosterlitzky looks at the wound on Buck's cheek. "It appears one bullet came very close," he says.

Buck touches his cheek. "Yep. Almost got a face-to-face with old Scratch himself today. The bugger who did it wasn't so lucky." He looks at Kosterlitzky. "I'm not saying that I ain't grateful, but how did you come to pop up here, right when we needed you?"

"You should know that little that happens in this region of Mexico that I am not aware of," Kosterlitzky says. "In fact, it is my business to know. I am President Diaz's eyes and ears in the north. I have known for some time about Torres' aspirations. Unfortunately, the President did not have the troops to spare to oppose Torres directly. It was left to me to do what I could, to watch for a key moment when I could act."

I look at Kelzel. He's standing there with his arms crossed, his expression stone. "I thought you weren't going to get involved. How did he change your mind?"

Kelzel smiles. It doesn't reach his eyes. If a hawk could smile, it would look like that. "He pointed out that Torres cannot be trusted."

"Which I did also."

"But he was able to make an offer you couldn't. A permanent deed to the land we live on now."

I ask Kelzel, "Do you think he will honor it?"

Kelzel looks at Kosterlitzky and shrugs. "We'll see. But if he crosses us, Diaz will have more problems in the north, and he already has all the problems he can handle."

"I would advise the President against such a decision," Kosterlitzky says. "Kelzel is a formidable opponent. It is preferable to have him as an ally." His eyes switch to me. "I have the President's authority to extend the same to you."

"What are you saying?"

"For your help in defeating the rebels, Pa-Gotzin-Kay will be deeded to your people. You need no longer hide."

I try to keep my mouth from dropping open. This is something I never would have imagined happening. "We'll take it."

Kosterlitzky says, "It seems you have a way of turning up in the middle of interesting circumstances, Ace."

"I've noticed that too."

"Hmm." He looks me up and down, measuring me it feels like. "So far each time you have been on the right side of the line."

"That's somewhere I'd like to stay."

"This is the second time you have aided my president. Two generals hungry for power that you have helped bring down."

"I think Diaz needs to cut down on his generals. I feel like I can't turn around without tripping over one."

"Hmm, yes." He's still studying me. I'm starting to feel uncomfortable. He rubs his chin. "Would you consider joining the

Rurales? I could guarantee you a commission. You would soon lead your own squad."

Of all the things I expected him to say, that wasn't one of them. This time my mouth does drop open. "You're offering me a *job*?"

"Indeed."

"Uh…let me think about it."

I walk off to go check on Tom. What's going on here? My clan wants me to be chief. Kosterlitzky wants to make me an officer. Whatever happened to being a no-account drifter?

53

After the dust settles I send every man who is healthy enough to ride back to Pa-Gotzin-Kay. Even though the general's out of the picture, I'll feel better knowing my people are protected. Buck sends one of his men to fetch the wagon from his ranch so they can haul Tom and a couple of the other injured men over there.

About that time a lone rider comes trotting in. It's Chee.

"Is he still alive?" I ask him anxiously. I can't read anything on Chee's face, good or bad.

Chee nods. "He was when I left Basaranca. The doctor said he's never seen anything like it. He said by all rights Hi-okee should be dead."

When I hear that a big weight I didn't realize was there is lifted from my shoulders. "Thank you."

Chee looks around at the sprawled bodies of the Mexican soldiers and the shattered wall. "Looks like it was a close one."

"Closer than you know."

By the next day Tom looks a lot better and he's laughing with Marla and giving Buck a hard time. A couple more days pass and he announces that he's had enough lying around and wants to get back to the stronghold.

"Take my wagon," Buck says.

"Buck, there's no way in hell that wagon is making it up to Pa-Gotzin-Kay. You know that," Tom says.

"Of course I know that," Buck replies. "But it'll get you close and you can switch to a horse then. You almost died a while back, or did you forget already?"

"You're being dramatic," Tom says, but after I start in to pressuring him too, he agrees to ride in the wagon "for a spell."

Buck loads up the wagon with food and other supplies. I protest, telling him we don't need all that much, especially since the Tarahumaras will be moving away now. Diaz granted them land of their own as well. He won't listen to me and soon the wagon is so full there's practically no room for Tom in it.

"I could always get out and walk," Tom says wryly.

Last of all Buck gives me something long and wrapped in cloth. I unwrap it to find a new Winchester 1873. "That's some rifle," I say. I hold it out to him. "I can't take this."

"You can and you will. Without your help, I'd have lost my ranch."

I nod. "True." I pull my old rifle from its scabbard and put the new one in.

"If you folks ever need anything, I mean anything at all, you let me know, okay?" Buck says.

"That goes both ways," I say. I mount up. "One more thing. What do we do about Riggs?"

Buck gets a dark look on his face. "You let me worry about Riggs. I've had a few riders back and forth to Slaughter and the others over the last few days. We're cooking up an unfriendly surprise for him. He'll soon learn that backstabbing your friends is no way to survive around here."

We ride away. "I'll be sending a man up your way in a couple of weeks," Buck calls after us. "With an invite to bring everyone down for a big shindig celebrating our victory. You be sure to bring the women and children too. Bring everybody."

I holler back and wave.

"I told you he'd come around," Tom says. "All you had to do was give him time."

"You mean all I had to do was nearly get myself killed, don't you?"

"That didn't hurt," he agrees. "Where'd you put it?" he asks.

I know what he's talking about. "It's right here," I say, patting my coat pocket. Inside is an envelope with an official-looking paper giving my clan the ownership of Pa-Gotzin-Kay. One of Kosterlitzky's men delivered it yesterday. He said the formal one with the President's seal on it will arrive in a couple of months. "You think I'd take a chance on losing it?"

"Your mother's going to be excited to see that," he says.

The wagon slows us down and it's late afternoon before we make it back. Men come down the steep trail to gather up everything Buck sent along with us. I help Tom up onto his horse for the ride to the top. Mother and Dee-O-Det are waiting for us when we enter the *rancheria*.

"Welcome home," she says, hugging me.

I go over to Tom to give him a hand dismounting. He slaps my hand away. "I don't need help, Niño. I'm not that old yet."

"But your injury…"

"It's hardly a scratch," he sniffs. "Nothing to it."

Nevertheless, the pain shows on his face as he climbs down. My mother takes his arm and he doesn't slap her hands away. "Once again you have proven yourself a great friend to my people, Taglito," she says.

"It was nothing," he says gruffly. "I only went along to keep Ace out of trouble. He needs someone to look after him, you know."

"Your bed is ready for you."

Tom shakes his head. "I did enough lying around the last few days." He looks at Dee-O-Det. "You got any whisky squirreled away? I'm parched from the ride."

Dee-O-Det gets a sly look on his face. "Maybe. Come with me and we'll look."

"And if I'm not mistaken, I smell some chow cooking. I could eat, too," I hear him say as the two of them walk away.

I take out the envelope and hand it to my mother. She looks at the paper inside. She doesn't read much, but she understands enough to figure out what it is. She holds it to her chest and gets tears in the corners of her eyes. "We're not the Nameless Ones anymore," she says.

"You know, Tom said the same thing."

"What you have done for your people…"

"I had a lot of help. And a lot of luck."

She smiles. "Every leader does. Didn't you know that?"

"It turns out there's a lot I don't know."

"And that is the beginning of wisdom, my son. Knowing that you do not know."

I think about how close I came to getting all my men killed. "It gets better, doesn't it?"

"It does. It happens faster if you listen to your mother." She smiles as she says the last, to let me know she's teasing. Then her expression gets serious again.

"There is someone here to see you. He showed up a few days ago."

Something in her tone alerts me. "Who?" I ask, looking around. I hope it's not Geronimo. He and I really don't get along.

"First I want you to give me your word you will not do anything hasty when I tell you."

"Who is it?"

"Your word, Ace."

Right then I see a man come around a nearby wikiup. Instantly, without me even thinking about it, my pistol is in my hand.

"*You*!" I hiss.

54

It's Mickey Free. He puts his hands up. I keep the pistol trained on him. I'm about an eyeblink away from shooting him. Without looking away, I say to my mother, "What's *he* doing here?"

"He wants to speak to you."

"The last time I saw him, he was trying very hard to kill me. I told you about that, didn't I?" Oh boy do I want to shoot this man.

"Please, Ace. Listen to him. You will want to hear what he has to say."

I raise my pistol and point it at his head. "Come to finish the job?" I snarl.

He hesitates, then nods slightly. My finger tightens on the trigger.

"But not like you think," he says quickly.

"How did you know I was here?"

"You're a wanted man in the Territory. Where else would you go?"

"Why are you here?"

"Like your mother said. I came to tell you something."

"That's a lie. You came to collect the reward on my head." Why am I still talking to his man? I should shoot him and be done with it.

"No. I'm not. You proved a worthy adversary, the most difficult one I have ever faced. That was all I really sought, a true challenge."

"That and the reward," I sneer.

"The true reward is the chase. The money has always been secondary."

"What did you come here to say? Spit it out fast and go before I shoot you."

He nods. "I've come to tell you that you do not need to fear the law in Arizona anymore."

"What? That's impossible." I did break out of the Yuma prison, after all. A thought occurs to me. "Did you find the Apache Kid? Did he confess to killing those settlers?"

"No. The Apache Kid is gone. You know this as well as I." He mimes wings flapping with his hands.

"Then how can I not be wanted anymore?"

"Simple. You're not wanted because the law believes you are dead. After our…scrape, I returned to Yuma and told them I had killed you, but that your body fell from a cliff into the river, and I couldn't not retrieve your head. They believed me."

I'm stunned. I lower my pistol. "Why did you do that?" I ask finally.

"I wanted you to be free. You should be free."

I holster my pistol. I'm still having trouble wrapping my mind around this. This is good news. It will be nice to be able to go back to Arizona and not have to look over my shoulder the whole time. But I can't simply discard the fact that this man standing here before me tried to kill me not that long ago.

My mother intervenes. "Why don't we go see if the food is ready yet?" she says. To Mickey Free she says, "Will you join us?"

"Thank you, but no," he says. "I have places to go." So saying, he touches his hat and walks away.

55

The next morning there is a council meeting and when it is over, my mother asks me if I will walk with her. We walk down to the springs. The whole way she doesn't speak, and when I try to say something, she quiets me. When we get there, she spends a couple of minutes staring into the water before she turns to me.

"I was wrong," she says simply.

I'm confused. "About what?"

"I told you your place was here, that it was time to give up your wandering and take up your responsibilities as chief of this clan."

At first I misunderstand her. "I don't understand. Is it something I've done? Did the council decide I would not make a good chief?"

"That's not it at all. You have led us through a dangerous time. You've done everything asked of you and more."

"Then why are you saying this?"

"Because I can see that your heart is not here. Not now. Perhaps not ever, though I hope that it will be someday. I can see that you are not done searching for whatever it is you seek. It was wrong of me to try and tie you here before you are ready. It would only make you unhappy with me."

"That would never happen."

"You don't know that. I let your father go, Ace, because I could see that he didn't belong with us. Had I tried to keep him, it would have turned him against me in time. Even the most loving chain is still a chain. Besides, we are entering a new time. We are no longer the Nameless Ones. We don't have to fear that we will be discovered and attacked. We have a deed from the government. And if that is not enough, we have our new friends among the ranchers and our allies among the Yaquis and the Tarahumaras. The world has changed. Maybe it is time for us to change as well."

She leaves me then and goes back to the *rancheria*. I stay and sit by the water, thinking. I realize that her words have lifted a great weight from my shoulders. I feel shamed by it, but the truth is I do not want to stay here and be a chief. There's too much I still want to see and do.

I hear the sound of hooves and turn to see Coyote walking up. He nudges my shoulder, then knocks off my hat. When I don't stand up, he nudges me again and whickers softly.

I stand up and stroke his neck. "Are you trying to tell me you're ready to go?" I ask him.

He tosses his head and pulls his lips back from his teeth. After all this time he is still surprised at how stupid I can be.

We don't leave right away. There's no rush, after all. And I don't want to miss the party Buck promised us.

A few weeks pass and one morning when I get up I know it's time. I head over to the wikiup where my tack is stored. Tom's sitting outside it and he smiles at me.

"Is it time?" he asks.

"It is."

"I thought so." He gets to his feet. He's still a little stiff, but he seems to have healed well. "I'll ride along with you back to Arizona, if you don't mind."

"It will be good to have your company." I whistle for Coyote, and he comes trotting up. When he gets close a sudden gust of wind blows through the *rancheria*. The wind blows Tom's hat off his head. It sails over and lands at Coyote's feet.

Coyote looks down at the hat. He picks up one foot.

Tom groans. "I was getting fond of that hat."

Then Coyote puts his foot back down. Not on the hat.

"I told you he was warming up to you," I tell Tom with a laugh.

The goodbyes don't take long. My mother smiles, but there is a wetness in her eyes. She holds me close for a long time. Hi-okee comes limping out of his wikiup and embraces me. Chee pats me on the back.

As Tom and I are riding out of the *rancheria*, I see Dee-O-Det standing beside the trail. He still has the withered crow foot sticking out of his headband. He gives me a crooked smile.

"The spirits aren't done with you yet," he says. "You'll see."

The End

How about going on Amazon and reviewing *The Hidden Fortress* now that you've read it? Your comments are very much appreciated!
(Page forward to find notes on the history behind this story.)

Find more of my books at:
Amazon.com

Afterword

As I said at the beginning of this book, there is quite a lot of actual history here. First of all, if you've read any of the other Ace books, you know that Ace is very loosely modeled after Ciyé "Niño" Cochise, who was the grandson of the great Apache Chief Cochise. The whole idea for this story comes from Ciyé's autobiography, *The First Hundred Years of Niño Cochise.*

First off, though I've changed a great many things in the interest of storytelling, the basic events outlined here actually happened. In northern Mexico in the mid-1890s, Governor General Luis Torres and General Joaquin Terrazas did "raise the red flag" of revolution. Their plans were thwarted by an alliance of Apache, Yaqui, Tarahumara and Opata Indians, along with American ranchers, Pancho Villa, and Colonel Kosterlitzky and his Rurales. (I'm sorry I didn't get to include Pancho Villa in this story as he was actually quite an interesting character. I simply didn't have the space. Perhaps Ace will run into him in a later book?) Afterwards, President Porfirio Diaz granted lands to the Yaqui, Tarahumara and Opata Indians in gratitude for their help. (Strangely, Ciyé doesn't say if anything was granted to the Apaches.)

One of the main reasons I wanted to write this story is because it fascinates me. I grew up thinking that the Old West was cowboys fighting Indians, with some cavalry thrown in. To find out that there was a time when cowboys and Indians actually banded together for self-preservation really blew me away. I think it's a wonderful, inspiring story and one that more people should know. It just goes to show that the Old West (along with just about every other time in history, I expect) was a much more diversified, unpredictable place than most of us realize. (If you've read books 2 and 3 in this series you know that old one-eyed Lou and Beckwourth—a woman who drove mule teams and pretended to be a man for years, and a freed slave who became a renowned scout and trapper—were also based on real characters who defied the stereotypes of the men and women who settled the West.

The other reason I wanted to write this story is Ciyé's mother, Nod-Ah-Sti. In real life, she was Cochise's daughter-in-law, rather than his daughter. In my mind, she was a true hero, one forgotten by history, and I wanted her story told. Let me tell you what I know, pieced together from references to her by her son in his autobiography.

From the autobiography:

"Tahza (Ciyé's father), the hereditary chieftain, with something of an omniscient mind, foresaw dark days ahead for his people and, although he led his tribe to San Carlos—so that the Chiricahui could not be blamed for breaking the treaty—he adroitly arranged for his own clan of thirty-eight to disappear enroute. Under the leadership of his young wife, Nod-Ah-Sti, (who took in the group me, their only son, Niño Cochise, and the aging shaman—Dee-O-Det), the family clan escaped and fled into Sonora, Mexico, disappearing into legendry. They were never again entered onto any reservation list."

Tahza later died while in Washington, D.C. The clan had no chief until Ciyé came of age, but was instead ruled by a council.

From bits and pieces I have gleaned throughout the book, it is my belief that Nod-Ah-Sti was the clan's nominal leader, or at least a respected voice of authority, for over a decade and a half. Certainly, according to her son, she led them as they escaped the cavalry accompanying them to the new reservation and fled to Mexico. (Where they lived until the early 1900s, when Pa-Gotzin-Kay was gradually abandoned, as the people living there dispersed into the larger world.)

Surviving all those years at the old hideaway was a monumental achievement. Simply making it through the first winter in the mountain snows, when they had no food stores, no guns, only weapons and traps that they made themselves, was an impressive feat. But that was only the beginning of the challenges those people faced.

For one, the Chiricahua Apaches were not a very agriculturally-minded people. They were hunter-gatherers and raiders. But if they were to survive where they did, they could not raid or they would inevitably have been wiped out. Nor could they reasonably follow the hunter-gatherer lifestyle, which requires the ability to move with the different seasons. That meant Nod-Ah-Sti's clan had to plant crops and take up animal husbandry in what was, and still is, a pretty rugged environment.

In addition, they had to deal with periodic visits from those Apaches who were still fighting against the US Government, the most notable of whom was Geronimo (Nod-Ah-Sti's brother). The fighters would show up when they needed a place to rest up and heal, and Ciyé notes in his autobiography how nervous such visits always made his mother. She could not refuse them, but she knew what would happen if the Army ever followed them to the stronghold.

Also, despite living at a fairly simple level, the clan still needed many things from the larger world, such as guns and ammunition, flour, beans, coffee, cloth, pots and pans, and so on. Periodically, they would take mules and go to one of the towns in southern Arizona, usually Sasabe or Bisbee, and load up. These trips presented a number of dangers. For some years there was a law in Arizona that said no Apaches could be off the reservation unless accompanied by a responsible white person. So when they went for supplies they had to dodge the Arizona Rangers and, when they got into town, they had to pretend to be Mexicans. They also had to worry about people noticing the gold they were spending and trying to rob them. One time they were ambushed after leaving Sasabe and had to fight their way free.

All in all, I believe that Nod-Ah-Sti was a hero in her own right, though perhaps not what we commonly think of when we refer to heroes. She helped guide her clan through an incredibly difficult time and allowed them the freedom to live their own lives on their own terms while throughout North and South America other indigenous peoples were having everything stripped from them. It's an amazing story and I think it deserves to be told.

Other historic figures

Tom Jeffords was an Army scout, an Indian agent, and a prospector, among other things. He met Chief Cochise in 1871 when he rode alone into Cochise's camp to set up a meeting with General Howard for peace talks. The two men became friends and later he and Chief Cochise became blood brothers. According to Ciyé, the Apaches called him Taglito, and he visited Pa-Gotzin-Kay several times.

Jeffords was with Niño when they found Buck Green nearly dead of a gunshot wound. Jeffords knew Green and he and Niño patched him up, using wild honey which helped slow the flow of blood and acted as a natural antiseptic. Green told them how he'd been tracking stolen cows when he was ambushed, but the place where he was ambushed was miles from where the two men found him. At first Green thought it was Apaches who'd shot him, as he knew there were some who lived up in the mountains, but then he realized it was Yaquis. It was Green's belief that the Yaquis shot him and carried his body closer to Apache territory as part of a plan by Torres to get the Apaches and ranchers to fight each other.

I haven't found a lot of information on Chief Kelzel outside the autobiography. I know that he was a man who Ciyé feared and respected. They had their conflicts, but ultimately they were able to fight together against the soldiers.

Alchise, Boa Juan, Kersus, Deya, Chatto and Nakai were all Apaches who Ciyé mentions in the autobiography. However, it was Eugene, not Nakai, who lived in Basaranca. He was married to a Mexican woman and he actually did work in the gunpowder factory. Ciyé arranged for him and his family to flee under the protection of one of the ranchers shortly before the fighting started. However, some miles from town, Eugene suddenly jumped down off the wagon and disappeared. Several hours later the gunpowder factory blew up. Ciyé believed that Eugene blew up the factory because he felt guilty about what the gunpowder would be used for.

A man named Jim Ticer showed up at the stronghold one day. He was injured and claimed to have been set on by bandits. Ciyé let him stay and eventually the real story came out, that he'd gotten a furlough from Ft. Huachuca and went to Tucson. There he won some money and got terribly drunk for ten days. When he woke up from it, he was a deserter and fled to Mexico. He turned out to be a real boon for the clan, because he knew how to mine. Under his direction, they bought old mining equipment that allowed them to crush the ore and smelt it into ingots, which were much easier to use as currency. Perhaps even more valuable, he taught them English, which doubtless helped in their eventual integration into the larger world. Ticer lived at the stronghold for years until he died helping the clan in a battle against bandits.

Chief Jemez and the Tarahumara Indians arrived at Pa-Gotzin-Kay in 1896 as the revolution was heating up. They had been chased from their lands by soldiers and were starving and beaten.

Ciyé took them in and gave them land on the shelf to use for growing crops, along with horses, cattle, seed corn and other supplies, many of them donated by the ranchers, who they were allied with by then. A number of the Apache men married Tarahumara maidens, including Ciyé himself, who married Jemez's daughter. She was later killed when she followed Ciyé into a battle with the soldiers. Ciyé mourned her greatly and never remarried, though he lived past a hundred.

Other tidbits

The part where Ace notes that Green's missing finger helps mark him as a cowboy? That's an actual thing. After roping an animal, the first thing the cowboy does is wrap the end of the rope around the saddle horn a few times so he can hold onto it. If you accidentally get your finger in there while you're doing that, you'll lose it. That never happened to me, but I did lose part of my little finger when it got caught in a rope and a thousand pounds of horse hit the other end. Pinched it right off.

Pa-Gotzin-Kay is a real place (the name means Stronghold Mountain of Paradise) and it was actually an ancient Apache stronghold. The description of it is taken from Ciyé's autobiography. I tried to be as accurate as I could. There was a vein of gold ore on the shelf that the Apaches did mine. Someday I would dearly love to go to Mexico and see if I can find the place.

The shaman soup, made from a whole elk, was a real thing. It sounds horrible.

I got the idea for the shadows on the cliff face from an experience I had in Copper Canyon (a huge canyon in the Sierra Madres, over 7,000 feet deep at its deepest) many years ago. I was in my twenties, backpacking the canyon with a couple of friends, when we came across a National Geographic expedition down in the bottom of the canyon. It is tremendously rugged country and, in the early '90s at least, almost no one went down into the deep canyons other than the Tarahumaras who live there. So we were pretty surprised to see them, as they were us. Anyway, that night they were camped around a bend in the canyon and they had a big light set up to draw in insects for the entomologist on the expedition to study (Yes, they had a generator, carried by one of the local men they'd hired. Oof. I'm glad I wasn't him. I could barely manage the trip with my backpack, it was so rough and difficult). The light was shining toward this huge cliff face, probably two hundred feet high. And whenever anyone walked in front of the light, they cast a huge shadow seventy or eight feet tall. It was very cool.

In his autobiography, Ciyé recounts a time when bandits took over the town of Basaranca. The Apaches had become friendly with a doctor in Basaranca, who treated Ciyé one time when he was injured badly, and so they came to their aid. A big gun battle ensued and when it was over the bandits were all dead and the Apaches had some new friends.

Remember when Coyote kicked Guzmán in the stomach and knocked him into the horse trough? Well, that actually happened to me when I was a kid, though I didn't get knocked into a horse trough.

Well, that's about it. I hope you enjoyed the story. If you have any comments, hit me up at eric@erictknight.com. I'd love to hear from you.

ABOUT THE AUTHOR

Born in 1965, I grew up on a working cattle ranch in the desert thirty miles from Wickenburg, Arizona, which at that time was exactly the middle of nowhere. Work, cactus and heat were plentiful, forms of recreation were not. The TV got two channels when it wanted to, and only in the evening after someone hand cranked the balky diesel generator to life. All of which meant that my primary form of escape was reading.

At 18 I escaped to Tucson where I attended the University of Arizona. A number of fruitless attempts at productive majors followed, none of which stuck. Discovering I liked writing, I tried journalism two separate times, but had to drop it when I realized that I had no intention of conducting interviews with actual people but preferred simply making them up.

After graduating with a degree in Creative Writing in 1989, I backpacked Europe with a friend and caught the travel bug. With no meaningful job prospects, I hitchhiked around the U.S. for a while then went back to school to learn to be a high school English teacher. I got a teaching job right out of school in the middle of the year. The job lasted exactly one semester, or until I received my summer pay and realized I actually had money to continue backpacking.

The next stop was Australia, where I hoped to spend six months, working wherever I could, then a few months in New Zealand and the South Pacific Islands. However, my plans changed irrevocably when I met a lovely Swiss woman, Claudia, in Alice Springs. Undoubtedly swept away by my lack of a job or real future, she agreed to allow me to follow her back to Switzerland where, a few months later, she gave up her job to continue traveling with me. Over the next couple years we backpacked the U.S., Eastern Europe and Australia/New Zealand, before marrying and settling in the mountains of Colorado, in a small town called Salida.

In Colorado, after starving for a couple of years, we started our own electronics business, because electronics seemed a logical career choice for someone with a Creative Writing degree.

Around the turn of the century we had a couple of sons, Dylan and Daniel (I say 'we', but when the hard part of having kids came around, there was remarkably little for me to do). Those boys, much to my surprise, have grown up to be amazingly awesome people, doubtless due to their mother's steadying influence during their formative years, and not to the endless stream of bad jokes and puns spewing from their father.

In 2005 we shut the business down and moved back to Tucson. I am currently writing full time.

Made in the USA
San Bernardino, CA
28 January 2019